"There is so much brutal, raw, and beautiful power in these stories. I kept wanting to read and know more about these characters' lives, how they ended up where they ended up, how they would get out, how they wouldn't. It is difficult to be so honest, and funny, and sad, at once, in any kind of work. Reading this book, I literally laughed and cried."

—TOMMY ORANGE, author of *There There*

"Morgan Talty's *Night of the Living Rez* is a beautifully crafted, raw and intimate book about youth, friendship, and family on the reservation. These stories are profoundly moving and essential, rendered with precision and intimacy. Talty is a powerful new voice in Native American fiction."

—BRANDON HOBSON, author of *The Removed*

"*Night of the Living Rez* is an indelible portrait of a family in crisis, and an incisive exploration of the myriad ways in which the past persists in haunting the present. I loved these sharply atmospheric, daring, and intensely moving stories, each one dense with peril and tenderness. Morgan Talty is a thrilling new talent."

—LAURA VAN DEN BERG, author of *I Hold a Wolf by the Ears*

"*Night of the Living Rez* is a fiercely intelligent and beautifully written set of stories—a spectacularly visceral and moving account of the experience of a member of the Penobscot Nation in today's America—as well as a wrenching meditation on family and familial dysfunction. Morgan Talty is a master of the way dependency and pain transition from one body to another; the way both separating and refusing to separate become modes of saving ourselves; and the way, for all of our failures, we never stop doing what we can to provide each other hope."

—JIM SHEPARD, author of *Phase Six*

"*Night of the Living Rez* is true storytelling. It's a book so funny, so real, so spirited and vivid it brought me back to my own rez life and the people who made me."
—**TERESE MARIE MAILHOT**, author of *Heart Berries*

"I am not predicting literary success for Morgan Talty, I am guaranteeing it. He is a fascinating and powerful and singular writer."
—**RICK BASS**, author of *For a Little While*

"*Night of the Living Rez* delivers stories that combine the otherworldly with the everyday in ways that startle and sing. Morgan Talty portrays Maine and his Penobscot characters in language and images both beautiful and inventive. With equal parts humor and haunting, this book will linger."
—**TONI JENSEN**, author of *Carry*

"Morgan Talty's *Night of the Living Rez* is a marvel. The experience of diving into that work was like first picking up a novel by Marguerite Duras, or like reading Denis Johnson's *Jesus' Son*. The prose is masterful. It's brutal and funny and smart and has a genuine warmth that's rare, especially in contemporary fiction. Talty's book has done a lot to restore my faith in the future of literature."
—**CARA HOFFMAN**, author of *Running*

"While soaked in pain and broken promises, *Night of The Living Rez* delivers with a grace and dignity on par with the writings of Craig Lesley, Dawn Dumont, James Welch and Joseph Dandurand. Morgan Talty delivers on so many levels and proves that this is why Indigenous Literature continues to be its own unique and sacred blessing. I loved this book. Loved it. And I can't wait to see what Morgan Talty does next. I am a fan for life!"
—**RICHARD VAN CAMP**, author of
The Lesser Blessed** and **Moccasin Square Gardens

NIGHT OF THE LIVING REZ

Published by Tin House, Portland, Oregon

Distributed by W. W. Norton & Company

Library of Congress Cataloging-in-Publication Data

Names: Talty, Morgan, 1991– author.
Title: Night of the living rez / Morgan Talty.
Description: Portland, Oregon : Tin House, [2022]
Identifiers: LCCN 2022000557 | ISBN 9781953534187 (paperback) | ISBN 9781953534255 (ebook)
Subjects: LCSH: Penobscot Indians—Fiction. | LCGFT: Short stories.
Classification: LCC PS3620.A586 N54 2022 | DDC 813/.6—dc23/eng/20220107
LC record available at https://lccn.loc.gov/2022000557

First US Edition 2022
Printed in the USA
Interior design by Jakob Vala

www.tinhouse.com

NIGHT OF THE LIVING REZ

MORGAN TALTY

TIN HOUSE / Portland, Oregon

CONTENTS

For Mom (1959–2021)
And for all the women who raised me

BURN

Winter, and I walked the sidewalk at night along banks of hard snow. I'd come from Rab's apartment off the reservation. Rab— this white guy with a wide mouth and eyes that closed up when he laughed—sold pot. He was all no-bullshit too. I had asked for a gram, and after he weighed it and put it in a plastic baggie and held it out to me, I reached into my pants and jacket pockets looking for the cash among the cigarette wrappers and pocketknife, and he didn't believe me as I acted the part and kept saying, "Shit shit shit, it must've fell out on the walk over here." He shook his head, took the weed out of the baggie, and put it back into his mason jar. "I ain't smokin' you up," he said, and so then I said, "Fuck you, Rab, I really did lose the money, you'll see, watch when I come back here in thirty minutes with the money I dropped, you'll feel stupid then." He shrugged a *Sorry, man*, and I slammed his door shut as I left.

At the bridge to the reservation, the river was still frozen, ice shining white-blue under a full moon. The sidewalk on the bridge hadn't been shoveled since the last nor'easter crapped snow in November, and I walked in the boot prints everyone made who walked the walk to Overtown to get pot or catch the bus to wherever it was us skeejins had to go, which wasn't anywhere because everything we needed—except pot—was on the rez. Well, except Best Buy or Bed Bath & Beyond, but those Natives who bought 4K Ultra DVDs or fresh white doilies had cars, wouldn't be taking the bus like me or Fellis did each day to the methadone clinic. That was another thing the rez didn't have: a methadone clinic. But we had sacred grounds where sweats and peyote ceremonies happened once a month, except since I had chosen to take methadone, I was ineligible to participate in Native spiritual practice, according to the doc on the rez.

Natives damning Natives.

The roads on the rez were quiet, trees bending under the weight of snow, and when I passed the frozen swamp a voice moaned out. I stopped walking. Nothing, so I kept on going on the sparkling road until I heard it again.

"Who's that?" I yelled. The moan came again. It was a man, somewhere in the swamp. I got closer, listening. There it was: a low and breathy noise, and with my cold ear I followed it.

The swamp was frozen solid, the snow blown in piles, and so I slid over the ice, looking for the source of the noise. Moonlight through bare tree limbs lit the swamp, and caught among the tree stumps and solid snow was a person sprawled out on the ground. He was trying to sit up but kept falling back, like he'd just done one thousand crunches and was too sore to do just one more.

It was Fellis.

"Fellis?" I said, standing over him.

He tried to sit up, but something pulled him back down. "Fuck you," Fellis said. "Help me." He groaned, shivered.

He didn't say how to help him, so I had to squat down to get a better look. I flicked my lighter and his purple lip quivered.

"Hurry," he said.

"Fellis, I can't help you if I don't know what's a matter with you."

"My hair," he said.

I looked at it with the lighter's flame. "Holy," I said, and I laughed. Instead of the tight braid that shined, Fellis's hair had come undone, and it was frozen into the snow.

"Get me out, Dee," he said. "Dee, get me out."

At first I tried to pull the hair out from the snow, tried to chip the snow away. But his hair wouldn't come loose, so I yanked, and Fellis screamed.

"Lift your head up," I said. I opened my pocketknife, and at the click of the blade Fellis spoke.

"Wait, wait," he said. "Don't cut it."

"What do you want me to do? Tell the ice to let go?"

Fellis spit. "Go to my house and get boiling water."

I closed the pocketknife. "Fellis, by the time I got back here the water would be chilled."

He was quiet. As if something walked around or among us, the ice cracked and echoed somewhere in the swamp. The moon shone bright, and I looked. There was nobody but us.

"I have to cut it," I said. "You ain't getting out if I don't."

Fellis asked if I had a cigarette, and when I told him no, he cursed. "Fucking bullshit, fucking goddamn winter, what the fuck."

I laughed.

"It ain't funny, Dee."

"Look," I said. "You want me to cut my braid too?"

Fellis took a deep breath, and he coughed and gagged. "No," he said. "Just cut it. I gotta get home. I'm sick."

I opened the pocketknife again, grabbed his hair in a fistful, and cut. When I got through the last bit of hair, Fellis rolled over and away from where he'd been stuck. He rubbed his head like he just woke up.

I helped him stand, and we slipped all over the ice on our way out of the swamp. Through dry heaves, Fellis said he'd missed the bus this morning to the methadone clinic—"No shit," I said, because I didn't see him on the bus or at the clinic—and he thought some booze would be good before he got sick from not having any methadone. He'd had a bit of booze left that afternoon when he decided to go see Rab to get some pot, and on the way he'd stopped off in the swamp to feel the quiet that came with too much drinking, and when he plopped down in the snow he'd dozed right off. When he woke up, his hair was frozen in the snow.

I got him to his mom's, Beth's, where he still lived. He walked fine by himself to the door, but I walked with him up the steps.

"I never thought I'd scalp a fellow tribal member," I said.

"Fuck off," he said. He fumbled in his pocket for his house key.

"You wanna smoke?" I said.

"Didn't you listen? I didn't make it to Rab's." He unlocked the door.

"I'll go for you," I said. "Give me the cash."

Fellis looked at me.

"Twenty minutes," I said. "I'll run there and back while you warm up your pretty bald head."

He gave me thirty bucks, and I didn't ask where he got it from. Yesterday he said he didn't have any money.

"Twenty bag," Fellis said. "And stop at Jim's and get some tall boys and a bag of chips. Any kind but Humpty Dumpty chips."

Down Fellis's driveway I imagined the look on Rab's face when I gave him the money. What I tell you? How about that gram?

"Dee!" Fellis yelled. "One more thing. Bring me my hair, so we can burn it. Don't want spirits after us."

"We're damned anyway," I said. "But I guess I'll get your hair."

I kept going, wondering, Hair or pot first? Pot made the most sense. It would look strange having to set the hair and ice down like a soaked mop on the counter at Jim's while I reached in my pocket for Fellis's money. Jim—that old wood booger—would say, "We don't take those anymore." I'd look him square in his sagging face and say, "I ain't trading no hair, you old fucker," and I'd smack down on the counter a ten-dollar bill for the tall boys and chips. With the change jingling in my pocket, I'd walk to Rab's and he'd say, "Get that hair out of here, it's dripping on my floor," and I'd have to plop the hair on the muddy white floor in the hallway while Rab reweighed the same nugs he'd weighed for me earlier.

No. I'd grab Fellis's hair from the swamp on my way home. With Fellis on his unmade bed, me on a torn beanbag in the corner, each of us with a tall boy and the pot smoke hazing gray the room, we'd keep poking and squeezing the hair, waiting for it to dry, waiting to burn it.

IN A JAR

I no longer had a fever, but Mom worried I was still sick and told me to take it easy. All throughout my first morning in our new home, she sat me on the couch with a bowl of cereal and half a piece of toast while she unpacked and fixed up the whole house, nailed her brown shelves to the white walls, and spread out atop the shelves all her colored knickknacks, miniatures of larger things like wooden bowls filled with wooden painted fruit, tiny glass soda bottles, little porcelain turtles, and a set of tiny, tiny books with real pages, all blank. When my food was gone, I sat wondering about Mom's hair. She had gotten a haircut, and I had no idea how she had time to get one. When she finished with the house, we went outside, where I sat on the concrete steps and played with my toy men, the ones I kept in a black plastic tub and the ones my father bought me each time he returned from the casino. I had a lot of toy men. As I played, Mom worked in the shed. She organized and stacked extra boxes from our move to the Panawahpskek Nation. Maybe *move* was not the right word. All I knew was that we left our life down south with my father and sister. I had asked countless times, but Mom never said if Paige was coming.

I wasn't at play long before I lost one of my men to a gap between the stairs and the door. It was a red alien guy, and although he wasn't my favorite, I still cared. Looking behind the steps, my knees were wet when I knelt in the snow, and my hands were cold and muddy when I held myself up. The sun beamed on my neck, and a sliver of sunlight also shone behind the concrete steps, right at the perfect angle, and in the light I thought I saw my toy man. But when I reached for him I grabbed hold of something hard and round. I pulled it out.

It was a glass jar filled with hair and corn and teeth. The teeth were white with a tint of yellow at the root. The hair was gray and thin and loose. Wild. And the corn was kind of like the teeth, white and yellow and looked hard.

"Mumma," I said. "What is this?"

"David," she said from inside the shed. "Can you wait? Please, honey."

I said nothing, waited, and examined the jar. My hand was slightly red from either the hot glass sitting in the sun all afternoon or the cold snow I crawled on.

Mom came out of the shed, squinting in the light.

"What's what, gwus?" she said. Little boy, she meant.

I held the jar to her and she took it. I watched her look at it, her head tilted and her brown eyes wide as the jar. And then she dropped it into the snow and mud and told me to pack up my toys. "No, no, never mind," she said. "Leave the toys. Come on, let's go inside."

She got on the phone and called somebody, whose voice on the other end I could hear and it sounded familiar. "I'll be by," he said. "I can get there soon. Don't touch it, and don't let him touch anything."

Mom hung up the phone and lit a cigarette.

We waited for a long while. Mom stayed quiet, and with no talk or toy men to occupy myself with, I tried to remember the move to our new home, which was not some faraway memory and was only a day back. But because of the fever, I remembered only fragments. Miles of highway, miles of pine trees. I remembered riding in the front seat of our white Toyota as I burned up. Mom had held her long Winston 100 up to the cracked car window, and at eighty miles per hour the passing air sucked the smoke out. "We left Paige," I kept saying. "We left her, Mumma." Mom took her eyes off the road and looked over at me. She held her hand to my sweaty forehead. "You poor thing," she said. Mom had driven fast. Real fast, and she watched me most of the time during the drive, as if I had been her road the whole way to our new home.

Mom's voice startled me. "Stop biting your fingernails," she said. She lit a second cigarette while we continued to wait. "He said not to touch anything—that includes your mouth." For quite some time I tried to remember our arrival, tried to find the exact memory of my mother putting together a bed, making it, and putting me under the blankets. But I couldn't remember any of that. All I remembered was that at one point the night before I had a dream where I crawled out of bed and into the darkness of the unfamiliar house, and I grabbed at a doorknob that wasn't there, tripped over boxes that cluttered the short and narrow hallway that led straight to the kitchen and small living room where a man's voice spoke to me, telling me to go back to bed. I'd asked who he was but he didn't answer. He guided me back to my room, his boots echoing down the hallway.

At the noise of a truck and its engine cutting off, Mom said, "Finally," and she stood from the table. When the man came down the driveway and up the stairs and stepped over that gap, I knew at once it hadn't been a dream. The man Mom called about the jar was the man who put me to bed last night. He was dark like Mom, and unlike Mom he had long black hair, and little black whiskers on his upper lip. He wasn't fat, but he had a pudge to him I hadn't noticed in the dark, and his jeans were faded and baggy. He wore a red-and-black flannel button-up.

"Gwus," Mom said. "This is Frick. He's a medicine man."

"He was here last night," I said to Mom, and then to Frick I said, "I saw you."

"Who do you think hooked up the woodstove?" Frick asked.

I thought Mom.

"Let me see your hand," Frick said.

I held my hand out to him and he took it and rubbed my palm. He let go and talked to Mom about the jar. "It's bad medicine," he said, and Mom wondered who would put it here. Frick had no answer. "Could have been anyone on the rez. I'll take care of it."

He left the house. I wondered why you couldn't throw it away, wondered how Frick would handle it. I asked Mom, and she got all annoyed.

"You can't throw it away," she said. "Frick's a Native doctor. It needs to be properly disposed of."

I asked why again, and she said that what I'd found had been meant to hurt me. To hurt us.

"But I feel fine," I told her, to which she said, "Just in case."

Soon Frick opened the door and said he was ready for us. Mom took me outside and to the back of the house and down into the woods where a tree had four cloth flags hanging: red, white, black, and yellow.

"It's the four directions," Mom told me.

"What's it for?" I said.

"It's to heal us."

"But my fever's gone," I said. "I'm not sick."

"Yes you are," she said.

Frick knelt in front of the tree with the four flags, and he was mumbling words in skeejin. It was strange hearing another person use skeejin besides Mom and Paige and Grammy, when Grammy would come to visit. But I couldn't hear what he was saying, and I still couldn't make out the words when smoke rose around him and he stood holding a giant seashell the size of a baseball glove filled with tobacco and this long, thick, bushy thing I'd later learn was sage that burned and smelled calm, like salt water.

In his hand he held a giant feather—eagle, Mom said—that was beaded at the quill. He moved toward us, still mumbling, and Mom said he was praying. "He's smudging us. It's good medicine. Watch how I do it, gwus."

Frick stepped forward and tripped over a hard root and he dropped the smoking sage.

"Shit," he said.

I laughed, and Mom let out a sharp shush and I shut up.

Frick picked up the sage among the soft mud and melting snow and he walked and stood in front of her. He had to re-light the sage. The smoke rolled up and around him, and with the feather he brushed the smoke over my mother. He started on her head, pushed the smoke with the feather over her and through her short hair, and then he moved the smoke to her chest. She turned around, and he did her back. She turned around, facing him, and she lifted her arms. His face looked serious. He smudged under her arms and in her armpits. Then down her legs. Mom lifted her feet and Frick pushed the smoke under her. He stepped away from her, and he mumbled a few more words, returned to the tree with the four flags, which blew in a slight breeze, and then he knelt again and spoke more words louder. He stood and then smudged me over in the same way he had my mother.

When he finished, he smudged my toys, too, and the steps and the back door. Then in the house he smudged everything, and I watched our home fill with a burning fog. I coughed once. He finally finished and returned to the tree out back while Mom and I sat at the kitchen table.

In time, Frick came through the door, and in his hand he held something red. At first I thought he'd gone behind the steps and got my plastic alien figure, but then I realized it wasn't my toy. It was thin yellow straw, wrapped in a red cloth bound in twine.

"Can you get me a wall tack?" he said to Mom, who got up and dug through a kitchen drawer yet could not find one. She went to the empty bedroom that I hoped Paige would soon fill and came out and handed a tiny green tack to Frick. He pinned the yellow straw in red cloth above our door. "It'll keep bad medicine out," he said to Mom and me. "Also, I have this."

He dug in his pocket and pulled out a small deer-hide pouch that was sewed shut. It was no bigger than a quarter, and an open safety pin stabbed through the middle.

"Come here," he told me. I stepped forward, and he knelt on one knee. Clenching the pouch, he stuffed his hand up my shirt, and in front of my heart, he stabbed the pin through the cotton and clamped the pin shut.

"Can I have one?" Mom said, and Frick pulled another from his pocket. Mom took it and pinned it on.

"It's a medicine pouch," Frick said. "I made it."

"How does it work?" I asked.

"It just does," he said.

The pouch was itchy, and I didn't care for it. I planned to take it off and stuff it under my bed the moment I was back in my room. At least what he hung and pinned above the door wasn't physically bothersome. Distracting, certainly—it looked like a toy, the way it was wrapped in that red, and every time I walked down the hallway or when I left the house I thought of my lost plastic guy who was getting sucked deeper and deeper into that thawing mud.

. . .

It seemed that Frick had moved in just as fast as Mom had unpacked the whole house. He'd be there all day, sitting with her on the couch or at the kitchen table, and he'd be there when I went to bed, both of them drinking wine from a box. In the morning, he drank black coffee and smoked cigarettes with Mom. Soon his hairbrush was in the bathroom, strands of hair floating unflushed in toilet water, and his toothbrush was in a cup next to mine.

I had heard Frick say the jar was an old curse, and most likely not done right, that some skeejins were messing with Mom and me, but it had been best to be safe and pray and smudge and bless the home.

I felt fine, even before the smudge when I had held that jar, so I agreed with Frick that it probably wasn't done right, but Mom wasn't so sure. "I don't know," she kept saying, not really to me, but to Frick, who would shake his head. "Only time will tell," she said.

At the end of March, I started up at school, and after school I spent the afternoons until dinner at the community center—rusted roof, yellow walls—playing basketball on the concrete floor with some of the kids in my class, and it took no time falling into that place, feeling that I had been there my whole life and that I'd not been plucked out of my bed in the middle of the night with a fever and driven way, way north to where Mom had grown up.

If Dad was mad about our disappearance he never said anything to me, but I heard Mom fighting with him on the phone late at night, and one time I heard Frick get on the phone and yell at him. "You gamblin' man," Frick had said. He slurred his words. "You lost a big hand." On the nights I heard them on the phone, I often fell asleep dreaming of my lost alien figure behind the steps.

I talked to Dad after dinner almost every night, and he always asked the questions Mom never asked: "How was school?" "What'd you have for breakfast?" "What'd you have for lunch?"

"What'd you play today?" "Get any homework?" "What's your favorite subject there?" Sometimes he'd say he'd send me up a toy. "When this next job goes through I'll send you up that space-ship." He always gave me some hope about something, and when I'd forgotten about the toy and moved on, some small action fig-ure would show up FedEx on our slanted concrete steps and then make its way into my black plastic tub with all my other men. The tub was getting full, the lid barely able to click shut.

. . .

For months, Mom mentioned the jar at least once a day. "There's something about it," she'd say. "I don't think we've seen the last of it." Eventually Mom stopped talking about it, because Frick told her to, but then she brought it back up again at the end of the summer when the air got sharp cold at night and Paige showed up in her tarnished Volkswagen. I'd heard the car before I saw it, heard the way the engine whistled and then thumped when she drove it in first gear. Mom and Frick were sitting at the kitchen table drinking wine from a box in hard plastic cups. I ran down the hall and into the kitchen and past Mom and Frick drinking and flung open the door.

"I told you she'd come," Mom said. I was so happy Paige arrived that I didn't even care that Mom lied: she hadn't said Paige would come.

In bare feet, I ran over the sandy sharp-pebbled driveway to Paige and hugged her waist and she hugged me back, ruffled my hair, and kissed the top of my head. "You got taller, you know that, chagooksis?" Chagooksis. Her little shit.

15

"Well your ears still stick out," I said. She made a face, wrinkled her nose at me, and then kissed the top of my head again.

Inside, Mom hugged Paige hard, and Frick stood, shook her hand. Paige didn't say anything to Frick, and after he left I realized Mom hadn't said anything to Paige about him. I was sitting on the couch, eating an Italian ice and watching *The Simpsons*. Mom and Paige were smoking cigarettes at the kitchen table, and whenever a commercial came on I listened to them.

"Who even is that guy?" Paige said.

"Frick," Mom told her. Since Mom was young when she'd had Paige—they shared a closeness—Paige had a way of getting Mom to open up, be something other than a mother. Sometimes, when Paige was around, I wondered if Paige wasn't in fact my mother's sister, given the way they spoke to each other and the way they fought and the swears they flung toward one another.

"Frick?" Paige said. "What the fuck is a Frick?"

Mom laughed. "His name's Melvin, but everyone says when he's drunk he's always saying, 'fricken this, fricken that.'"

"Does he?"

Mom's lighter flicked. "Does he what?"

"Say *fricken* when he's drunk?"

Mom was quiet, thinking. "Yeah, I guess he does."

"He's weird," Paige said. "He didn't even talk when I got here. He shook my hand and then sat back down, didn't even say anything else and got up and left."

"Oh, he's just shy."

"If you say so."

16

Mom pushed her chair back and the legs squeaked against the floor. I heard the fridge door open. "Gwus," she said. "You want something to drink?"

I told her no, and then she asked Paige if she wanted a cup of wine. I stared at the television as Homer choked Bart, Bart's pink, worm-looking tongue flapping in the air, and I was laughing and laughing all by myself, my empty plastic cup of Italian ice bobbing up and down on my belly. And then a commercial came on and I stopped laughing and there was this moment of immense silence, and then Mom was on Paige like Homer on Bart.

"Whose is it, Paige? Huh?" Mom was yelling.

"Would you calm down?"

"I ain't going to calm down." She slammed her plastic cup down. "That's why you come up here, isn't it? You little bitch. Little bitch!"

I peeked around the corner and into the kitchen, and Mom was standing over Paige, and then Paige stood and leaned into her, yelling back, cursing, pushing her with her body.

This was nothing new—the racing heart—but I still panicked and screamed and slapped the wall. "Stop it!"

Mom didn't look at me. "Go to your room, gwus. Right now."

I hurried down the hallway, Mom's words buzzing in my head, and I heard Paige before I shut my door: "He's going to grow up to hate you too."

. . .

I stayed in my room, playing with my plastic men, while they fought with low voices over the running kitchen-sink faucet.

Mom slammed plates and cups and silverware while she did the dishes. Half the time that was how she washed dishes. Every so often Paige's laughter hit my ears and I knew it made Mom angrier and angrier. After about an hour, the house was quiet. But that they weren't talking didn't mean the argument was over.

I put my plastic men away and opened my bedroom door, crept down the hallway into the kitchen. Mom was wiping the kitchen counters and the back door was open, and through the screen door I saw Paige outside on the steps, smoking, her knees pulled up to her chest.

"Boy," Mom said. I stood still. There was one word that told me Mom's mood, and that was the word. *Boy.* There was something about it, the way she'd call me *gwus*—which meant boy—or the way she called me *boy.* Maybe it was the tone she said it with.

"Boy," she said again. "Go tell your sister that smoking's bad when you're carrying a child."

"Go tell her?" I said.

"You heard me." She scrubbed the stovetop, which shook the burners, a rattling metal. She tossed the rag down and picked up her plastic cup and finished what had been in there. She went to her room.

Through the screen door I said, "Paige?"

She didn't look at me. "I know, David. Go watch TV."

Mom didn't come out of her room for the rest of the day, and Grammy showed up after Paige cooked me dinner. Grammy always popped up unannounced, and on more than one occasion Mom would see Grammy pull in the driveway and would shut all the lights off and take me to her room and tell me to be quiet, that she didn't feel like visiting that day, and I had to sit there on the itchy carpet with her and listen to Grammy knock and knock and knock, and I imagined she was putting her face to the little window on the door, looking in, looking for us. "We went for a walk" was what Mom always told Grammy when she saw her next.

The door was open, and so Grammy came in. I hopped off the couch. "Hi, son," she said. I gave her a hug. Paige turned off the sink faucet and dried her hands.

"When'd you get here, doos?" Grammy said to Paige.

"A little while ago."

Grammy walked over the linoleum with her shoes on and gave Paige a hug that said *It's nice to see you.* "Where's your mom?" she said.

"She's not feeling well."

Grammy looked up the hallway.

"Something she ate," Paige said.

Grammy said, "Mm-hmm." She stood in the doorway, and Paige asked if she wanted to sit down. "No, no," Grammy said. "I was coming to see if David wanted to go to the evening service at the church." She looked at me, and in looking at me I was compelled to say yes. She was my Grammy after all. But I didn't want to go alone with her, not because of her but because it was church.

"I'll go if Paige goes," I said. Paige dropped her head and shoulders, shook her head. She went to her bedroom and changed.

Grammy's car was a puttering, two-door piece of rusted metal. I'd thought Paige's car was bad, but Grammy's was something else. The engine made this whining sound every few minutes, like a bomb siren. Her turn signals worked, but on the dashboard it didn't say if they were on or off, so sometimes she drove with her turn signal on for miles. Maybe she knew; maybe she was messing with other drivers. Also, the radio turned on and off by itself, and after we drove in silence past the small health clinic and the large tin-looking community building and the tribal offices tucked behind thick pine trees and the tan-brick school and the football field, we pulled into the church parking lot and the radio kicked on and blared out Meredith Brooks's "Bitch," and Paige bobbed her head, telling Grammy to turn it up, but she flicked the radio off.

"Michaganasuus," Grammy said. This shitty thing.

We got out of the car, and Grammy hurried in front of us. Paige walked by my side and whispered about Goog'ooks. Evil spirits. "They follow Grammy around," she said to me. "That's why the radio turned on."

I tried not to be scared, but I was. Paige always talked about Goog'ooks, and one reason why I never stayed at Grammy's house was because Paige said it was haunted, and when I told Mom that, she said the whole Island was haunted, that years and years and years ago our people used this place as a graveyard, that even late at night she heard Goog'ooks tapping on the walls. Mom told me not to be scared.

In the church we took our seats, and I thumbed through the Bible in front of me. Other than that, I didn't pay attention to anything, just watched people here and there, some with their eyes closed, some open. I didn't think Paige was listening either—her head was turned sideways, eyes half open, like the priest's Word was putting her to sleep.

After we'd lined up to receive the body of Christ—which I wasn't allowed to ingest and instead received a pat on the head from the priest because Mom hadn't had me baptized—we returned to our seats. Paige nudged me. Grammy watched, hand on her chest, as Paige broke her cracker in half and gave it to me. It dissolved in my mouth, and it tasted like a chalky cracker that had gotten wet and had dried again.

Paige saw the disgust in my face, and she whispered, "It's the best Jesus could do."

"Jesus made this?" I said.

Paige had her arms crossed. "I know, right?"

Grammy told us to shut the heck up.

Church dragged on. When we had to kneel, we knelt; when we had to sing, we sang; when we had to pray, we prayed. Grammy probably prayed for God to forgive Paige, and Paige probably prayed for a cigarette. Me, I prayed for the safe return of my alien figure in his red space suit. I still felt bad that he was all alone under those steps, buried in the cold mud, and I prayed that the change in seasons would churn him out to the surface, and I'd find him one day.

Toward the end of the service, we knelt one last time, saying one more prayer, but I didn't pray for anything because I couldn't focus: I smelled a stinky pigadee, a fart. I had my eyes cracked open, looking, and I felt Paige looking too. We made eye contact, and she leaned toward me.

"David," she whispered, and she pointed at the upholstered cushioned wood we knelt on. "You ever wonder why they call this a pew?"

I puckered my lips, felt my face getting hot. I bit my tongue, using the pain to distract me from laughing. Grammy was looking at us, shaking her head, and it looked like she, too, was trying not to laugh, and when Paige saw Grammy's face, Paige let out a little croak of laughter, loud enough for the priest to hear, loud enough to turn heads, loud enough for the person who ripped one to know they were caught.

. . .

Grammy dropped us off, reminded me once again that I could stay at her house anytime I wanted, and I told her okay. Frick was there, his truck pulled right behind Paige's, but we didn't see him or Mom. I walked down the hallway to my room, and I looked at the base of Mom's door. There was no light. There were no voices.

I got ready for bed, put on my pajamas, and went to Paige's room. I stood at her open bedroom door, trying to get her attention. She was lying in bed fully clothed still, head propped up with a pillow, reading the local Overtown paper with a cigarette between her fingers, the smoke clinging, rolling off the gray paper up to the ceiling. She moved the paper to the side and looked at me.

"Be-dee-gé, chagooksis," she said. Come on in, little shit.

I crawled on her small bed, tried to roll over but elbowed her in her side. "Ow! Would you sit still?"

She read. Smoked. Flicked her cigarette. Read some more. Snubbed her cigarette. Lit a new one. Turned the pages, crinkled them. Finally, she lay the paper flat on her stomach, and it looked like a little mound but I knew it was her clothes making that bump, not the baby. Paige blew out an extra-long puff of smoke, and then was quiet.

The fridge in the kitchen hummed, and then it grumbled low like a stomach and clicked off. A pipe in the wall rattled. A minute of silence before the fridge started up again, humming, grumbling. Click. Another pipe. Silence. This went on until a different tapping began, gentle knocks down the dark hallway, over and up the walls. They got louder, closer, and Paige must have felt me grip her arm, because she said it was a pipe, but the knocking got louder, seemed to tap right on her bedroom door, and I knew there were no pipes in that thin hollow plywood.

Paige opened her eyes and looked. The knocking stopped, and I heard the fridge click on again and the floorboard heater ping, but then it all stopped again and the next thing I knew Paige jumped up, which sent me flying off the bed, and she screamed, grabbing her thigh.

Paige's scream woke Mom and Frick, and Mom came out in her underwear and a long T-shirt, and Frick came out with his big brown belly hanging over his blue boxers, and in the light both Mom and Frick squinted.

"What the hell is the matter?" Mom said.

"Ow, shit!" Paige couldn't roll up her black pants, so she pulled her pants down, and Frick looked horrified at her doing it, but then his eyes widened. I was grabbing Mom by the wrist, holding on to her, looking at Paige's thigh. Something had bitten her—itty-bitty teeth marks.

"Move," Frick said to Mom.

"Could it be the jar, Frick?" she asked.

Frick ignored her, got close to Paige, knelt and looked at the bite mark. Paige told Frick and Mom what we heard, the knocking, and then the silence, and then the pain she felt in her leg. I still gripped Mom's wrist.

We were spooked, but Frick stayed calm. He went into Mom's room and brought out a little bag made of deer hide, and he told Paige to go with him.

"Just stay inside," Frick said to Mom and me. He still only had on his underwear, and I felt the chill come through the open door and nip through my pajamas. Mom and I sat at the kitchen table, and we were both in separate chairs. She was rubbing her head, and I asked her if she had a headache.

"A little bit, gwusis."

They were gone for a long time, and then Frick opened the back door with Paige following him, the cold following her. Frick held the seashell bowl and smoke was coiling up and it swirled and blew away when he shut the door behind him and Paige. He smudged the whole house—especially Paige's room—and then he smudged Mom and me.

When he finished, he blessed his seashell and tobacco and put it all back in the deer-hide bag. Mom didn't say anything. She gave Paige a hug, kissed her good night, and then did the same to me, but told me to get to bed.

But I couldn't sleep. All night I listened and listened for the knocking, which never came back, and I tried not to think about what it all was. What it all could be. At some point during the quiet night I got up and went to the floor and slid out from under my bed the black plastic tub, and when I pulled it out the medicine pouch Frick had given me dragged underneath the tub. Just in case it would help, I pinned the pouch to my shirt on the inside, and the pin pricked me. In the dark,

I didn't know if I was bleeding. I touched the skin, and it felt bloodless.

I opened the black plastic tub. I didn't take out the men—I looked at them there, a pile of plastic bodies in the moonlight that shone behind me through the parted black curtains draped over the window. I realized that I'd have to get rid of some of the men, have to make room for new ones. What to do with the old toy men, the ones fading in color, their joints clogged with dried mud and crud? I thought about my father before I closed the black tub quietly and got back in bed. As the hours passed—as I dozed on and off—my room lit up with cold dawn light pouring through my window. I felt for the pouch, but it had fallen off. I flipped my blankets and pillows and looked for it, then I looked between the bed and the wall. It was way back under the bed. I tried to reach for it, yet it was too far down there. I left it, and I went down the hallway and into the kitchen.

Mom usually poured cereal in a bowl for me the night before, and filled a small cup up with milk and put it in the fridge, so that way I didn't wake her and I could fix breakfast myself. But Mom had forgotten to do it, and instead of trying to dump cereal into a bowl and pour milk from a gallon jug over the food pantry cornflakes, I went straight to the couch and turned the TV on and watched cartoons. The house was cold, and Mom had told me not to touch the thermostat. Frick still hadn't shown me how to run the woodstove, so I covered up in a blanket and blinked at the television, which was on low, and during commercials I listened for Mom or Frick or Paige to see if they stirred, coughed, flicked their lighters.

After a few shows I heard a door open and the bathroom light flick on and the whir of the fan, and I heard pee hit the water hard, splashing down, and I knew it was Frick. He flushed, came out of the bathroom and into the kitchen and plugged the coffeemaker in. He didn't say anything; maybe he didn't see me.

In time, everyone was up, and Mom and Paige were talking about what to make for breakfast while Frick sat at the kitchen table smoking and sipping his coffee. Paige made scrambled eggs and Mom made some sausage, the stuff in a yellow box that cooked in the microwave. She made toast, but we didn't have a toaster so she put it in the oven, and the bread wasn't really crunchy, just stiff and stale.

Mom turned on the dusty gray boom box, inserted her Elton John CD, and played "Tiny Dancer." No one talked about the jar, the bite marks. Frick and I ate and listened to Mom and Paige laugh at each other and sing along, their mouths filled with eggs or a bite of toast, until we all finished eating and listened to the song three times.

"Damn," Mom said, rising, clanking together all of our plates and bringing them to the sink. "Those were some good eggs."

Paige turned in her chair. "You want to know the secret?"

"Love?" Mom sang.

"No, low heat and a stick of butter."

Mom looked at Paige slow, how I imagined the eggs had cooked, and in my mind I stared at the thought I'd been thinking earlier, that this morning had seemed like we all had traveled back in time to the day Paige pulled down the driveway in her tarnished Volkswagen.

Butter! A whole stick of it! I could've sworn my heart fluttered, all that fat, but Mom interrupted it all when she ripped open the fridge, the door swinging and banging, glass-bottled condiments shuttering on the rack. The door swung back and nudged Mom, whose head was in the fridge, her hands pushing aside dollar-store Tupperware covered in tinfoil. "That was our last stick," she said.

I didn't know what was louder: Paige's chuckling, the squeaky noise Frick's toothpick made between his teeth, Mom's loud stomping down the hallway to her room, or my heartbeat.

. . .

In late October, Frick started taking Mom to his camp on some skeejin land twenty miles north. They took me there once, and I didn't have a good time. All Frick and Mom would do was play cribbage and drink wine from a box while I was stuck walking around outside all by myself with a single toy man, Han Solo, whose blaster I had lost. (I couldn't bring my black plastic tub with me; only so much stuff fit in Frick's utility basket.) One afternoon at camp, Frick brought me hunting. He let me use his pump .22, and I enjoyed shooting cans—I felt like Han Solo. But when he brought me out into the woods, he pointed at this small rabbit standing still, this small white creature knowing we were there or knowing it was in the presence of something dangerous, and Frick said, "Go on, before it hops away." I readied the gun, looked down that small thin brown barrel at the white rabbit, but I couldn't pull the trigger.

"Go on, he's gonna run. Do it," Frick said. But I stalled too long and it hopped away. I was relieved until Frick said, "I might as well drop you off at Save 'n Shop, let you go hunt like white people." I never told Mom, but she knew I was upset about something. After that she let me stay home each weekend with Paige while she and Frick went up to camp.

After a few weekends staying home, Paige didn't want to watch me anymore. She said she needed a break. Not from me—maybe I was partly the reason—but from the world. Paige was like that: time and time again she slowly sank into some darkness, and then when it got no brighter she'd pack up and leave as if to chase the sun so it could never set. She always returned, though, and I liked to imagine that she'd gone around the world, never letting the sun dip below the horizon and out of her sight, until she finally made it around the globe and home again and was full of the light she'd chased. Each time she left I worried a little, and I always had this feeling that a time would come when she wouldn't return, that she'd disappear for good. But there was no way she'd leave now: she was pregnant, and so I felt she knew better than to run.

Since Paige didn't want to watch me, and since I didn't want to go to camp, Mom arranged for me to stay with a kid named Jay Pitch (but his parents and teachers and classmates called him JP) at his house. JP was a bit chubby, and when he kept his long black hair tied back he looked chubbier. I was happy about staying with him—we were always shooting hoops at the community center after school, and he had some cool plastic men too.

So most weekends I spent my days at JP's, playing men outside until it got too cold, eating dinner with his mom and dad and brother who was in high school, and at night JP and I would get yelled at by his mom when she heard us up way past twelve o'clock laughing hard at pigadees, or when we told or made up stories about our plastic action figures. JP told me about leaving one out during the summer once, and the sun beat down so hot that it melted his face, and we couldn't stop laughing at that deformed guy, couldn't get his funny-looking face out of our heads late at night while we lay in the dark. I always went to JP's house pretty tired, but come Sunday, when Mom and Frick picked me up, I left awake in a way I didn't when Paige would watch me.

I never told JP the story about the jar or the bite marks— not because I couldn't tell him (no one had told me not to talk about it), but because with him all that mattered was good weather and our action figures. And so I had forgotten all about the jar and the bite marks until one blue, cold Saturday when Mom and Frick picked me up a day early. "Go get your stuff, gwus," Mom said.

No one explained anything. Mom said something like, "I still don't know why he has to be there," and Frick told her, "Because it matters. It concerns him." When we got home, parked the truck in the driveway, Mom hurried inside and Frick and I followed her. She yelled for Paige, but Paige didn't say anything. She was in the living room, sitting on the couch with a blanket over her lap, spacing out, looking at herself and maybe at all of us in the reflection of the black-screen TV as we huddled around her.

"Honey," Mom said, putting her hand on Paige's shoulder. She sounded like she wanted to cry, but Mom never cried.

"Where is it?" Paige looked up at her, and then her eyes flicked to the hallway and to the bathroom. "Okay," Mom said. She turned to me. "David, gwus, go to your room. We'll get you in a bit."

I did, but I didn't want to be in my room. I wanted to help, to be part of it all. Whatever all of it was. On my bed, I set out my black plastic tub, took out a few men. I didn't play with them, just looked at them, waiting for Mom to come get me. The house was quiet, and my thoughts were quiet, too. Muted. I heard Mom and Frick in the bathroom. He was telling her they needed a case, something hard that wouldn't leak.

And then I knew how to be part of it all, how to make it concern me. I grabbed my black plastic tub and dumped all my men out onto my bed. Mom and Frick were in Mom's room, and I opened my bedroom door. Mom heard and hollered for me to get back in my room.

"Here," I said. "Here, Mumma."

Her feet were heavy on the ground and I felt the house shake when she stomped. She had crazy eyes when she came out of her room, but when she saw me holding out to her my black plastic tub her stare softened under her short hair and she smiled.

"Here," I said again. "You can use it. I don't need it."

Frick looked it over, said it was good, and he took it into the bathroom. Mom took my hand, guided me to the living room, and sat me on the couch next to Paige.

Mom grabbed a kitchen chair and brought it next to the couch, sat close to Paige, put her hand on her leg, and I did too, but she looked like she didn't want anyone touching her.

After some time, Frick came out of the bathroom and he carried my black plastic tub, water dripping down its side. He set it down on the floor and went to the bedroom, came back out with his deer-hide bag. "I'm ready," he said to no one, and I got up and Mom got up but Paige stayed sitting.

"Come, doosis," Mom told her. "It has to be done."

Paige got up slow, and the blanket fell off and she was in her underwear. The couch cushions were wet. Mom got her some pants and helped Paige into them.

There wasn't enough room in Frick's truck for all of us, so Frick told me to get in the bed, to lie down and stay down.

I got in but Mom told me to get out. "He ain't riding in the back there. I won't let you put him in there." She meant it.

So we all piled into the truck, Paige in the passenger seat, Mom in the middle holding the plastic tub, and Frick driving with me on his lap. "Keep your head down," he said. He smelled sour like old grape juice filled with snuffed-out cigarette butts, and the safety pin—stabbing through his medicine pouch and through his shirt—poked my back when we hit potholes. Maybe I should have brought mine.

We drove as far north as was possible on the Island, then turned onto a bumpy dirt road toward the riverbank. We got out. It was cold, and the sun was sinking fast behind dark pines across the river. A wind blew off the water and the hairs on my arms stood up. We followed Frick down a path and came out to a little sandy brown beach.

Frick told Mom and me to go find small pieces of dry wood, and I tried hard to find good pieces, but it was getting dark. I found maybe a couple of good pieces, and Mom thanked me in skeejin, and then set them in her big pile. Frick started a fire and knelt in front of it the way he had with the tree out back of our house, his arms to his sides and his face looking up into a bruised sky.

Mom pushed down on my shoulder, had me kneel beside Frick, and then she knelt. I looked at Paige. She stood, and in the glow of red flames from the fire her face was shallow and deep, and it shone like plastic wrap in the light. Frick reached in his deer-hide bag, pulled out his seashell, and poured tobacco into it. He lit it with a stick that he held in the fire. My eyes and nose burned from the smoke.

He smudged himself first, and then Mom. When he smudged me I watched his sweat glisten in the firelight, roll down his forehead over his nose and drip down into the seashell or onto the sandy beach. He finished with me and then smudged Paige, and Mom had to help her, had to lift her arms for her, had to help her lift her feet up. Then Frick set the seashell down and went to his truck.

The fire popped. A beaver slapped its tail somewhere in the river. I heard Mom swallow once, heard her clear her throat.

Frick came back with a shovel and he dug and then he stopped. "We have to take turns," he said. Mom made me shovel next, and it was hard work. Sweat dripped down my nose and it tickled me. I stopped to itch it, and Mom must've thought I was crying, because she took the shovel from me.

"It's okay, gwus. That's good enough." Mom shoveled, and she went at it, jabbing and jabbing the sharp metal tip into the sand, loosening all the hard ground, and then she scooped it up and tossed it into the woods. She didn't stop until that hole was dug.

"She has to do it," Frick said, talking about Paige.

Mom rubbed Paige's back, but Paige didn't say anything, just stared out at the river. Mom rubbed her back, whispered in her ear, hugged her, let go, hugged her again. Soon, Paige moved, looked down at the ground at the black plastic tub at her feet and she bent down and picked it up. She cradled it, brought it to the hole. She knelt. The fire spat yellow. She stayed like that for a long time, holding the tub, whispering to it. Then she spoke aloud. "I can't do it, Mumma. I can't do it." I wanted to rub her back the way Mom did, but when I stepped closer Frick held his hand out to stop me. Mom went to her, told her she had to. Paige set the tub in the hole and looked at Frick. "You're sure it's the right thing to do?"

"It's how I was taught," he told her.

Paige got up and Frick said she could go back to the truck, and I tried to follow her down the dark path, but Mom told me no. "We dug the hole," she said, "and now we fill it." She looked at Frick to make sure.

We were all on the ground and in the cold sand, using our hands to shovel the sand back into the hole and over the tub and when the sand fell it hit the tub, made thumping noises, and eventually the tub was gone, buried four feet under the sand, and I wondered if the river would undo our work when it rose up, ripping away the sand and sucking out my tub, taking it away forever and ever, carrying it downriver before dumping it out into the salty ocean.

GET ME SOME MEDICINE

A November rain battered the window above the kitchen sink, and a damp brown leaf pressed against the glass. Fellis was searching for the deck of cards. I sat at the table, and I slid away the ashtray with Fellis's cigarette smoke coiling into my nose.

Fellis slammed a cupboard shut and brought the cards to the table. "Shuffle these, Dee," he said to me. "I have to take a shit." He went down the hallway and into the bathroom. I shuffled the cards for a long while.

The past two weeks we did nothing but sit and binge-watch TV, and I was getting tired of it. I wanted movement. My neck was achy and stiff, and while I did enjoy having to constantly focus on the television, following along and paying attention, I felt that I was slowly forgetting something I needed to remember. Maybe I didn't need to remember—maybe I wanted to remember.

In August, Fellis had started school at the community college off the reservation. He said he only attended to get a refund check from financial aid, which was distributed around week three. After that, he checked out. Tuition was waived for us skeejins, and so since his mom, Beth—who he's lived with for twenty-six years—made crap teaching at the rez school, Fellis got this nice fat financial aid check that he wasted on Amazon: red-and-black Jordans, sixty—yeah, sixty—pairs of white ankle socks, a smart TV, and an iPhone that he stopped paying for. Now he only used the phone as a flashlight. He dumped the rest of the check on cigarettes, beer, and pot, which I didn't mind.

One night Fellis bought whip-its, and we huffed four boxes each, and I got so lost in fourteen straight that my father's voice spoke to me—he said my name—for the first time in nine years and I gave Fellis the rest of mine, and another night Fellis bought some coke from this skinny skeejin named Meekew, and Fellis bitched about him even though Meekew didn't rip him off. But anyway, all that stuff Fellis bought was a bargain—except the drugs—and since Fellis was a student Amazon gave him a six-month free trial to Prime, and so he never paid shipping.

But that Prime was the culprit in our binge-watching marathon, the reason why I was damn tired of sitting. These past two weeks Fellis and I dumped six, seven hours a day watching *The Sopranos* for free, and we only ever left his mom's house to pick up our methadone take-homes or to get smokes. And so when the series was over and Fellis was ready to start a new one, I said hold up, told him I was tired of sitting and said we should go to the bar, but he suggested we play cards. Something different, I suppose, but it was still sitting.

The toilet flushed. It flushed again. Then once more.

Fellis came out of the bathroom and down the hallway.

"I don't know what's more satisfying," Fellis said. "What I just did in there or that feeling you get when the car behind you also runs the red light."

Fellis went to the cupboard and grabbed the box of spaghetti we used as gambling chips. He shook the box of spaghetti and the uncooked noodles slid onto the kitchen table.

"Let's play with money," I said.

"You don't have any money," Fellis said.

"Loan me twenty bucks. I'll play with that."

"How you going to pay me back when you lose?"

"I'm not going to lose."

"But you always lose," he said.

I had no way to get him the money. I was laid off last summer, had been working tribal maintenance part-time and mowing the graveyard. I was on unemployment for about three weeks, but I forgot to send in the form that showed I was looking for work, and they kicked me off. The only money I'd seen lately came from bringing dead porcupines to Clara over on Birch Hill who paid twenty bucks a stinking carcass. She used their quills in her regalia.

"I'll find a way," I said. "I can do your chores."

"I don't have any chores."

"You got chores," I said. "You just don't do any. Your mom's always asking you to do shit around here. Take the garbage out, wash some dishes, chop some wood."

"She don't ask for any of that," he said. "She knows I'm busy with school and all."

I laughed, and so did Fellis.

"For real," I said. "She asks you to do stuff." I stood and went to the kitchen counter. I grabbed the white envelope with postage and waved it at him. "You remember Beth asking you to put this in the mail this morning before she went to that teacher's conference?"

Fellis stacked his spaghetti. "Fuck you," he said. He went to his room. When he came back he held cash. He always had money somewhere, yet he never said where it came from. I'd asked once, and when he wouldn't tell me I kept joking, kept saying, "I bet you're sick in the head and get disability." He got pissed, started saying shit like, "You're sick in the head, can't even apply for a fucking job, can't even go get an application." It was all a joke, but he got so upset I couldn't stop thinking that maybe he was on disability.

Fellis handed me the money. "If you lose you owe me twenty bucks. Deal the cards."

We played a few hands back and forth, and I was up five dollars. Fellis grabbed the cigarette that was now burned out in the ashtray, and when he relit it the paper flashed giant red. He took two drags and handed it to me, and before we killed the smoke I was up ten. "Hold on," he told me, and he went to his room for two more fives.

When he returned he asked for the cards. "I'm dealing," he said.

"You think I'm cheating?" I said.

"It's just strange you're winning all of a sudden." He cut the deck in fours and shuffled two at a time. When he had two piles, he shuffled them. "I think you stacked them," he said. "That's some shady Meekew shit."

"I ain't cheating," I said. "And would you shut up about him? He didn't rip you off."

"If I'd had a scale I would've known. Top of the bag was filled with too much space."

"It weren't neither," I said. "Deal."

"Bet first."

I bet ten. He matched and then dealt. I looked at the cards. Nothing. I bet like I had something, though. I raised the pot by ten and then discarded one card. Fellis went to his room and got more money.

"He's lucky I didn't go and find him," Fellis said, sitting down.

"He would have kicked your ass," I said. Meekew was skinny, sure, but he was wiry and long. He was a few years younger than us, did well at the university—"Dean's List," the tribal paper wrote—and he sold drugs to help pay his car loan (that was what I thought, but Fellis said Meekew sold drugs because he was a scumbag). Fellis never liked him. He said Meekew preferred white people to his own kind.

"No, he wouldn't have," Fellis said.

I gave a *Yeah, okay* look.

"He wouldn't have," Fellis said. "So shut the fuck up. And you better not have touched these cards while I was in my room."

Fellis snuffed out the cigarette. It smoldered in the ashtray. We bet, and then Fellis dealt one last time. I peeked at my cards. Barely better than nothing.

"Next time I see him I'm going to say something," Fellis said.

"You do that," I told him. "I'll watch you get beat up."

"You fucking would watch, wouldn't you?" he said. "You'd help him up after I beat him all to hell, probably bandage his face and bring him home. Bet."

I bet once more, leaving me with no more money. Fellis matched, leaving him with no more either. Fellis cracked his knuckles and fingers. The pot was at sixty bucks.

"Christ, Beth will be bandaging your face," I said, and I started laughing. "Look at those skinny arms of yours. You ain't beating no one to hell."

"Fuck you, Dee," he said. "Flip your cards over."

"You first, tough guy."

He flipped his cards over. A king, a queen, a jack, a four, and a seven. "Wait," he said. "What?" He searched the bottom of the deck.

I laughed and flipped my cards over. "A pair of twos beats nothing!" I said. I took the money and held out the four fives I owed him.

"I meant to keep these two." He showed me. "Shit! If you weren't talking my face off."

"You lost," I said. "Just like you'd lose to Meekew."

With one sweep of his arm Fellis sent all the cards and spaghetti onto the floor. He snatched the fives from my hand and went to his room.

I picked up the cards and stacked them on the kitchen table. I cleaned up the spaghetti—some rolled under the stove, so I left it there—and I put what I could find back into the box.

Fellis's door was open, his bedroom light bright like day. He sat on his bed, looking at the floor and rubbing the back of his neck as if something had struck him.

I leaned against his dresser. "You know how you can make the money back?" I said.

"I don't want the money back."

"But you know how?"

Fellis stood. "I don't give a shit." He opened his closet.

"We can go hunt porcupines and bring them to Clara."

Fellis said nothing. He grabbed his jacket from the closet floor.

"Where you going?" I said.

"To the bar."

I looked at the clock. "Last call's in an hour."

"Then let's hurry," he said.

My jacket was in the living room, draped over a box filled with old assignments that Beth always kept and filed away, like her young students would one day grow up and come looking for their old tests on fractions.

Fellis brushed past me and opened the front door.

"Hey," I said. "Put that envelope in the mail for your mother."

"Is the mail going to come between now and when we get back from the bar? Let's go."

It was raining. Fellis didn't speak much on the way to Overtown. When we crossed the bridge—the river moving below—and left the reservation, Fellis pointed to Jim's. He bought two packs of Camels and four tall Steel Reserves. I bought a pack of Marlboro Reds and a pint of Smirnoff. It felt good to buy something.

The door jingled shut behind us and rain hit my face. We crossed the street and kept on to the bar. Off in the woods, the river rushed by. But other than that rushing and Fellis's heavy breathing he did when he was mad, the night was quiet and cold and rainy. The roads were black wet. Ahead, a streetlamp flickered orange above a red For Lease sign. I didn't remember what used to be there.

Fellis pulled me by the sleeve off the road and into the woods for a drop-off. We went down to the riverbank, and

Fellis set his plastic bag of tall boys against a tree. The river flowed strong, and the wind sprayed water on our faces.

We went back to the road and shared my pint between us, and when we walked by the red For Lease sign we took a left on Falls Road.

The bar was quiet. Two people stood outside, talking. Inside, the lights were dim like honey. Fellis took his jacket off and hung it over a chair, and I did the same. Four men wearing soaked jackets were playing pool—the green cloth torn in spots—and a couple sat at the bar.

I felt bad Fellis lost the money, so I bought him a drink. "You're welcome," I said.

He sipped.

I was feeling hot—the alcohol set warm in my blood.

Pool balls cracked. The bartender called last round.

"Let's kill these and get one more," Fellis said.

We did, and I bought the next two again.

Pool balls cracked once more, a shot after the game, and the men leaned their sticks against the wall and zipped up their jackets. Two rows of overhead ceiling lights turned on, and the bar brightened like a bulb about ready to blow, and in the newly lit air I noticed that the wood table we sat at was filthy with straw wrappers and peanut shells and two used wet matches and blue gum that stuck to a pepper shaker.

I brought the cold glass to my lips and Fellis smacked me, spilling beer down my chin and shirt. I swore, and Fellis shushed me. He pointed at the four men walking to the door. One scratched at the back of his neck, and in seeing that I realized I was rubbing the back of mine. Next to him stood a fat man in a blue Ecko sweatshirt whose pants hung low, red boxers sticking out like a panting dog's tongue. Behind him another man shook loose a smoke from his pack, and he handed one to the man behind him, the man I recognized.

"He won't even look at us," Fellis said.

"Would you leave him alone?" I said.

"Why do you defend that fucking kid so much?" Fellis said, but before I could say, "Because he's not a dud like us," Fellis stood and yelled to Meekew, who was halfway out the door.

"Doosis," Fellis said. "Duna'gak?"

Meekew looked back, and then gave a nod. He said something to the three men, let the door shut, and then walked over to us.

"Who are those winooches?" Fellis said.

"Some guys from school," Meekew said. "They're cool. We came up to shoot pool."

Fellis finished his beer and he set the frothy glass on the table. "Pound that," he said to me, looking at my glass, and he stood. Fellis led Meekew outside.

But I drank my beer slowly, not wanting to deal with Fellis. With one sip left of my beer, I thought briefly about going out the back door, but from there I wondered where I would go. Not Mom's house—I'd been avoiding there since she left to get better, and I didn't want to hear the voice mails she left on her own machine wondering where I was, when I was going to visit her, and if I could please bring her cigarettes. And there was no way I was going to Tabitha's apartment in Overtown where I'd been staying and trying to pay rent with her. We were over, and she left me and that apartment, which, like Mom's house, I'd been avoiding too.

I wished the bartender would turn the light off until everyone left.

I put my jacket on and went out front. Fellis passed me his cigarette.

"Go do it after," Fellis was saying to him, and Meekew looked up at the dark sky and blew cold breath. "Just walk with us a little ways. Split off at the bridge."

And like that we started moving down the road to the rez. Fellis walked beside Meekew, and I walked sort of behind them, watching. Fellis was talking, asking him about the coke. Where he gets it from. How much he pays. How much he makes. Meekew didn't say who he got the coke from, but he told Fellis how much he ended up with in the end, and Fellis whistled.

"You think about expanding?" Fellis said.

"Nah, man," Meekew said. "This is temporary until med school."

Over his shoulder, Fellis gave me a can-you-believe-this-Indian look.

We passed under the orange light and then by the red For Lease sign. Fellis stopped walking.

"Doctor Meekew," Fellis said. "Let's go down here. The woods are holding my beer."

"I got to get going," Meekew said. "I have three tests tomorrow."

"I want to buy some of that medicine," Fellis said. "It'll only take a minute."

"Fellis," I said. "Didn't you hear him?"

"One minute," Fellis said. "Just one minute."

The riverbank was dark. Fellis took out his iPhone and turned the flashlight on and looked for the bag. He pulled out a tall boy and cracked it open and offered it to Meekew, who said he was all set.

"Don't say I didn't offer," Fellis said. He then tried to give it to me, but I flashed him my pint and then took a small burning swig.

Fellis drank the tall boy and then he shone the phone's light in Meekew's face. He squinted, and like the squirrel he was named after, Meekew had no indent between the bridge of his nose up to his brow.

"Let me get a gram," Fellis said. "Sixty, right?"

"I'm not selling grams right now," Meekew said. "Only balls. You were the last person I sold grams to."

Fellis set his beer against a tree. "Is that why the bag was a little light?" he said.

I pulled from the pint.

"What are you saying?" Meekew said.

"I bet you don't rip white boys off," Fellis said.

Meekew waved a hand and turned to leave.

"I'm messing with you," Fellis said, and I started laughing. Fellis was full of shit.

"Find me another time," Meekew said.

"Just wait," Fellis said. He reached into his pocket and took out his money. "Dee, front me some cash."

"I'm out," I said. "Spent the rest on your beers."

Fellis counted what he had. Meekew waited between two crooked pines. "Here," Fellis said. "I got seventy-one. I have more at my place and I can get it to you tomorrow."

"I don't sell that way," Meekew said. "You know that."

Fellis stepped toward him. "Take it," he said. He stuffed the money into Meekew's pockets, and when Meekew took it out Fellis wouldn't take it back. I sipped the Smirnoff.

"Here," Meekew said.

Fellis backed up. "No."

Meekew threw the bills in Fellis's face, and Fellis jumped forward and grabbed him by the arms. Back and forth, their bodies rocked and smacked together. Punches flew one after the other. Fellis fell down and picked up a stick and swung, but Meekew dodged and rammed his shoulder into Fellis's stomach and lifted him into the air and slammed him down so hard that all the air in Fellis shot out. Meekew turned to leave, but Fellis wasn't done. He kicked Meekew's knees and he buckled. Fellis was tired—his punches were slow and had no power. Meekew wasn't, and with great ease he grabbed Fellis, turned him around, and held him in a headlock.

I was about ready to step in, but I wanted to see Fellis get his ass kicked. Fellis's phone had landed in the mud, but the light pointed away and shined on the wet trees so it was difficult to make him out. I could see that Fellis was on his knees, hands trying to peel Meekew's forearm from his throat. Meekew stood strong behind him, and he kept squeezing. Fellis was talking shit—"fucking white boy, fucking punk"—so he must have had his chin tucked down good, preventing a sleeper.

I was laughing, sipping my pint. In the semi-dark, Meekew pulled his fist back and drove hammer-handed into Fellis's thigh. Fellis let out a horrendous, high-pitched scream that muffled the rushing river.

"He's stabbing me, Dee!" Fellis yelled. "Dee, he's stabbing me!"

I moved quick. I grabbed the plastic bag of Steel Reserves and swung it over my head and brought the three heavy cans down on top of Meekew's skull. Fellis broke loose and stepped back. Meekew dropped and fell forward, his face plopping into the mud. He rolled onto his back and held his head.

"Where's the knife?" I said. Fellis stood and then stooped, and he picked up leaves and sticks and mud and tossed it all over Meekew.

"Fellis!" I yelled. "Where's the knife!"

Fellis kicked the ground over Meekew, adding to the great heap of earth already covering him. With one hand I grabbed Fellis's arm and pulled him with me through the woods and in the other I gripped the plastic bag. On the road, we ran—Fellis behind me—and we hurried over the bridge and onto the reservation—slanting rain pelting our faces—and we kept going past the church and food pantry and around the small pond—streetlights on the far side casting light over the water and showing the thousands of raindrops plunking the surface and giving the illusion of a boiling pot of water—and when we saw the rusting community building bulging in the dark we turned away from it and slinked into the woods and followed the watery path to Fellis's road. It was on that road that the rain turned to mist.

We walked slow, out of breath. The bag was ripped, and the beers were gone.

Inside his house, we sat at the kitchen table.

"Let me see where he got you," I said, and Fellis started laughing.

"I got you," Fellis said. "Nice to know you got my back if someone's got a knife."

I got up quick and Fellis flinched. "What's the matter?" he said.

I threw the plastic bag away.

"What if he's dead?" I said.

"They're cans," Fellis said. "He probably woke up and went home. Fucking apple."

"We shouldn't have left him there," I said. "We shouldn't have."

"Well, I ain't fucking walking all the way back there. He's fine, Dee. Quit worrying. You hit the boy with some cans. What's the worst that can happen?"

I felt sick. I leaned against the sink, and on the window rain droplets raced down. I turned the water on and rubbed my face wet and let it stay wet. My head hurt. The pint on the table didn't even look good. Fellis's room up the hall looked close.

He asked what I was doing and I told him I was tired.

I spread blankets on the floor and undressed down to my boxers. Fellis came in, flicked off the light, and sat on his bed, his back against the wall and his gums flapping with talk. The room spun, and since I was on the ground I couldn't do that trick where you put one foot flat on the floor to steady yourself, steady the rotation of the earth. Fellis was talking, going on about his phone he'd left by the river. "I should have bought that waterproof case," he said. "It was on sale too."

I burped and gagged.

"You want a wastebasket?" Fellis said. He got up from the bed.

Again, I burped and gagged.

"Yeah," he said. "Let me get you a wastebasket."

. . .

I woke up to the sounds of Beth's cooking—the sizzling of a pan and the opening of the fridge. The red-lit clock read eight, and I sat up. Fellis was asleep on the floor, about an arm's reach away. The wastebasket was at my side. It was empty. I threw the blankets off me and dressed. The bottoms of my jeans were damp and cold and muddy. I dug around the floor for my lockbox that held my methadone. It was under a pile of dirty clothes. I opened it and took out my last bottle of that pink drink and sipped it slow like coffee.

I crossed the hall to the bathroom and I glanced at Beth in the kitchen. She was bent over and picking something off the floor.

In the bathroom, I peed and washed my face. I scrubbed my hands with soap three times. I turned the shower on but didn't shower. Sitting on the toilet, hands in my face, I said out loud, "That motherfucker better be alive."

The hallway floor creaked and creaked. A door opened and closed. Silence. I flushed the toilet and went out into the hall. Beth had gone into her room. In the kitchen, bacon spat in a hot skillet and eggs fried in another. The kitchen smelled of pepper and grease. I put on my jacket and laced my shoes. Fellis's Jordans were caked in mud.

The sun was hot gold in a cool sky. I hurried, cutting through the woods—I saw one beer from the ripped bag, but left it. I passed the community building and pond and food pantry and church. Father Tim was opening the double doors and I didn't say "Father," just passed by him and walked to the bridge, and halfway over I glanced back and saw no Father. A wind had blown shut the church doors he had opened.

I walked slow to where he'd been left, and I made sure no cars were coming when I dipped into the woods. I kept my head down, watching the ground, not wanting to know. Finally, I had to look. Meekew was gone, but an imprint of where he'd been remained in the mud next to the river, and the great heap of earth Fellis had covered him with was scattered about. I wondered how long it would stay that way.

In the mud was Fellis's iPhone. I picked it up. It was wet. The screen was smeared, and I tried to turn it on but it was dead. I thought about skipping it like a rock over the river, but then I'd have to tell Fellis that I didn't find it, and he'd be convinced that Meekew took it.

Halfway back to Fellis's house I was feeling sick again. I made it to his road, and up a ways something brown waddled over the sidewalk and into the woods. Money. I crossed the street and then ran after the porcupine, split through dense pine trees, and as I chased it, following its sound of crunching leaves, I had to stop and crouch down and puke. I spat. My head throbbed, and when I stood and wiped my mouth on my sleeve I heard nothing but a dull ringing in my ears.

Back at Fellis's, Beth was washing dishes. Fellis sat at the kitchen table, his hair pressed to one side, talking with his mouth full.

Beth looked at me as if she wanted to know where I'd gone, but instead she said, "You forgot to shut off the shower."

I stepped toward the hallway and bathroom.

"It's off now," she said. "Sit. I made you a plate. There's more toast too if you want it."

I thanked her—either for turning off the shower or for the food, I wasn't sure which—and I grabbed the plate and sat.

Beth got a broom from the pantry closet. She hit at Fellis's legs for him to move. She swept under the table.

"Why is there spaghetti everywhere?" she said.

Fellis took a sip of pink juice. He stood and demonstrated with a dirty rag. "Dee was holding the box last night—you know, to make a snack—and he got a big leg cramp and he goes, 'UGH!' and he threw the box up into the air."

Beth laughed. "You're ridiculous."

She leaned the broom against the wall and picked up the rag. She lobbed it onto the counter. Over the garbage she turned the broom pan, and spaghetti and dirt scattered.

I was chewing a bite of egg, laughing still, when Beth said, "What is this?"

She reached into the garbage and pulled out an envelope.

"Didn't I ask you to mail this?" she said.

"I forgot," Fellis said. He kept eating.

"Why is it in the garbage?"

"It must've fell in."

Fellis stood and grabbed more bacon from a white plate next to the stove.

Beth stared at him as he sat back at the table.

I got up and asked for the envelope. "I'll go put it in the mail," I said, but Beth wouldn't look at me.

"You want to get charged for your tuition?" Beth said. "If they don't know you're Native they'll process you like a white person."

"I ain't white." Fellis wiped his greasy mouth with his shirt.

"I'm surprised they haven't already charged you," Beth said. "You were supposed to have given the form to the school months ago."

"Beth," I said. "Let me see it. I'll go put it in the mail."

"I ain't white," Fellis said. "So they better not."

"No," Beth said to me. "You sit and eat. Fellis will do it."

"Dee said he'll do it."

"Put this in the mail!"

Fellis stood and snatched the envelope from his mother. He brought it to the trash and stuffed it down with the spaghetti and dirt and eggshells and bacon fat.

"I quit school," he said, and he sat back at the table.

"Quit?" Beth said.

"What did you expect?" he said. "I didn't know what I was doing there. I didn't even want to go. I did it to stop your nagging."

"You didn't even try," Beth said.

"For fuck's sake," Fellis said. "I didn't belong there. For two fucking weeks I sat in that philosophy class with that short fuckwit of a professor—who all he did was sit in a chair in front of the class swishing cough drop after cough drop around in his mouth—and I tried to pay attention but when I realized I'd spent two weeks—two fucking weeks!—thinking we were talking about that clothing brand—what's it called," he snapped his fingers, "—Aeropostale, yeah, that's it—but we were actually talking about some guy named Aristotle, I knew I was screwed. So I bolted midclass. Even left my books."

We were quiet. My eggs were cold.

"And my notebook, too," Fellis said. "The one Aunt Alice bought me."

I wanted to feel bad for Fellis. Really, I did—he'd never told me that was what happened. Why would he? He'd made it out to be all about the money. But seeing how bad he treated Beth lit my temper and got me burning.

Beth picked up Fellis's napkin and threw it away. She left the envelope in the garbage. She turned to say something but didn't. Down the hallway, I expected her to slam her door, but she let it close with a gentle click.

Fellis rose and stood at the sink. "What did she expect?" he said, eating a strip of bacon. "She did all my homework for me throughout high school. Fucking bitch."

I brought my plate to the sink. My hands shook and the fork on the plate rattled. I rinsed the plate and slid it under a dirty bowl. There was one piece of bacon left and I wanted to eat it, wanted to chew on it and release a primal rage, but Fellis took it before I could and he stuffed it into his mouth.

He smiled at me and I broke his fucking nose.

. . .

For four days—the air cold and moist and the sky continuously pale, the feeling of the first snow coming—I searched for porcupines along the sides of the rez roads. I'd not spoken to Fellis, and so each day I was on my own, hunting porcupine, searching the woods (one day was wasted on the bus route up to the methadone clinic). But on those days I was out looking I found nothing. Porcupines—dead or alive—were not easy to find. At night, tired of searching, I slept in the boiler room out back of Mom's house. I went inside only to get food or to use the bathroom or to change my clothes. The phone on the kitchen table blinked red, but I never checked it, and I never heard the phone ring. The house was clean: the dishes were put away, the floors were swept except for what I dragged in, and the place smelled as if it had been aired out, the way houses do when nobody's been using them.

Early each morning, right as the sun was coming up, I set off to look for porcupines to make some money. My body hurt from sleeping on the hard concrete in the boiler room, and as each day passed my bones felt closer to breaking. By the fourth morning—it was about 3:30 AM—I got up, went inside, and unplugged the phone. I slept on the couch, and when I woke up it was noon. The first thing that came to mind were the Steel Reserves. I said, Fuck that porcupine, told myself I wasn't going to find it, and I switched my attention to those missing beers.

That afternoon I only found one, and the can was dented and smeared with dirt. I kept on through the woods, picking up kindling and cradling it, and I came to the river. It was high and scraped the bank as it flowed by. Under the darkening sky, the river looked black.

I found a little patch of ground with no vegetation growing—hard, chilled soil and rocks—and settled onto it and built a small fire. I chugged the Steel Reserve to rush the buzz. The river flowed like a sound machine and I spaced out, watching the cold ground. Like looking at the stars, there were various rocks stuck in the mud that seemed to outline a figure. Once I saw it, I couldn't unsee it, and it got me remembering a story my mother told me.

It was after the tribe had forced my father to leave. I was no more than ten, eleven—he'd come up, had driven ten hours to take me for the summer. Mom wouldn't let him, kept saying, "That's what you get when the money's late!" I remembered it: the police charging in and dragging him away from the bedroom door—"I have rights to my son!"—behind which my mother had barricaded us. It wouldn't have come to that if we'd gone to camp with her boyfriend—or if her boyfriend had been around—but that was how it ended up. She'd covered me with a blanket and had hidden me in the closet among her upside-down shoes and snapped plastic hangers.

She'd told me the story after all that, after he'd been banned and visited me through the phone for some time.

The story was about the stone people. I remembered standing on a chair that had been pulled to the sink. Mom washed dishes, and I dried them. She made conveyer-belt noises as she passed me a dish. At some point—perhaps when the noises grew less funny—she told me about Gluskabe, the man from nothing. I never understood—and I still didn't—how Gluskabe was from nothing since Kci-niwesk—the Great Being—had created him.

He'd come from somewhere, I said to my mother, and she laughed. "Honey," she said, maybe passing me a plate or a spoon to dry, "men are so self-absorbed and so proud they would like to think they created themselves."

Before Gluskabe got us right, or close to being right, my mother said, before he shot an arrow into an ash tree and split it in half and out poured us into first light—the people of the dawn—he made beings out of rocks. For a time, he walked among them and tried to teach them. But they were cold stone, aggregates of minerals, and when they walked, their joints of quartzite sparked and created fire that caught the dry grass and spread to the oak ferns and then to the shagbark hickory and birch bark and oaks until the world was half burning. One stone man pointed to the sky—to the sun—and then he pointed back to the earth as if predicting.

The stone people couldn't feel the heat, couldn't feel pain, and so Gluskabe accepted he'd failed. One by one, he set out to smash them, to destroy them, to start over. But some of them ran off to the mountains and hid. Occasionally, my mother said, the stone people come out and walk among us.

. . .

The fire was out, and I felt embarrassed for having remembered such a story. I stood and brushed the back of my jeans off and stretched. I grabbed the beer I'd chugged and took a sip of an eyedropper's worth of booze from the bottom and then chucked the can into the woods. After stepping on the fire and making sure it was out, I started for the boiler room, even though I was thinking about the couch.

It was dark, but I found the path and followed it. Every few feet, I tripped over large roots or jutting rocks. The path forked, and I went to take the left so I'd come up behind home, but I heard footsteps down the other way, heard branches snapping and the sound of rummaging. I went right.

It was way darker down that path, as if all the trees were pressed too close and the bare stripped branches too tightly tangled together so as not to permit any light, even from the moon, which was up above behind the clouds that periodically broke away to light the place in a blue hue. I walked slow on the bumpy dark path toward what sounded like someone cursing.

He was nothing more than a standing shadow, swinging a stick back and forth in the air at a tree.

"Meekew?" I said.

The shadow jumped and dropped the stick. He bent down and picked it up.

"No, you fucking idiot," Fellis said. "Get a stick and help me."

I asked what for, but he didn't answer me. I kicked around the ground for a stick. Three times I thought I found a good one, but they were each short and wet and brittle.

"There's no good sticks," I said.

"Christ," Fellis said. "Use mine."

He handed it to me, got close to me, and in the dark I could not see his face but something else.

"Fellis," I said. "I'm sorry about your—"

"Don't worry about it, Dee," he said. "Don't worry about it. Just swing that stick."

"Swing it at what?" I said.

"Look up in the tree."

I looked.

"You looking?"

"Yeah, I'm looking."

"What do you see?"

I looked hard. The moon came out and shone but not enough to see anything but blurs of branches. "Nothing," I said.

Fellis rustled around the ground for a stick. Finally, he found a long one—at least fifteen feet—and when he turned holding it I had to back up out of the way.

"Watch this," he said. He hoisted the stick above him and pointed it right up in the tree. He sent it flying, and it crashed through the branches until gravity pulled it back down. Debris fell over us, and the stick whacked the back of my neck.

We looked up, and I finally saw the prickly animal sitting on the highest branch. It looked down at us, terrified.

"Did I hit it?" Fellis said.

I told him no, that it was there staring at us.

In the dark, Fellis leaned against an oak.

"We can wait for it to come down," I said. "What else do we have to do?"

Fellis lit a smoke, and in the lighter's flame I saw his swollen, puffy nose, saw the corners of each eye filled with a dense, thick red. He took two deep, deep drags, and with each inhale the orange glow grew brighter. He handed me the cigarette and set to making a fire. When it was blazing, I pitched the butt into the flames and sat next to Fellis.

"You want to bet how long it takes for him to come down?" I said, and Fellis laughed.

"No," Fellis said. He took out from his jacket pocket an opened bag of something. He reached in it and took whatever was in there and then he handed the bag to me, and against the fire's light I saw it was that thick foggy plastic filled with a stack of saltine crackers.

A can opened. Fellis slurped and handed me some of the other Steel Reserve.

"Why not?" I said. "You afraid you'll lose again?" I took a sip and passed the can back to him.

"It's not that," he said. "I'm afraid that neither of us would win." He tossed a stick at the tree. "I have a feeling that fucker ain't coming down."

FOOD FOR THE COMMON COLD

The snowy graveyard looked to be burning. Gray branches swayed like smoke against dark pines. The farther I got down the hard dirt path, the more I wanted the smoke to be real, wanted to see the place engulfed in flames, so the matter between Mom and Frick would be settled.

They'd been going at it when I left in the late afternoon. Well, they'd been going at it for five years, but that afternoon they fought about the headstone. Frick had said the graveyard needed to go, that the one and only headstone needed to be ripped out and smashed, that we needed to bring back the old way.

"What old way?" Mom had said, and Frick tried to remember, or tried to summon some answer that sounded good, but he'd been drinking too much. He was a medicine man who had been forgetting to pray in the mornings and at night, forgetting to feed the spirits once a month. "That headstone will stay forever," Mom said, and Frick looked at me, then at Mom.

"I wonder what will stay longer," Frick said. "Me or that headstone."

That was what made Mom run to the bathroom and cry privately. That was what made Frick get another drink. And the whole thing was what made me grab the slingshot my father had sent up for my eleventh birthday—the slingshot Frick hated and called the "little white-boy toy"—and go on down to the graveyard to shoot at the headstone, as if all our problems weren't buried cold below but were actually right there on the surface, facing us all.

The headstone was a solid mass of black granite, no engravings. It was rounded at the top like a little door, and it leaned a bit to the left, not unlike the door to our house, whose foundation had shifted over the years. For a while, I fired at that crooked headstone, the slingshot's rubber pull cracking in the cold, and I worried I'd snap it, but I had to let those balls fly. I missed maybe ten times before I found my groove and couldn't miss, kept blasting one after the other until the metal balls were gone. I tried to find them in the snow around the headstone, but they were buried. The stone had not one dent.

I made my way back home, and our house's chimney smoke coiled into the sky.

Inside, Frick was still sitting at the kitchen table, face hard, his hand wrapped around the same cup of wine he'd been drinking when I left. He stared up the hallway at Mom, who came out of her bedroom—or maybe he had been staring up that straight hallway, and he seemed to look at her only because there she was, eyes bloodshot, swollen. Mom went to the kitchen sink and started on the dishes, a few of which we'd eaten pasta and eggs off of last week.

"What's for dinner?" I said, hoping the answer could put us back together for just a moment.

But before Mom could speak, Frick said, "Whatever you killed with that slingshot."

He wouldn't look at me and stayed staring at Mom. I remember wanting to say it was just a graveyard, a headstone, but I felt it was more than that.

Frick looked over his shoulder at me, looked at my empty hands. "Not even a chipmunk?" When he laughed his double chin popped out, revealing his wine-red teeth.

"Leave him be," Mom said.

A chipmunk diet would be good for you, I thought, and right as the thought smoked out of my brain, Frick rose in a way that made Mom and me look at him, like he was about to take the slingshot from my hands and throw it away or commit a darker, unforgettable thing.

His hair was unbraided, the way it always was when he drank in the early morning. "I'm going to check on camp," he said.

Mom didn't say anything while he laced up his boots. I turned on the TV in the living room. I didn't hear the back door close but I heard his truck start and groan. For a while, I heard the sink still running, and Frick's truck was still grumbling in place in the driveway. I wondered why he hadn't left yet, and so I looked through the living room window at the truck. Mom was standing at the driver's-side window, looking sorry. Over my shoulder, in the kitchen, drops of water dotted the linoleum from the sink to the open back door.

Finally, with Mom hanging from the window, Frick backed the truck up and yanked her along with him until Mom let go and fell to the ground. On her knees, she was crying and watching him as he put the truck in drive and pulled away.

For as long as she stayed on the ground I stayed at the window and watched. Two cars drove by, and each time the driver gave my mother a passing glance. When she finally got up, she wiped her hands on her jeans and then wiped her eyes, and she came down the driveway. She must have seen me there watching her from the window, but she acted as if she didn't, and when she came into the house she went right back to the sink without a word or a sniffle.

Mom finished the dishes and then she cooked. Moose meat, peas, and boxed couscous. When the food steamed from the sideboard, Mom made herself a plate and set it next to the microwave for later. She still didn't say one word, and it looked like she still had tears buried somewhere in her.

At the kitchen table, I blew on my hot food, but I hoped it'd stay hot forever because I wasn't hungry. I turned in the chair and looked at Mom wiping down the sideboards.

"Mumma?" I said. She didn't look at me, and I recall needing her to look at me.

"Mumma?" I said again.

"What, gwus?" She sprayed the counter with cleaning solution.

Ever since I'd met Frick, since he'd moved in those five years back, I always felt his anger or passive-aggressiveness was due to my existence. And while I could often combat that feeling with Mom's happiness, with her cooing over me or her comforting reassurance about whatever childlike anxiety I had about some issue, some worry, her distance that day left me too alone. But if I had known that that was growing up, I wouldn't have asked: "Is he mad at me?"

Mom's reaction didn't settle me. She burst out crying again and didn't try to hide it. The last time Mom cried twice in one day was when my sister lost her child. No, she cried twice in one day too when my sister lost another one and up and left, leaving behind only a note that read she'd lost something and that she was off to find it.

I stood, nauseated. I asked her what I had done.

She came over and sat me back down with wet hands. "You didn't do anything. Just eat."

That she looked at me was enough to calm me. Still, I wasn't hungry, at least not for food. Mom finished the sideboards and went to her bedroom. When her door clicked shut, I took my food, covered it, and set it next to the microwave by Mom's.

I fell asleep on the couch with the TV on mute, and I woke up in my bed. It was around dawn, and a pale-pink light glowed outside, lighting my bedroom. Hushed voices came down the hallway from the kitchen.

"You're going to have to tell him, doos," the voice said. It was Grammy.

"He'll leave if I tell him," Mom said.

"Good," Grammy said. "He's no good."

"He is good. Recently he's been not good."

He was good at one time, but Mom was right: Frick had gotten meaner ever since he stopped being a part-time medicine man and started drinking full-time.

Grammy coughed. "You're going to have to tell him," she said. "When he comes back, you say it. You can't have children. And then you go from there."

Children?

"Miracles can happen," Mom said. "But I don't want to risk what happened before."

"Doos," Grammy said. "You can't have children. Face it. You tell him that, and that's the end of the discussion."

"He'll leave," Mom said. "He will."

"Are you forgetting you have a son?" Grammy said. "And a daughter?"

"A daughter," Mom said. "I almost forgot."

"She's still grieving," Grammy said. "And she's her own person. A grown woman. She can go and do as she pleases."

Mom said nothing to that first part. "She is a grown woman," Mom said. "Frick wants us to have our own."

"Michigun," Grammy said. "He wants a dark baby all for himself. That's what those western Natives always want—dark babies. Pass me that ashtray."

Mom didn't say anything.

"Go ahead," Grammy said. "Don't believe me."

A chair squeaked against the floor.

"I told you what I can," Grammy said. "You have to figure the rest out."

"You're not staying?" Mom said.

"I have to go to church," Grammy said. The back door opened. "Doosis," Grammy said. "Something smells funny in here."

"It's probably that garbage," Mom said.

"No, no," Grammy said. "It smells fishy."

"I don't smell anything like that," Mom said.

I took a whiff in my room, and I agreed—I didn't smell anything.

"I don't know, then," Grammy said, and as she left she repeated to Mom that she should tell Frick, and when Mom thought she was all alone she said it again: "I don't want to risk it."

Risk what? Children? Is that why Frick didn't seem to like me, because I wasn't his?

I got out of bed. From the hallway I watched Mom at the kitchen table sipping coffee. I went to the bathroom, and when I came out to the kitchen, all that remained at the table was the rest of the coffee and a freshly snubbed-out cigarette that glowed red in the ashtray.

I knocked on her bedroom door.

"I'm sick," Mom said. "Go watch TV."

I turned the TV on, but didn't watch it. I picked up the phone and dialed Dad's number.

It rang once and only once and he answered right away, eager to talk to me like always with his "Hey, buddy!" and I didn't even let him say his "How's my buddy today?" before I asked him why Mom didn't want to risk having another baby, why Grammy said Mom couldn't.

"What?" he said.

"Why can't she?" I said.

"Put your mother on the phone," Dad said.

I looked up the hallway to Mom's room, and her door opened.

"Who are you talking to?" Mom said.

"Dad," I said.

"Is that your mother?" Dad said. "Put her on."

"Hang that phone up and come here," Mom said.

"Let me talk to her, David," Dad said.

I hung up.

Mom came down the hallway. "What did you ask him?"

"Why you can't have babies," I said.

"That's none of your business," Mom said. "That's nobody's business but my own."

I took the phone and slammed it down on the table three times and yelled that it was my business, that if Frick wants his own but if there is only me then he's going to keep hating me and you and this place. "No one's ever going to be happy," I said.

The refrigerator clicked on, growling, and the kitchen light buzzed. The phone rang. Mom answered it and immediately hung it up.

Mom's knees cracked when she sat on the floor, and she pulled me shaking onto her lap.

"We'll all be happy," she said. "Every single one of us."

I looked at her, but she turned away from me and stared at the back door. And so did I. From the angle I was at in my mother's arms the door looked straight, like no foundation had shifted over the years, and I believed her—that I'd be happy, that she'd be happy, that Dad would be happy, that even Frick would be happy—and that I believed all that made it feel attainable, even if it was only for those brief minutes in my mother's arms before she stood me up and I saw dead on that our door was crooked.

. . .

Since the day Frick left, Mom hadn't cried once. She ate dinner every night with me at the kitchen table, and two nights in a row she dug out Monopoly, which we didn't play properly and instead took wads of colored money and walked around the house pretending we were at Tiffany & Co.

A week went by, a week in which happiness seemed to course through our veins like blood, but since then I've come to think that it wasn't happiness but instead numbness. At least for Mom. On a Thursday, I came home from school and Mom wasn't home. And she wasn't home when night dripped over, and so I heated up leftover rice and chicken and stared at the mess of food on the plate until midnight. When Mom didn't come home, I set the food in the fridge and I stayed up all night, waiting, sometimes sitting in the living room, sometimes going outdoors and sitting on the cold concrete steps.

By the time the sun came up, I felt like I had to get ready, had to start the day, had to go on. I showered, dressed, ate cornflakes, brushed my teeth, but when the school bus stopped in front of the house, I stood at the back door, hand on the knob, not able to go, not able to pull open the crooked door, and eventually the bus pulled away, its white fumes thick in the cold air.

After the bus was gone, I opened the door, heading to the only place I thought had answers: the maintenance garage where Frick worked part-time for the tribe. I knew he'd be there. During the cold months, he was paid to sit around in the maintenance garage and sip water from the water cooler. His duties during the warm months were to mow the tribal buildings' lawns and weed-whack the tall grasses growing around all the chain-link fences surrounding the Island school and the graveyards. But it was the end of winter, and so he had nothing to do but shoot the shit with the guys in the garage and wait for the snow to melt.

I sprinted the whole way there and only slowed when the garage came into view, men sitting in metal fold-out chairs away from where ice dripped water from the garage's roof, each sipping coffee or water or something else in little cups. They all looked at me when I got close, and then one of them yelled to Frick.

"Your boy's here," a man said.

I didn't go any closer, not wanting to talk to anyone but Frick, and when Frick came out he stayed back like he didn't want to talk to me.

"Why ain't you in school?" he said.

"Mom's gone," I said. "Since yesterday she's been gone. I don't know what to do."

He looked at me and then at the ground, then looked behind him at the garage, at all the men who had gone back to talking and sipping their drinks.

"Come on," he said, and he started for his truck.

He didn't say anything, just started driving, and I thought he was taking me to school but we drove right past the long tan-brick building and red playgrounds. He wasn't driving fast—Frick never did, was always so careful on the road—and at each street he slowed, looking, and finally I realized he wasn't taking me anywhere. He was looking for my mother, and I got this feeling that he felt bad for something.

We checked every road on the Island, and then Frick parked his truck on the bridge to Overtown, the river flowing under us, carrying ice sheets toward the dam. Even in the warm truck I was cold.

We stayed on the bridge until lunch, and we didn't speak one word to each other until my stomach rumbled.

"Let's go eat," he said, and then he put the truck in drive and drove over the bridge. He took a right—there was nothing to the right except camp, so that was where we were going. I hadn't been there since I was nine, since the time Frick had finally made me put a bullet in a rabbit's head that hadn't even turned fully white, this little thing in between changes, in between something larger than simple molting, simple brown to white.

The way to his camp used to be a path that we had to walk, leaving our vehicles a mile behind, but Frick had had the way cleared, wide enough for his truck, and like all camp roads, the one to Frick's was bumpy, jagged, the dirt solidified like a rough sea frozen. The road was straight, but then it curved, and once the curve was turned, the road went straight again, and another curve popped up—there was a never-ending feeling to the road, like the ocean. And the road only ever ended when the camp—unfinished, a blue plastic bucket upside down to step on to get through the yard-high door, the inside walls pink cotton-candy insulation—appeared unexpectedly, and stood wrapped by pine trees.

The chimney bellowed out clouds that disappeared among the tall oaks and pines. Parked next to the camp was Mom's white Toyota.

"Found her," Frick said, and when he parked his truck he rubbed his eyes. "Shit," he said.

When I got out of the truck, so did Frick. He put his hands on his waist, waiting. The camp door opened, and Mom looked at Frick.

She held square Kodak pictures. "What are these?"

"None of your business," Frick said. "Put them back, take your son, and go."

Mom stepped down on the blue bucket and then onto the ground. "Who is this?" Mom said. She pointed at the picture. It was a girl, no older than I was. A shawl was draped over her shoulders. She was dancing.

Frick stepped closer to Mom, grabbed her wrist, and twisted.

I yelled louder than Mom, and then I ran full force to try and shove Frick, but he used my momentum and pulled me past him so I flew onto the ground.

Mom got up, and then got me up. She pulled me to the car.

Frick picked the pictures up off the ground, wiped them, and then stepped up onto the bucket and went into the camp.

"It's my daughter," Frick said, and he shut the camp door.

. . .

Mom drove fast over the bumpy dirt road.

"I'm sorry I left you," she said.

"It's okay," I said, even though it wasn't. "Where'd you go?"

Mom was silent, which meant she didn't want me to know.

"He helped me look for you," I said. "I didn't know where else to go, so I went to the garage. He helped me look for you."

"Nice of him," Mom said. She drove with her knee and rubbed her wrist.

When we finally got to the end of the camp road, Mom pulled a U-turn on Route 1 and pulled back onto the road we'd just left. "He's going to talk," Mom said, not to me, not to anybody. "Yeah, he's going to talk."

Mom parked behind Frick's truck. She told me to stay. She balanced on the blue bucket while she shimmied her food stamp card in between the latch and doorframe, and when the door swung open Frick was right there and he pulled her in. But there was no noise. Neither screamed or yelled. I rolled down the window, the cool creeping in, and I tried to listen for their fighting. Nothing, so I got out of the car and sat on the hood. The faint smell of rotting guts rolled out from the small shed where Frick skinned his kills. I turned away, and no noise came from the camp. Nothing was banging, rattling, smashing in the way Mom sometimes got. And Frick wasn't saying his, "Come on, now! Come on!" There was none of that. Crows cawed somewhere off in the trees. The little stream down past the camp dripped by. The hood under which I sat dinged. The immense quiet was uncomfortable, and I wished that they would yell, or that something would crash.

Frick opened the camp door. "Go," he said. "Just go."

Mom had one foot on the bucket and the other still in the camp. "I didn't know that," she said. "Frick, I didn't know that."

"Now you do," he said.

"You can talk to me," Mom said. "You can talk to me."

"Talk to you about what?"

"I know what that loss is like," she said.

"No, you don't," Frick said, and he pushed the door shut but Mom pushed back.

"Goddamn it," she said.

The door stayed open between them.

"I do know what it feels like," she said. "Like the whole world is warped, like something is off balance that will never be balanced again. And guess what? It won't ever be balanced again. Every morning's deformed, the day so close to spinning out of control, but you have to find your footing, your own balance."

"Well maybe you're throwing off my balance," he said. "You ever think of that?"

"Listen," she said. "You need to understand I can't give you what you want. And even if I could, it wouldn't fix anything. I know that."

Mom looked at me and then at Frick.

"Why can't you?" Frick said. "I want to know."

Mom stepped off the bucket. "You want to know?" she said. "You really, really want to know?" She started for the car. "Come on," she said. "I'll show you why."

And Frick started to follow, stepped down off the blue bucket and onto the ground. I was at the car door, opening it, and then Frick stood still.

"He's hungry," Frick said, nodding at me.

"I can wait," I said. I remember feeling ourselves closing in on something, something important, some unnamable thing that like a jointer could straighten the boards upon which we walked.

But Frick insisted, and I felt he pulled us away from it. He already turned back to the camp door, stepped up on the bucket, and pulled himself up.

"He has to eat," he said. He stood in the camp by the door, waiting for us to follow, and when we did—Mom first and then me—he closed the door.

Frick boiled fiddleheads and sautéed salted pork on the gas stove, and while the fat sizzled and the water gurgled and the window screen next to the table where Mom and I sat whistled in the sharp wind, a pipe banging somewhere underneath the cabin, our silences rested deep amid the noise of cooking and breathing.

"Corinne was thirteen," Frick said. His back was to us while he cooked. "She was like David," he said. "Hated hunting. Wouldn't talk to me when I brought back deer or elk or moose or geese or swan. Especially swan. Only hunted it once." Frick laughed. "She told me and her mother that she wouldn't eat meat, that she heard of other ways that didn't include death. Where would a six-year-old hear that?" Frick laughed again, stirring the fiddleheads.

He cleared his throat. "A few weeks after her mother disappeared, we were on were on Rosebud."

Frick flipped over the salted pork and it seared and smoked.

"I was guiding nonmembers on hunts, and Corinne was with me full-time. One afternoon, I was supposed to take out this guy, Charlie, that was his name—I'll never forget it—but Charlie didn't show, which wasn't unusual. Those white guys were always jerking us around. They'd get their permits to hunt on tribal land, but then they wouldn't show.

"So Corinne was out there with me, waiting, freezing. Absolutely freezing. It was raining, so the dirt roads in the woods were mud and slick. We waited in my truck for Charlie to show, and an hour passed. I wanted to hunt, but Corinne was shivering, even with the heater on. It was like she couldn't get warm. Maybe it was her mother having disappeared."

Frick drained the water from the fiddleheads and then dumped them into a large metal bowl. He salted them, and then he put the salt back in the crooked cupboard and he pulled out vinegar and drizzled it over the steaming fiddleheads. The salted pork was sizzling slow, hardening.

Mom's cigarette smoke wandered toward me.

"I was mad," Frick said. "Damn mad. I wanted to hunt, but Corinne was there, shivering. Kids don't always know everything, don't know how hard it is to make enough money to buy food instead of hunting. And we were low on both—money and food."

The pork began to burn, smoke, hazing the camp, and Frick kept flipping each piece over and over.

"I should've hunted. I should've killed more time. But I only had my 9mm with me—it was the gun I carried when I guided—and I got out of the truck and sprayed every bullet I had into the rain and sky and then I reloaded twice, ran through two clips in thirty seconds."

Frick dumped the salted pork into the fiddlehead bowl. He mixed it up with his hands, like a salad.

If it weren't for my mother's smoking, I would have forgotten she was there. She got up from the table and went to Frick. He fluffed the fiddleheads and salted pork together, and Mom held her cigarette out to him, and he took a drag from it. Then one more. Mom came back to the table.

"It's funny," Frick said, blowing smoke. "The things you remember, the things that come to you throughout the day. Little things. The tiny details like the mud and bullet casings and the rain and the guy's name you were supposed to be guiding out there on a hunt, out there to kill. That was why I had to leave Rosebud, because I'd kill him, even though he didn't deserve it.

"You see, he did show up, but he was late—way late—and we were leaving. If someone's an hour late why think they'd show up? Even Indians know better, with all that 'Indian time' crap. Corinne had fallen asleep—she'd crawled down below her seat and was tucked right against the blower motor. I drove slow, because the dirt road was long and wet and slippery. Half-way down that road there was a sharp curve. I took it quick all the time, had one of them spinners clamped on the steering wheel, used to crank right around that turn—no matter how mad Corinne was, she always laughed at that, made me turn around two, three times to do it again."

Frick used both hands to set the bowl of fiddleheads and salted pork on the table. His face glossed and shined. He went to the cupboard and grabbed three bowls and three cups.

"But that dirt road was narrow," Frick said. "I was going slow, but Charlie wasn't."

Frick sat. He looked at me, looked at Mom, and he shook his head. And then he stopped shaking his head, and started to nod, like he'd come to some conclusion, some agreement that could only be made with himself and the details.

"She was sleeping," he said. And then again, "She was sleeping."

Frick took my bowl and filled it high, then he set the bowl in front of me. Then he filled Mom's bowl, and then his own. I held the bowl, warming both my hands. Frick scanned the table, look-ing for something, and his looking made me look too, made me think that what we were looking for was important, so important, and we were both searching for it together, looking sometimes at each other and then back at the table, trying to learn if something was missing or was in fact right there at the table with us.

It was Mom who figured it out.

"I'll get them," she said, and she went to the drawer by the sink and got three forks.

. . .

In the evening, after Frick fed the spirits—there by the shallow stream, under the gray-blue sky, mumbling a prayer he'd never let me hear—Frick's truck wouldn't start, and so we left it there with the locked-up camp and drove back in Mom's car, Mom driving, Frick in the passenger seat. I leaned my head against the cold window.

"I don't need to know why," Frick said to Mom. He watched the trees go by as we drove down the dirt road.

"But you do," Mom said. "I'll show you tomorrow."

"Show me what?" Frick asked.

But Mom said, "Tomorrow." She drove with both hands on the steering wheel, and she went slow, and rightfully so. When we hit Route 1, I realized no one was going to speak, just sit and ride, and I wondered what Mom would show us. I wondered about tomorrow.

When we were almost home, riding over the bridge to the Island, I sensed that even though their problems were their own, there was no escaping how those problems shaped us all, no escaping the end, like the way the ice melts in the river each spring, overflowing and creeping up the grassy banks and over lawns, reaching farther and farther toward the houses until finally the water touched stone, a gentleness before the river converged on the foundation, seeping inside and flooding basements, insulation swelling, drying only when the water has receded. What remained was a smell, a reminder that the water had come and risen up and would rise again, in time. I would never forget that car ride or that night at home: because we all found that smell, literally, and it was not subtle.

"What is that?" Mom said. We smelled it before we got indoors, and when we were indoors, the stench was so terrible that we were laughing as we stood in the house. "Oh my God, what is that?"

Frick walked around the house in his boots, looking for the smell. "Holy Jesus," he said.

"Smells like chagook," Mom said, and she looked in the garbage, took a big whiff, and shook her head. "David," she said. "Did the house smell this morning?"

"Not really," I said, covering my nose. "It smelled like it always does."

"Christ," Frick said, and he looked at us in the kitchen. Then he squatted, put his nose to the floor, and smelled.

I laughed, and so did Mom.

"What's funny?" Frick said. He smelled another part of the floor, following something.

"You're smelling the floor," Mom said. She had her hand over her nose.

"And?" Frick said.

"And you look ridiculous," Mom said.

Frick wasn't laughing. He was smelling the floor, and Mom and I watched him crawl up the hallway on all fours, sniffing like a dog. He made it down the hall and sniffed the closet. Then he opened the door and kept sniffing, stuck his head between hanging clothes.

Mom was cracking up, and in between laughs she started to gag, and when she gagged I gagged and then Frick said, "Don't," and he started gagging. He got up off the floor and dry-heaved in the bathroom.

"The hell's a matter with you two?" he said. We were still laughing, and for a second he looked to smile, but then he gagged again.

He took a deep breath. "I'll be back," he said. He grabbed a flashlight from under the sink, and he went out the door and around back of the house.

Mom and I stopped laughing when we heard him under the house, crawling about, cursing. When he stopped moving, we listened, and the silence was broken by one giant gag, and Mom and I started up again, banging our hands on the table.

"Listen to him!" Mom said.

I was laughing hard, but not at Frick: Mom was hysterical, tears coming down her face, and she was hyperventilating, trying to catch her breath, and her laughter made me laugh.

"And to think—" Mom laughed so hard she wasn't making noise, was shaking in the chair. The phone rang and she hung it up. "And to think I clean this place every day! What's the point! Shit just creeps right in! Tend a nice house, my mother always said. What does she know! Oh God, it stinks." She stood. "It stinks so bad."

The phone rang again, and Mom let it go to voice mail.

"Shh, shh," Mom said, a finger to her mouth, stifling her laughter. We listened as the voice mail spoke the caller's message.

"Yeah, it would be nice if someone WOULD CALL ME BACK!" Click.

"Your poor father!" Mom said, and she exploded with laughter. "If only he could smell it!"

Mom rose from the table and went outside, and I followed, wiping tears from my eyes, and in the silent cold we stood in the driveway, waiting for Frick.

Mom started up again. A slow laugh at first, then it built and climbed up higher and higher—she couldn't stop. I didn't find it funny anymore—she looked like she was about to collapse.

Frick came from out back and stepped into the porch light. He held out and away from him something large and oval like a saucer sled. It dripped, and the smell came right at us again, stronger than in the house.

"Found it," Frick said.

"What is it?" I asked.

"A snapping turtle," Frick said. It was decomposing, rotting from inside its shell. "Must've crawled up there and died. How it got in, don't know."

"It died in our house!" Mom said. She was breaking—it was that kind of laughter. "The house killed it!"

"You all right?" Frick said, and he brought the turtle to the side of the shed and dropped it into the hard snow.

I looked at Mom: she leaned on the car and shook and shielded her eyes with her hand like a light somewhere was blinding her. And then the laughter turned to tears and she cried hard, the kind of hard tears you laughed at after.

"What's a matter?" Frick said. He moved closer.

"It's dead," Mom said.

"Way dead," Frick said, and he nodded at me to go inside. He pulled Mom from the hood of the car, and followed after me into the house, where he guided Mom down the hallway and into her room and put her to bed.

The house still smelled. Not a little—a lot. It reeked, but it smelled better than standing outside while Frick held the rotting turtle in front of us.

Frick took a shower, and when he came out I smelled the sweet shampoo.

"Good night, David," he said from the hallway, and I heard Mom's door click shut. In the quiet, I looked at the clock, but I couldn't see the time. I spread out on the couch, wondering how deep we'd all rest, wondering, again, about tomorrow.

. . .

In the morning, Frick cooked breakfast. Fried eggs, moose meat. Mom made biscuits and gravy. The sun burned bright, and the sky was a crystal blue. The house smelled a bit of the turtle, but it was hard to distinguish between it and the cooking and woodsmoke.

Mom and Frick joked about the turtle while they made breakfast together. I sat at the kitchen table. My chest was feeling heavy, a pressure building up—the beginning of a cold.

"I thought you were done for," Frick said. "The way you were laughing."

"I don't even remember seeing the turtle," Mom said. "Was it big?"

Frick turned, eggs splattering. "You want to see it?"

"No way," Mom said. Then she turned to me. "David," she said. "Take this knife and go get some turtle meat. It'll go good in the gravy."

I smiled a little. My chest hurt, and I had to cough, and I did, and Mom heard the cold.

"You sick, gwus?" she said.

"I'm all right," I said. "A cold."

"That don't sound good," Frick said. He turned to Mom. "You want to finish cooking this? I'll make him tea."

Frick mixed honey and lemon juice in a mug with hot water. "When you finish it," Frick said, "don't cough. Just hold it down, let the tea settle."

I sipped the tea while Frick set the table.

At some point during breakfast, Mom said, "Today. After we eat."

When we finished, both Mom and Frick cleared the table, and Mom told me to get ready. I put on jeans and a T-shirt. I felt hot.

"Put a jacket on," Mom told me before we left the house.

I followed her and Frick out the back door and into the day and onto the briny asphalt. I went to the car, but Mom said no, that we were walking there.

We walked to the end of the road together, and then onto the bumpy brown path.

"I don't go up there often," Mom said.

"Where?" Frick said.

"The graveyard," Mom said.

Frick stopped walking. "Do you have something to show me?" he said, and he spit. "Or does this have something to do with what I said, about ripping that headstone out? You know," he said, pointing at her, "you would bring this shit back up. You wouldn't leave it be. You want me to say I'm sorry? Is that it? Come on, now."

"No," Mom said. "Well, maybe. I'm trying to show you that I know what loss feels like."

I was hot, burning—couldn't speak on the road to the graveyard.

Mom sat on a fallen oak, the river thawing at her back. She looked at Frick and told him a story I never knew existed. I listened as best I could, the heat of my body radiating so hard that it took my attention. It was like my vision was narrowed, a pinhole looking outward at the passing of experience.

I heard her say there should have been two, that they were healthy for the whole time, but after he, me, after he came out, the other one, the other one wasn't whole, was a tumor with hair and teeth sprouting out.

Frick had taken off his jacket and put it over my shoulders, which reminded me I was there, with them.

"The tumor spread throughout me," Mom said. "That's what they said, the doctors—he'd spread throughout me." Mom laughed. "And my mother, my mother wouldn't let the doctors keep the tumor. Her convenient Indian came out, said it was improper to dispose of it the way they were going to. A few weeks after the hysterectomy, my mother and I came up here. The church wouldn't bury the child, so we did. The headstone was already there. Maybe that's why I go up there sometimes, to see if it's still there, to make sure no one other than him has been buried under it. And maybe that's why what you said upset me."

Ice scraped against the riverbank, and out in the middle of the river an ice sheet cracked and echoed downriver.

"So I can't give you what you want," Mom said. "It's impossible."

I coughed up mucus and spit it out.

"Let's get you home," Mom said to me. She put her hand to my forehead.

Mom guided me down the road, and Frick followed. We'd not go to the graveyard—we'd all been there before, and we'd all be there again: Frick, when he had to work after the snow melted; me, when I ran out of metal balls for the slingshot and knew where to find some, scattered there in the mud; and Mom, when she went to say hello, or good-bye.

We emerged out from under the thick dark pines that shrouded the path we just walked, the path that led to a place we'd never return to, but that was the point. Up the hill, our chimney smoke rose up in quiet plumes before dispersing into a flat gray haze against the hard blue sky. Down our driveway, Mom covered her nose, the turtle decomposing on the side of the shed. I couldn't smell anything. My nose was stuffed up. We'll all be happy, I thought, even if it's for a moment.

Frick stayed outside. He tied a bandanna around his face to cover his nose, and he began to gut the turtle, planned to keep the shell. I watched him through the kitchen window as he dug his blade into the turtle's opening, scraped out the insides.

Mom made me another tea and set it on the kitchen table. The phone rang and she answered it, said hello, and then handed me the phone.

"How's my buddy today?" Dad said. I sipped the tea—steam swirling and warming my face, and over the rim of the mug I saw Frick through the window gutting and scraping and gagging—and I told Dad his buddy was good. A little sick, but his buddy was good.

IN A FIELD
OF STRAY
CATERPILLARS

All the staff—the psych techs, the nurses, the doctors—kept asking if I was searching for an exit. I wasn't. I had to pee. The ECT waiting room, where I'd been waiting for Fellis and trying to remember the third thing that needed to be done that afternoon, didn't have a bathroom. There was one around the corner but it was being cleaned, and the janitor took his sweet time plopping the mop in the yellow bucket, and after ten minutes of my waiting for him to finish I pushed off from the wall where I'd leaned and walked the short and narrow and not-too-bright halls looking for another bathroom. As always, I got all turned around. The hallways spread out from the main building in every direction like spider legs, except unlike spider legs they crisscrossed and forked and even intersected a few times, open junctions with numerous paths to outpatient services like Mood and Memory. Every worker I encountered was like, "Are you looking for a way out?" It was a stupid question, because each and every hall ended with a red exit sign above double doors that opened to the bright outside as if the place knew how confusing it was. If you got turned around, you could burst through those exits and walk around the sprawling building to the main doors and start over for what it was you were searching for.

That was how mental health therapy worked, I was pretty sure.

Hallway after hallway, I wasn't finding a bathroom. A vacant one, anyway. I retraced my steps back to the ECT waiting room, and when I got there the janitor was still cleaning. He was on one knee, and with a dirty white cloth he wiped the silver handicapped-toilet bar.

"You going to be done soon?" I said.

"In a minute," he said, without looking at me.

I tapped my foot. I was used to waiting. For the past four months I was seeing this girl—Tabitha, who I'd met at the clinic—and I stayed at her place in Overtown. One bedroom (always an unmade bed), one bath (makeup everywhere), tiny living room with blue walls (Christmas lights above the couch, even though Christmas was over), and a narrow kitchen (the brown cupboards never stayed shut). She worked retail all day for T.J. Maxx, and so I was stuck at her place watching TV or searching for work on her small laptop (UPS never got back to me). One night I made her dinner—one-pot pasta with broccoli and carrots—and even though she ate it I knew she didn't like it. "That was pretty good," she'd said, but with the same voice and scrunched-up face used to say, "That was pretty bad."

The janitor switched the knee he leaned on. "Almost done," he said.

"Don't worry about it," I told him, and he started to clean behind the toilet.

Even though I spent a lot of time waiting for Tabitha, it was worth it until that day I brought her to the Social on the rez.

Before that, we would stay up late and watch Netflix, eat junk, lie in bed and share cigarettes and read Ask Reddit threads on her laptop. But after the Social, we started to fall apart. She didn't do nothing—it was me, my attitude, and I knew it. This was about three months back. It had rained that day, so the Social was held in the community building. Drum groups spread out across the basketball court (so many Native dudes wearing baseball caps backward, their braids pulled through the back hole), and small vendor tents circled the out-of-bounds lines. Tabitha loved it all, kept asking me to show her how to dance to this song, to that song. I showed her once. I was never good at dancing. When an honor song played—an elder had died not many weeks back—everyone sang around one drum, and while Tabitha could say a word here and there but didn't understand, she still cried at the end. After that, we walked around some—smoked a cigarette outside—and I bumped into one of Mom's friends, Cheryl, and she ignored Tabitha, kept asking how I was, how Mom was (which I didn't know—we barely talked), and then at the end she pinched my arm and said, "You should find yourself a nice Native girl," and walked away. I bet my mother put her up to it.

After Cheryl said that, Tabitha and I sort of split. Not physically, but mentally. We did our own things. At night, when she'd come home from T.J. Maxx, she would shower and eat in bed and watch *Gilmore Girls*. I'd usually sit outside and smoke or go for walks until I was tired. That routine started to drag on, but then a few weeks later I started taking Fellis to his appointments, and it saved me, got me away from Tabitha's and gave me some purpose. His mom, Beth, couldn't take him. During the summer, she worked at Family Dollar for extra money on top of her teacher's salary. The only other person who could take him was his aunt Alice, and she did for a little while until her daughter Lily started up at the tribal day care (Lily's father was a bum, lived up north on some other rez), and Alice got a job as the "secretary to the chief's secretary" (tribal citizens wondered where our money went), licking envelopes and sealing them shut. When Beth called Tabitha's place and asked that I take Fellis every other day, I took one look at Tabitha sitting up in bed, plate of Thai Lean Cuisine noodles in her hands, laptop open, and I told Beth no problem, that I'd be there in the morning.

A male nurse passed by as I leaned on the wall. He'd stopped me once before. "You haven't found the exit yet?"

I pointed to the bathroom.

He kept on walking.

When I'd gone over that first day to pick Fellis up, he was sitting in bed and watching TV, and it reminded me so much of Tabitha that I started to regret my decision. But he looked so beat up. An ashtray crammed with butted cigarettes sat on his lap. His eyes were half shut, his expressions plain and simply devoid of any life, kind of like if you'd put two black dots and a straight line on an orange and called it a face. But after that first ECT treatment I witnessed, Fellis seemed to be more awake, more alive.

The janitor flushed the toilet and let out a groan as he stood. He put the dirty white cloth in his back pocket. When he came out the door, he did a double take at me.

"You from the rez?" he said.

I didn't look too Native, and so I said, "Yeah, how'd you know?"

"Your shirt says 'Native Pride.'"

I looked down at my shirt, and the janitor started talking again.

"Is it true what they're saying in the papers?"

"Depends," I said. "What are you talking about?"

"The caterpillars." He squeezed dirty brown water out of the mop and into the yellow bucket.

"Yeah," I said. "Looks cool with them all there on the road, but it don't smell that great."

He was saying something about going to check it out—like the rez needed another visitor—but I quit listening. I slammed the bathroom door shut behind me. With my foot I lifted the toilet seat and accidentally smeared dirt on it.

After I peed and flushed the toilet and wiped the mud off the seat with a paper towel and washed my hands and opened the door to the hallway, the janitor was gone. I went back to the ECT waiting room. Except for the woman typing behind the sliding glass window, the room was empty. I sat on the couch and rubbed my hands over my arms. Every five minutes the central air blasted. Some days I got so cold in that room I had to go to the end of a hall and take an exit, go stand in the sun or walk to the bus stop and bum smokes from those waiting, and it was always awkward when the red bus showed up and I didn't get on, the driver looking at me like, "Are you coming?"

Five, ten, fifteen—the minutes passed. I grabbed a space edition of *National Geographic*. I didn't read it, just looked at the pictures of the purple cosmos and bright stars and pluming yellow gases. I closed the glossy magazine and tossed it onto the table in front of me. I shut my eyes and leaned my head back. After his appointment, Fellis and I were supposed to return *Transcendence* to Redbox, which we hadn't even watched yet. And then we were supposed to go to Indian Health Services to get Beth's Adderall and Alice's blood pressure meds. There was something else, though. I was sure of it. What the hell was the third thing that needed to be done?

The woman behind the sliding glass scooted her chair back and the noise shook me. I looked up, watched her stand. She disappeared through a door, and someone said, "Go slower."

The door opened into the waiting room and out came Fellis. A woman in a white coat guided him by the arm into the room and she rubbed his back. In the corner of the room was the wheelchair. I got up and opened it.

Fellis took small steps. I watched his face, the one I'd seen each time his treatment ended. Droopy, but not like he was high or anything—etomidate was the anesthesia, and it was a non-barbiturate since he was on methadone—but droopy and soft yet sharply focused, as if the electrical currents searing across his brain had awoken something, something that had rested for far too long and was now awake with a dedication to look through Fellis's eyes and relay to the brain everything as pure sparkle and gold, even if what it saw was only a cold waiting room with bland white walls and old magazines and me standing there scratching my ass while I waited for Fellis to get into the wheelchair.

The woman told him to take it easy.

"They need to put your voice on an alarm clock," Fellis said. "I'd wake up to it every day."

The woman didn't smile, crouched down, pulled out the footrests of the wheelchair, and lifted each of Fellis's feet onto them. She said Joan would schedule the next appointment, in a few weeks: he was done with the every-other-day regimen.

Joan came out and handed me an appointment card and as usual the clipboard with the agreement that I would stay with Fellis all night. I signed my name, dated it, and then handed it back.

I pushed Fellis in the wheelchair through the door and he said, "Bye, Joan." The janitor was back at the bathroom like he'd forgotten to clean something, and we passed him and went around the corner. The hallway declined, and Fellis said, "I'm done for a while, let me fly," and so I let go of the wheelchair but kept pace alongside him. Before he could crash into the wall, I grabbed the wheelchair and stopped him but the momentum flung him from the seat and he fell forward onto his hands and knees.

A small nurse and this big burly man in flannel came hurrying over. "Is he okay?" they asked, and both Fellis and I didn't answer them because we were laughing. Fellis got back into the wheelchair and said he was fine, and before the nurse could say anything about what had happened I stopped laughing—or tried to anyway—and said, "We're looking for the runway. Which way's the exit?"

. . .

Out in the parking lot, I rushed Fellis in the wheelchair to his truck, Einhell. That was what we'd named it. The chassis was green, but the underbelly was red in spots. In order to pass in-spection, Fellis had welded sheets of metal from a broken lawn mower over the rust, and the brand Einhell was in fading black right under the driver's door.

I helped Fellis into the truck, had to give him a boost.

"You want me to buckle you in too?" I said, and he laughed.

I'd gotten used to driving. I didn't have my license—and I was always nervous behind the wheel—but I had no choice. I reversed the truck, slipped it in drive, and took off to the main road. We had to wait over five minutes for the traffic to break away. When a narrow space presented itself between two cars, I gunned it, tires skidding. The person I cut off honked.

Fellis stuck his hand out the window and either waved or gave the middle finger to the honker.

I continued north to I-95 and I didn't hit a single red light. Off the freeway and down cracked gray roads left and right we came to a stop and directly across the way arched the steel bridge, the river flowing below, to the reservation. A yellow flashing sign at the beginning read "Drive Slow, Use Caution." This—not the sign, what lay beyond it—was what that janitor was asking about. Right over the bridge the road boiled with caterpillars. Some were dead, run over by cars and trucks—it sounded like pop-corn popping when we drove over them—and others were alive, crawling among the gooey dead in search of trees with leaves that they hadn't already eaten, or of tree trunks that the Department of Natural Resources hadn't wrapped in duct tape and smeared with petroleum jelly to save what leaves remained.

I drove slow over the road, which was slick with caterpillar guts.

"Shit, that stinks," Fellis said.

The place smelled of bait, of something chewed up and spit out or even shit out, and when the wind blew just right the smell moved about the rez. Fellis and I covered our noses.

I parked Einhell next to Beth's house along the road. When we got inside, the landline phone was ringing. Neither of us answered it. We passed through the living room and into the kitchen, and we poured some iced tea. With our sweaty glasses we went out back of the house and sat in rusty fold-out chairs in the cool shadow cast by an oak tree.

I fell asleep in the fold-out chair for a few minutes, but was awakened by the phone ringing again.

Fellis leaned forward for his iced tea and took a sip. His chair squeaked when he set the sweaty glass back in the sparse dirt-grass at his feet.

The wind blew, bringing with it the smell of bait.

"Jesus," Fellis said. "I'd rather you hold me down and pigadee in my face for an hour than have to smell that smell."

Fellis leaned back in the chair and farted. He closed his eyes and put his hands on his head. "What time do we have to get going?" he asked.

I reached for Fellis's smokes and took one. "Get going where?"

"I don't know," he said. "Didn't we have to go somewhere?"

I was going to tell him his memory was still shit, was going to tell him where we had to go, but the phone rang again. Fellis got up and walked to the back sliding door. I brought my wet glass of iced tea to my lips, and a burnt blade of grass floated in the murky tea. I set the glass down.

In the blue sky clouds rolled through and grayed the sun. A wind blew again, and with it came the smell of bait.

The glass door slid open and again screeched shut. Fellis walked back over.

"I remember what we have to do," he said.

The phone rang again.

"For fuck's sake," Fellis said. He went back in the house, and he wasn't gone too long.

"It's your girl," Fellis said. He left the door open.

"Isn't she supposed to be at work?" I said, and then I remembered: today was her day off. There was something else, though.

"How the fuck would I know?" Fellis said.

"Tell her I'll call her back. Tell her I'm in the bathroom."

"I already told her you were outside."

"Well tell her you were wrong, that I wasn't outside but in the bathroom."

Fellis went and told her, and when he came back out I got up and headed to the house.

"You're calling her back now?" Fellis said.

"I need some water."

I went inside. On the kitchen table Fellis had scribbled some notes, fragments of sentences, on a piece of paper. He'd written *addies* and *blood presure* and *DVD*, then below he had new stuff: *gabage* and *wash dishs*. At the very bottom he wrote, *Call Tabittha*.

I poured a glass of water and leaned against the counter. Next to the sideboard the garbage was full of old coffee grounds and silver cans and food scraps like rice and peas and broccoli stems and a thick blob of grits that Fellis had nuked too long, and on top of it all was a red liquid. I could smell the garbage, but it smelled sweet like the sugar Beth put in her tomato sauces. I finished the water and set my glass in the sink.

I took the garbage outside to the bins. I washed what little dishes there were—two plates, four cups, several spoons and forks and butter knives with peanut butter glued to the blade—and I set them to dry on a damp white towel. Dishes were a small price to pay when you spent so much time at someone's house.

I went down the hall and used the bathroom, and when I came out and into the kitchen, Fellis seemed to be looking for something.

"You seen my smokes?" he said, and I told him no.

Fellis leaned over the table and pulled the note to himself, and then he went to the sink and then to the garbage.

"I did them," I said. "Took the *gabage* out too."

"Fuck you, I can't spell."

"Go get that Redbox movie so we can take it back."

Fellis went up the hall to his room, and I hollered after him. "And then we'll go get those meds!" It was well past lunchtime, and they'd be ready.

Once we left the house, the phone rang again, and it really set Fellis off. "You better call her later," he said to me. "I don't want her blowing up the phone all fucking day." He went to the phone and hung it up. Then he took it off the hook so nobody could call.

We hopped in Einhell—Fellis drove, even though I told him he shouldn't—and we went to Indian Health Services on the rez for the meds. Fellis didn't say much—he said he had a headache, and while he drove he leaned his head against the window.

At IHS he parked the truck and got out. He walked to the maroon building and then disappeared through the doors that used to open automatically but no longer did. He wasn't in there but thirty seconds before he came back out and said that the pharmacy had faxed both meds up to Save 'n Shop.

"We gotta go there anyway," I said.

The day grew red hot, and the closer we got to the head of the Island the stronger the scent became. The caterpillars cooked in the sun. The smell was worse at this time of day. People were usually out walking, but nobody was down this way except us.

Fellis passed the first sign that flashed "Caution," and he drove the truck with one hand on the wheel while he put the other over his nose. The smell was worse than ever. I buried my face in my shirt. The road looked to be moving under us, and I wondered if Fellis put the truck in park and we sat there unmoving, whether the thousands of caterpillars would lift us up and carry Einhell on their backs to our destination.

Halfway through that road the place looked almost season-less. Some trees were bare, and the limbs swayed naked like trees in the fall, but it wasn't fall, and the road was slick like packed-down ice, but it wasn't winter. The area looked half dead like spring, except it wasn't spring. It was summer, and hot.

The truck tires skidded and Fellis let off the gas. The tires caught, and he pushed the truck on toward the bridge right there in front of us.

Then Fellis gagged, and it made me gag.

"Are you gagging from the smell?" I said. "Or are you sick?"

Fellis waved a hand at me and breathed deep. We were almost by the tribal museum, almost to the bridge and out of that rotting place, when Fellis pulled over.

"Can't you wait?" I said. Fellis got out of the truck and dropped to the ground, hands and knees among hundreds of dead caterpillars, and he vomited.

The smell took over the inside of the truck. I gagged and went to open the door but it would not open. I pulled the handle time after time but the door stayed shut. "Fellis!" I said. "Fellis! Open my door, I'm gonna be sick—" But it was too late. I threw up on the floor of his truck, and as I heaved once more Fellis came around the truck and opened my door and he said, gagging, "Oh, man," and I pushed him out of the way and heaved once more onto the street, which appeared to be squirming.

I sat back in the truck, eyes watering.

"We have to clean that up," Fellis said.

"Drive," I said. "We'll clean it up at the store."

"I ain't driving with puke in my car."

"Well if you didn't lock me in here," I said.

"I didn't lock you in here, shithead, you have to jimmy the handle up and down for it to catch the latch in the door." Fellis spat onto the caterpillars. "You know that."

"Let's go," I said. I tucked my face into my shirt.

"Clean it first," Fellis said.

"With what?"

Fellis looked in the bed of his truck but found nothing.

"Throw the fucking floor mat out then," he said.

I grabbed the wet floor mat and threw it on the side of the road.

We drove to Save 'n Shop twenty above the speed limit with the windows rolled down, and every minute or so I'd find a caterpillar crawling up my leg and I'd flick it out the window.

The parking lot to the store was full, and Fellis parked far out, the truck facing away from the store and toward a cornfield. I got out of the truck and went to the bed and lowered the hatch and sat on it. I didn't see Fellis leave the store—I was watching this older woman lift her bags from her shopping cart and into the trunk of her blue car—but I noticed him halfway back to the truck, because he was swearing and waving a hand in the air. He held in one hand two white bags and in the other hand he held the Redbox case.

He got in the truck—so did I—and he threw the white bags onto the dashboard. He slammed the door shut.

"I forgot to put the fucking DVD in the case."

I said we could go get it and bring it back, but Fellis said no, that we could do it another day.

"What's one more late fee for Beth?" he said.

At the intersection Fellis turned left, and I asked if he remembered which way was home.

"I'm taking the highway and then the long loop back," he said. "Air this fucker out."

The long loop made no difference. We had to drive through that rotting road again, but before we hit the bridge we stopped at Jim's and Fellis bought a pack of smokes, two thick cheap cigars, and two tall cans of Arizona Iced Tea. Before he pulled Einhell onto the bridge he parked along the road and we each lit one cigar and let the cab of the truck fill with thick smoke. We drove in a self-made fog that was nowhere but inside this machine, and it helped ward off the smell of bait enough for us not to gag, but we were gagging from the thick smoke by the time we got to his aunt Alice's, and the clouds of smoke rolled out of the truck as Fellis got out and put the meds in her mailbox. He raised the little red flag.

. . .

I called Tabitha when we got back to Fellis's. I leaned on the wall by the back door. Fellis was looking around the house for the Redbox movie, *Transcendence.*

"You were in the bathroom long enough," Tabitha said.

"Fellis didn't know what he was talking about," I told her. "He gets like that after his treatment."

Fellis yelled something at me from the living room, but I ignored him.

"Well where were you?"

I told her what we did, but she had nothing to say about it.

"When are you coming back?" she said.

"Tomorrow," I told her.

"Come home tonight," she said. "I want to talk."

I switched the phone to my other ear. "I have to watch Fellis. Why don't you come over here?"

"I don't want to go over there," she said.

"They ain't like that here," I said. "It's different in this house."

"Please come home tonight," she said. "I just want to talk. We need to talk."

"Look, I gotta go, I'll call later."

"Dee," she said. "Today's our—"

I hung up and then removed the phone from the hook.

. . .

Beth got home four hours early. Fellis and I were on the couch, watching reruns of *The People's Court* and sipping warm Arizona Iced Tea. The sun was still shining, and when I heard the car door bang shut I thought it was Tabitha and I got excited, but then I saw it was just Beth.

She came into the house and clunked her keys onto the table by the back door.

Fellis turned down the TV but didn't take his eyes from it. "You quit?" he said nonchalantly.

I thought that shit was funny and I cracked up. Quit!

"I didn't quit, dummy," Beth said. "The whole store had to shut down for the day. Something's wrong with the septic, and all the aisles smell like chagook. Worse than those caterpillars."

"No way," Fellis said, and he turned the TV back up. A new episode was starting. "Dun nun nun," Fellis said. "Tktktktktk-tktktkt, dun dun dun DUN."

I laughed.

"That show's so stupid," Beth said, and she left us and went into the kitchen.

While we watched *The People's Court*, Beth baked chicken and made a green bean casserole, and while each cooked, she'd come into the living room and watch the show with us. Every case that came and went, Fellis would say, "Guilty!" and he'd slam his hand on the coffee table between us and the TV. "That motherfucker is guilty!" It didn't matter if the people were innocent or not.

As the cases came and went—as Beth walked back and forth from the living room to the kitchen—Fellis and I said, Fuck Judge Milian. We'd deliver the verdicts. A young mother in a pink blouse and jeans was suing her neighbor, a tall pale man, for running over her daughter's bike. When the judge pulled the young daughter up to the stand and questioned her, the judge discovered that the little girl had left her bike in the road on accident.

"Lock her up!" Fellis yelled.

"Give her life!"

"That young lady's trouble!"

"Why's the phone off the hook?" Beth said.

"Hold on, Beth," Fellis said. "I need to hear all the facts to the case."

The moment that phone went on the hook it rang.

I hit Fellis's arm. "Turn that down, I want to know who it is."

"What the fuck," Fellis said, and he turned the TV down.

We listened, and Beth was talking but I couldn't hear anything.

"Satisfied?" Fellis said, and then he said, "Hey, what'd your girl want anyway? She coming over?"

"Turn the show back on," I said. Whoever Beth was talking to, it wasn't Tabitha.

Fellis turned the show back on, and Judge Milian banged her gavel. "Verdict to the plaintiff—"

"Fellis!" Beth said.

"For fuck's sake, Beth, what?"

Beth stood in the living room, the phone to her ear, its tan cord taut.

"You got your auntie all upset," she said.

"What do you mean?" Fellis muted the TV.

Beth spoke into the phone. "I'll come get you and Lily," she said. "I'll give you one of my Ativans so you can calm down. Yes, I'm coming right now."

Beth brought the phone to the hook and hung it up.

Fellis was standing up. "What I do? Why does she need an Ativan?"

Beth slipped her shoes on and grabbed her keys. She opened the front door, and I smelled the dead caterpillars. "You gave her my Adderall," she said.

. . .

Fellis was all worked up while Beth went and got Aunt Alice, yet I didn't have much to say to calm him down. He wasn't worried about her health—he just didn't want her to yell at him, because unlike her sister, Aunt Alice could rip into Fellis.

The phone rang while Beth was gone, and I went to it and picked it up, yet nobody said anything. "I know it's you," I said and hung up.

In the living room, Fellis had the TV off and he was sitting upright rubbing his face. I sat down next to him.

"It was an accident," I said. "Quit worrying."

"What is that?" Fellis said.

"What?"

"You smell that?"

The chicken and green bean casserole was on fire in the stove, and Fellis went to the cupboard under the sink and grabbed the fire extinguisher, and he squeezed the trigger but nothing came out.

"Remove the pin," I said.

He did, and he sprayed white into the stove.

The front door opened and then banged shut.

"Is that the chicken?" Beth said. Alice was behind her, coughing, and between the two of them little Lily peeked her head at us.

"It's out," Fellis said.

"Get me that pill," Alice said. She was fanning herself. "I can't breathe."

"Oh, calm down," Beth said. "You're overreacting. It's an Adderall."

"I'm not overreacting, Beth." Alice picked up Lily and put her on the couch. She turned on the TV but didn't change the channel from *The People's Court*.

"Get your auntie a Klonopin," Beth said, fanning smoke out of the kitchen and through the back sliding door.

Alice sat down in the kitchen, still fanning smoke from her face while Fellis brought her the pill and a glass of water. She took it, and water dribbled down her chin.

"I'm sorry," Fellis said. "I should have read the labels."

Alice set the glass down. "You should've, but you didn't. At least I got my bills done."

. . .

We ate McDonald's that cloudy summer night. Beth came back with three bags full of double cheeseburgers, fries, three four-piece chicken nuggets, and one fish filet with no cheese that was for Alice. Beth bought Cokes too, which Alice said she couldn't drink but she drank anyway, and after we ate at the kitchen table among the greasy wrappers—after Fellis bitched and bitched about his treatments, how the nurses said he might have to get a chest port because it was difficult to find a vein—Beth cleaned up the garbage and Aunt Alice put Lily to bed and Fellis went all around the house looking for *Transcendence*, and when he found it he slid it into the DVD player in the living room, and as he and Beth and Alice sat on the couch—"God, I hate Johnny Depp," Aunt Alice said, to which Beth said, "Why? He's a hot Navajo," and the two argued whether or not he was Native—there was no room for me with them on the couch, and so I told them I'd be right back and went outside to get a chair, but while there in the dark I stepped on something hard. Fellis's pack of smokes he'd lost. I took one but didn't have a lighter, and so I stuck the smoke behind my ear and looked at the fold-out chairs in the dark, and I said out loud under the swaying oak, "You should be ashamed of yourself." I was and I wasn't. I'd made my choice, knew what I was going to do, yet I didn't want to do it. It wasn't the right choice either. Keep on with her or don't—neither was right.

"Movie's starting!" Fellis yelled to me, but I was already around the side of his house, heading to Overtown, and I wondered if there was a way around those dead caterpillars and the smell of shit, of bait. But I knew there wasn't.

THE BLESSING
TOBACCO

Grammy slid the pack of Misty 100s across the kitchen table. Under the ceiling light the age spots on the back of her hand looked like sprinkles of dirt, and like the dirt, the age spots hadn't always been there.

"Help yourself to a smoke, Robbie," Grammy said. "I'll make us some coffee."

Grammy was sick. Not cough-cough sick, the way some old people got before they slid over to the other side like a pack of smokes. Well—maybe she was cough-cough sick, but not in her lungs. The cough came from her brain, from below the soft gray stuff, burrowed deep in tissue, something tickling her there in an indescribable way. And like a thick, hacking chest cough, the one from Grammy's brain was bad.

"Go on, Robbie," Grammy said. She poured water into the coffeemaker and then dumped the old coffee grounds into the wastebasket with a thump. "The lighter's in my purse."

I dragged the pack to me, the back of my hand dirtless. With my fingernails, I pulled out the cigarette. It smelled like mint and was longer than my fingers. When I put it between my lips, it dangled there, the tip of the cigarette so far away.

"Robbie," Grammy said, "I know you do it. Mom knows you do it. The lighter's in my purse. But please—don't get me in trouble." Grammy went to the fridge and opened it.

Robbie had been Grammy's little brother, and he'd been dead since before us skeejins even had rights. I never knew him. To me, he was only a relative who left young and stayed young. Little Robbie. Little Great-Uncle Robbie. He'd been my age—twelve—when the river took him, keeping him little forever.

"Are you hungry?" Grammy said.

"No," I said. "I'm all set, Frances." Mom had sent me down to see if Grammy needed firewood brought in—that was why I was here—and before I left Mom told me to play along if Grammy's brain coughed. Mom didn't say "brain cough," though. She said, *David, if Grammy starts up, go with it.*

Grammy's purse hung on the side of the kitchen chair. With the Misty hanging from my lips, I unzipped her purse and dug through papers, receipts, some braided sweetgrass, loser scratch-off tickets. Dirt in the bottom of her purse lodged itself under my fingernails. The loose change stuck to my hand. Two times I pulled from the purse what I thought was a lighter, but was actually lipstick and mascara. I took the purse from the chair and set it on the table under the light, and dug my face in there until I finally found the lighter. A purple Bic.

I sat back down, the cigarette filter all wet and slimy and damp in my mouth. The coffeemaker gurgled, then steamed and hissed, and finally water tunneled through the fresh grounds and sputtered out and into the stained coffeepot.

The lighter warmed the longer I held it, and I wondered how I should smoke or who I should smoke like. I could, maybe, smoke like my sister, Paige, cigarette always held close to her face between drags. Or I could smoke like Mom's boyfriend, Frick: take tiny, tiny puffs, but expel the largest cloud of smoke. Then there was Mom, who only lit her cigarette, took one drag, and then forgot she even held it until the ash bent and then she flicked it, barely making the ashtray.

But then I realized I couldn't smoke the way they did, because I was supposed to be Grammy's little brother. *Go with it*, Mom said in my head.

I took the cigarette from my mouth, dried the moist filter as best I could, and then put it back between my lips. As I did with the woodstove at home, I flicked the lighter, except instead of putting flame to birch bark or newspaper, I touched the flame to tobacco. It caught, sizzled, and smoke rose up, stung my eyes. Smoke dived down, burned my throat.

Don't cough, I told myself. Don't cough.

The coffeemaker stopped dripping.

And then I coughed. Grammy laughed.

"Think you'd be used to it," Grammy said. "Mom did say you were digging into the family's blessing tobacco. Said she couldn't catch you, but knew you were doing it."

She was talking to Robbie, so I didn't say anything.

I tried the cigarette again. It was easier on the throat, but it was coarse, like swallowing sand.

"Mistys are my favorites," Grammy said. "Harsh but not too harsh."

"I agree," I said.

Grammy laughed. She reached in the cupboard and took down two white mugs, red lipstick faintly staining the rims.

"Sugar? Cream?" she said.

"Both," I said.

She fixed the coffee, set mine in front of me, and took a seat. My ash was getting long, and so I flicked the cigarette over the ashtray. The ashes flung up and over and landed on the other side of the table, and Grammy swiped them to the floor.

Grammy lit her own cigarette, took a drag, and set it down on the table, the lit end dangling off. She picked up her coffee, blew on it sharply, and sipped.

I could have smoked more of the cigarette, but I butted it. I didn't even sip my coffee twice before Grammy offered me another Misty.

"Go on," she said. "Help yourself."

"I'm okay," I said. My throat hurt.

"No, no," she said. "Please. Have another."

"That's okay, Frances. Really."

Grammy sipped her coffee and then set the mug down. "Have another," she said.

By the seventh cigarette, I realized Grammy was setting me up. Or setting Robbie up. I was sitting in that chair, watching Grammy grow angrier and angrier, forcing cigarette after cigarette.

"Smoke another," she said after I butted each one.

I was being stubborn—I could have run home. But I stayed until my body couldn't take it anymore, until my head was banging and banging, until the coffee acid in my stomach begged to rise up and out.

I didn't know how many I smoked, but finally I shot up—the chair tipping over—and I bolted for the front door.

"That'll teach you to steal the blessing tobacco!" Grammy said.

Down the road, I dry-heaved into some brush.

My knees shook and my eyes watered. Everything was blurry. I weaved into the woods, split through sharp pine branches, stopping to lean on an oak every so often to try to puke before bobbing and bobbing—branches scratching my skin—farther and farther from Grammy's house.

On the riverbank, my knees in mud, I tried to throw up but could not. It was in there—so much was deep down in there—but it would not come. I burped and gagged and burped, but only saliva dripped from my mouth, sending ripples through the river when it hit, making it harder to see in the brown water what I looked like.

I was thirsty, but the river was a brown watery grit, filled with poison from the mill up north that sent down wads of pink and shit-colored bubbles that eventually dumped out into Penobscot Bay. I needed a drink, so I cupped my hands and dipped in, and I slurped the water. It tasted fine, but sickened me. I tried to throw up once more, but I couldn't, and I almost fell into the river, had to catch myself, hands all muddy.

Before standing, I splashed water on my face. My headache was fading, but that nausea in my gut was trapped.

I hurried back through the woods, hoping I didn't look ill, hoping I looked fine. Excuses are easier if you look fine.

At home, Frick was outside under the hood of his gray truck, swearing, and I ran past him and up the concrete steps and through the back door. Mom was where I'd last seen her, at the kitchen sink with a bottle of Connoisseurs Silver Jewelry Cleaner, freshening what she hoped to sell at the pawnshop in

Overtown where Paige had started working when she randomly showed up back home, and the smell of that cleaner—of old pennies—made me wonder if everything was going to smell worse than it actually was.

"Did she have enough wood?" Mom said.

"Yeah," I said.

I kicked off my shoes, and through the hole in my sock my big toe stuck out. I put it back in and hurried down the hallway to my room. Paige came out of hers and bumped into me.

"Jesus," she said, waving her hand in front of her nose. "Grammy smoke you out over there?"

"A little."

Fully clothed, I crawled into bed, my muddy knees staining the white sheet.

. . .

Paige was in my room, watching me over my bed when I woke. It felt like I'd slept forever.

"Chagooksis," she said. "Are you okay?"

Maybe she saw the worry in my face, or maybe I didn't look so fresh, like a butted cigarette or old jewelry, because she sat on the bed and massaged my scalp.

"You don't feel well?" she said.

I shook my head. I no longer had a headache, but my stomach gurgled, and it felt as if something moved about my insides.

"You were making a lot of noise in your sleep," Paige said.

"Did Mommy hear me?"

"No, she's gone. She's been at Grammy's."

"Don't tell her," I said.

"Tell her what?"

"Listen, just don't tell her."

And then I pushed Paige aside and burped and gagged off the side of the bed. Paige grabbed the wastebasket but I told her no.

"It won't come up," I said.

"David," Paige said. "You're freaking me out. Why are you sick?"

"Listen," I said, and I told her what happened. Paige stopped rubbing my scalp and instead stared at me, her face scrunched up like she was trying to make out something in the distance. I ended the story by asking, "Am I going to die?"

Paige laughed and shook her head. "How many cigarettes did you smoke?"

"I lost track after fourteen."

"Fourteen!"

"Am I?" I said.

"No," she said. "You got pretty sick from the nicotine."

Paige went to the kitchen and brought me back a ginger ale. "Just sip it and burp," she said and started for the door.

"Where you going?" I asked.

"To smoke a cigarette and get ready for work."

While she smoked in the bathroom and combed her hair—the snapping of tiny brown knots—I sipped the ginger ale in bed. The condensation dripped off the can onto my shirt and seeped cold through the cotton onto my chest.

Every few minutes Paige came in and checked on me. I had to pee already, and even though I was starting to feel better, I knew if I got up my stomach would spin out of control.

Mom came home, and Paige met her in the hallway. I could smell their smoking.

"Aren't you late?" Mom said, and she didn't let Paige answer. "Look what my mother gave me. Four silver necklaces, this gold locket, this silver watch, and ..." She stopped, rummaging through a paper bag. "Look at these rings. How much you think I'd get?"

"I can't pay you more because you're my mother," Paige said.

"But the watch is in great condition."

"It's stainless steel," Paige said.

Mom crinkled the bag. I didn't think she liked Paige's job. Actually, I thought Mom hated that Paige had a job while Mom didn't.

Paige came to say good-bye. She stood in my doorway, wearing black pants and a red blouse.

"See ya later," she said, and then she laughed and mouthed, "Feel better."

When Paige was gone, Mom came down the hallway and into my room.

"Why are you in bed?" Mom said.

"I was tired."

"Too tired to fill your grandmother's wood box?"

"She said never mind about the wood," I said.

"Why are you fibbing? Grammy said you didn't even show up. Where were you?"

I sat in bed, and I felt nauseated. "I was there," I told her. "Grammy wasn't herself."

Mom stared at me. "She started up? Well, you should've listened to me and filled that wood box. The river may be thawed and running again, but it gets cold at night."

"Was she okay when you saw her?"

"She was sleeping when I got there, but I woke her up after I saw the wood box was empty."

I sipped the ginger ale. "Did you fill it for her?"

"That's your job," she said. "Get up."

"Really?"

"Yes, really. It'll take ten minutes."

Mom left the doorway and went down the hall. I got up from the bed, the trapped feeling in my stomach loosening up and slipping out. My legs shook. Something bad seemed to be my fault. I guessed it was the smoking. I didn't want Mom to know about it, just in case she snapped on me. Or even worse, on Grammy. I couldn't do that to Grammy.

My sheets were muddy and I covered the mess by making my bed.

In the bathroom, I scrubbed the smell of smoke away until my hands were red.

At the front door, Mom handed me a heavy garbage bag. "Take this out, too." She kissed the top of my head, opened the door for me, and sent me out. Frick was still working on the truck. As I passed him, he lay awkwardly in the passenger seat trying to disconnect something from under the glove compartment. "Shit, shit!" he said. "Fucking piece of *shit!*"

On the walk there I kept trying to push from my mind the woman I'd met earlier, but I couldn't. I prepared for wickedness.

Grammy's house was dark. The porch light was off, and the door was wide open. When I went inside, I made sure it clicked shut behind me. The only light—blue and white—that was shining came from the TV in the living room. Grammy sat in her recliner with her arms on the armrests, lit cigarette between her fingers, smoke coiling to the ceiling.

"Grammy?" I said.

"Oh, chagook!" she laughed. "You scared me."

I stepped into the living room.

"Mom told me to fill the wood box," I said.

"She won't stop about that damn wood box. Go ahead, I suppose."

I went back outside and around back of the house to where a dark green tarp covered a cord of wood. The tarp crinkled and dumped water when I lifted it. I stacked seven logs of ash in my arms and carried the load back inside. The bark was digging at my forearm, and I felt a piece slipping loose, so I hurried down the hallway and came to the wood box, and as I got close to it, the pieces started to fall, but I lunged forward so all the wood fell directly out of my arms and banged and rattled into the box.

"That's how it goes," Grammy said. She smoked her cigarette. "Don't carry so much next time."

I filled the wood box in two trips.

"Well, I have to—"

"You eat?" Grammy said.

"No," I said. "I should get home and do that."

"I'll cook you something. Go on, have a seat."

I didn't want to stay, didn't want to be alone with her too long, but I decided to remain with her, and I was glad I did. She turned more lights on in the house and I sat at the kitchen table and she fired up the stove and fried me up two greasy eggs and drippy strips of bacon and two slices of toast with raspberry jam on it and told me a joke about a brown bear wiping its ass with a white rabbit. And after I ate the food, after I made her tell me the joke one more time—my laughter making her laugh—and after she took my plate and rinsed it and covered the dirty dishes with a cloth as was our custom to tell the spirits to stay away—that there was no food for offering—she handed me a freezer-burned orange creamsicle. And when she turned off all the lights and ushered me in front of the TV in the living room, I saw smoke, yeah, but I saw Grammy and myself under all of it, all of it hanging over us.

She turned on *World News Tonight with Peter Jennings*, but I wasn't paying attention. I was trying to figure out in the dim lighting if my creamsicle was dripping over the plastic wrapper and onto the couch, and so I ate the creamsicle as fast as I could so as not to make a mess. My mouth was cold and numb.

Grammy had her eyes partly open, dozing, a cigarette wasting away between her fingers, like Mom. I turned my attention to the news, holding the wooden creamsicle stick and the wrapper in my hand. Peter Jennings was gearing up to a segment about NASA and *Pioneer 10*, how it sent its last signal, and how NASA had no plans to contact *Pioneer 10*. No plans! None. The metal ship was going to keep on going way out there in quiet, quiet glides of black, and since it was a thing, a machine, it couldn't see like us, and we way back here would never, ever know if the machine was okay. I wished that the near impossible would happen: that a passing space rock would collide with it, shatter it to pieces, and send it broken toward the stars.

The news ended, and while the TV went black I wondered when Grammy would send her last message. In her recliner, barely rocking, she snored, her cigarette ash long, bending, slipping from her fingers. I saw to it, plucked the cigarette from Grammy's fingers, and when the ash fell to the carpet I rubbed it in with my foot. I didn't set Grammy's smoke in the ashtray, but instead I held it, looking at the filter and the red coal dimly lit, and I thought how I could take some if I wanted to, could commit to it. I put it to my lips.

Grammy was looking at me.

"It was gonna fall," I said. I put out the cigarette in the ashtray.

"Woliwoni," she said.

Grammy resituated herself in her recliner. Then she looked at the creamsicle wrapper and its dried wooden stick. "Go on," she told me. "Have another."

. . .

I walked out the front door and she closed it behind me and I heard the click of the dead bolt. The night sky was so packed with stars that I felt the urge to squint. My stomach was grumbling from the four creamsicles I'd eaten, and from the cigarettes, too. A day with Grammy, I thought. Smokes and sweets.

At home, all Mom's jewelry was spread out on the kitchen table. Mom and Frick were in the living room, watching TV, three empty Barefoot bottles of wine on the coffee table. As I stood there in the living room, waiting for Mom to say something, Frick spoke for her.

"You were at your grandmother's?" he said.

Yes, I told him.

The house was scrubbed clean and smelled like bleach, the way it did when Mom was upset and had scrubbed the floors like she was trying to erase them.

I brushed my teeth, and my tongue was bright orange, and no amount of scraping with the toothbrush removed it.

"Good night," I said from the hallway.

"Good night," Frick said.

"Good night, mumma," I said.

In my room, I undressed, slipped on a pair of gym shorts, and pulled the blankets down and got in.

At midnight, when Paige returned home from work, their bickering woke me up.

"It's the way you said it," Mom said. "And in front of all those people."

"You asked for it," Paige said. "I offered you way more than what they were worth and you wouldn't take it."

"You were ripping me off," Mom said. "You're always ripping me off."

"Me? I give you most of my check, and then you try and come to my work and get more money than your junk is worth. And that's what it is—junk! Old crappy necklaces, a piece-of-shit watch that doesn't work, and tarnished silver rings."

"They're antiques!"

"Quiet, you two," Frick said.

Their voices lowered.

"You embarrassed me," Paige said. "You were rude and put me in a difficult spot, and I offered you more for the jewelry but you wouldn't take it."

"It wasn't enough," Mom said. "Just say it. You didn't want to give me more."

"I would have given you the whole store if that was how it worked, but it doesn't."

The phone rang. It was curious to hear the house go so quiet, to hear only the phone and nothing but the phone, and right then I realized that it was no longer the day Grammy made Robbie smoke all those cigarettes, but the day after. I never thought much of the hours between midnight and waking in the morning as being part of the next day. It had always felt like an in-between time, but there was no in-between. It was always now.

Mom answered the phone. "Who is this?" she said. Then again, "Who?"

A lighter flicked.

"She was found?" Mom said. "Where?"

I was sitting up, listening. I had the same questions as Mom. Was she found in the woods? Walking the roads? I kept imagining her in somebody else's house, watching TV on their couch or cooking in their kitchen.

"Oh God," Mom said. "Bring her here."

Mom hung up. Nobody said anything for a while, but the house sounded louder than when the phone had been ringing. The kitchen sink turned on, and water sprayed against the metal pan. The fridge opened once. Someone stepped on the part of the kitchen floor that creaked.

Then Mom spoke to Paige. "Is your bed made up?"

"Yes," she said.

"I'll get you blankets for the couch," Mom said.

Right outside my bedroom door, Mom and Paige were going through the closet, getting blankets and pillows for the couch. They worked in quiet reaches at the shelf. And because they were there, so close to my door, I decided to get up and ask what was going on.

"Get back in bed," Mom said. I knew she would get mad if I didn't listen, if I didn't give her what she wanted. "Go to sleep," she said.

Soon, from in my bedroom, I heard Paige say someone was pulling in. I pressed my ear against the bedroom door. The back door peeled open, and I heard Grammy speak. "I didn't mean to," she was saying, crying. "If I'd known."

"It's okay," Mom said. "Frances, come on. Come into the living room."

"Who are you?" Grammy said. "They said he's dead. Drowned!"

Grammy stopped crying and then she screamed, one short quick yell, and it sickened me more than all those cigarettes.

There were men's voices. Tribal police. EMTs. They spoke over Grammy's questions. It was hard to make out what was said. Something about her car being totaled, something about finding her shivering and screaming down by the river. The officer spoke louder, and I heard him much better. He said when they touched her, when they tried to gently pull her away from the riverbank, she pointed at them, asked them to help her find him in the water, asked them to call to him, and then she stuck her thumb and finger under her tongue and whistled to the stars.

And then Grammy whistled just like that in the house, and everyone quieted.

"Where is he?" she said.

"Grammy," Paige said. "Where's who?"

"Grammy? I'm not your damn Grammy."

When the officers and the EMTs left, Mom tried to get Grammy from the kitchen to Paige's bed, but Grammy kept on talking, kept on crying.

"I shouldn't have done it," she said.

"You're okay," Mom said. "Come on, now. Let's get you changed."

I tensed against my door. Footsteps walked closer to the hallway, closer to Paige's room.

"I can't!" Grammy said. "No one saw him today but me."

I pulled myself up off the floor by the doorknob, and I opened the door. Mom and Paige were on either side of Grammy, whose pants were wet and covered with mud. Mom stomped toward me, pointing to get back in the bedroom, but Grammy stopped her.

"Robbie," Grammy said.

The way she stared at me, the relief in her puffy eyes. I wondered what that felt like. You could see it, absolutely see it. But to feel it. Like waking from a dream in which something hunted you—not a little, but violently hunted you—and when you sat up in bed you took a deep, shivering breath as crisp as a glass of ice water.

"It's okay, Frances," I said.

Grammy moved away from Paige, past Mom, and came to me, held my face in hands that didn't look age-spotted, because the hallway light was off. "Why did they lie?" she said.

"Come on, Frances," I told her. Mom, Paige, and I brought her to Paige's bed.

"Don't go," she said. "Come here, gwusis. Abin." Sit, she said.

She wrapped her arm around me, pulled me in. She scratched at my head, massaged my scalp. She sniffled. Paige was standing there, watching, and Mom was coming back with the couch blankets. She dropped them onto the floor and made a bed large enough for her and Paige to sleep on.

"I'm sorry," Grammy said. "I shouldn't have done it. I shouldn't have done it."

I leaned harder into Grammy's holding. Mom's eyes were on me, wondering. "Frances," I said. "Everything's fine."

Grammy let go of me and leaned away. "But you shouldn't have tricked me," she said. Her voice quivered the louder she spoke. "That was not right."

"I'm sorry," I said, and I wondered if Robbie was sorry for dying.

Grammy shook her head. "You two need to leave," she said to Mom and Paige.

They stood in the hallway, and I heard Paige telling Mom about the cigarettes, and I tried to listen to how she told the story—because how it was told mattered—but then Grammy grabbed me by the shoulders and pointed her long finger in my face. "You think that was right, what you did?"

I grabbed the mattress hard; I couldn't go with it. I pulled my face away from her finger. "You're sick, Grammy."

"Jistowks!"

Mom and Paige looked in.

"Get out!" Grammy told them. "I said, get out!"

"David," Mom said. "Come on."

I tried to get up, but Grammy pulled me back down, and then I wiggled loose from Grammy's grip. When I ran she grabbed my leg, and I fell forward onto my face.

"That's enough!" Mom said. She was rough with me as she picked me up and pushed me out of the room and slammed the door.

In the living room, Frick sat in the rocking chair, dozing, a bottle of wine at his feet. When I came in, one of his eyes opened and he looked at me.

"You want a cigarette?" was all he said, and he laughed himself to sleep in the chair.

It wasn't until around 4:00 AM that Grammy quieted. I sat on the couch, Frick snoring in little bursts in the rocking chair, and I listened as Mom scolded Grammy. And all Grammy would say was that what Robbie did was worse, stealing and tricking, and that she would do it all over again. It was all sickness, the whole thing, something that couldn't be cured, but—and maybe it was because I was tired—I felt that I had done something terrible, like I had been the one doing the violent hunting, and I wanted to get up and right it all, but I didn't know how. Maybe that was how Great-Uncle Robbie had felt, like he had no choices, that no right way existed to fix anything at all. In the moments before my eyes shut, hearing Frick snore and the clock tick toward 4:00 AM, I felt like I knew Robbie, felt like I had memories of him where he took me fishing or hunting, and when I couldn't take the fish off the hook or when I couldn't kill the white rabbit, he told me that that was fine, and he unhooked the fish—its jaw popping, gills throbbing—and plopped it into the river, or he took the rifle from my hands, and after all that we walked away through mud or snow until I stopped walking but he kept on going and going and going out there in quiet strides through a dark-pined forest until he was gone.

SAFE HARBOR

I'm sitting at the weathered picnic table under the gazebo in back of the crisis stabilization unit, and it smells like rain. My mother's walking to get two cups of coffee. I don't watch her. I'm too busy watching the short and skinny exterminator walk along the grass against the building's foundation. He's dressed in a white coverall, and he's checking the black boxes filled with poison. Rodent bait boxes. I don't think he looks at me, but he knows I'm here. He has to see me. I wonder if he thinks I belong here.

The crisis stabilization unit is thirty minutes away from the reservation. To get to the unit, I pass McDonald's and a thrift store before I take the highway for most of the drive. Exit ramp. Red light. Always a red light. I have to turn left, so I always have to wait. Then I turn. Drive straight. School zone, drive slow. I cross a black-and-blue-tagged bridge before cutting through a brick city. One-way roads. Then some trees. More trees. The unit is coming up. Right turn. The unit is down a bumpy and cracked side road, away from the busy part of town. Against the woods, sharp pine trees clutter and lean into each other, and cardinals and finches flutter and jet from tree to tree.

The unit isn't large. Inside, there's the staff desk. To the right of it a long hallway filled with bedrooms. Rooms simple in decor that say *relax*. A bed with clean linen. A nightstand and a lamp and a dresser. Thin white curtains. To the left of the staff desk is the living room and kitchen and TV room with maroon chairs and a quiet room where people can paint and draw or sit and read. A whiteboard is screwed to the wall in the living room and in blue marker a quote is written: "A ship in harbor is safe, but that is not what ships are built for." Like human beings are ships, as if they were crafted things. Things that rock and bang or cruise smooth in an unpredictable ocean of salt and froth and depth. Out there is natural extermination.

The back door creaks open, then bangs shut. My mother's shoes crunch the grass. The exterminator is gone, gone around the building.

"Here." Mom hands me the coffee. It's too hot to sip so I blow and blow on it, but it doesn't cool.

"Thanks for the cigarettes," Mom says.

That's why I'm here: to bring her cigarettes. That's why I'm always here when she's here. To bring her cigarettes. I never don't bring her cigarettes.

I blow on my coffee again. It's too hot to sip.

Mom asks me if I heard from "your sister," and after I tell her no she makes a noise with her throat and then asks me what's new.

Nothing, I tell her.

And then she goes into it, why she's here again. The twelfth time in the past three months.

"I didn't want to be alone," she tells me. "The walls in my bedroom started to look black and grimy."

I ask her if she's out of her meds. Clonazepam. Benzos. She says she gets them filled tomorrow. Only sometimes she takes her meds. She runs out because she needs money. Always needs cigarettes.

"But I have Valium," she says. "It still won't help me sleep. I can't sleep."

She tells me she's been awake for three days. She doesn't look it, though. Her short gray hair is spiked. She's wearing little gold earrings. She's dressed nice. Casual. A white T-shirt and black yoga pants and white sneakers. She doesn't do yoga. All the white on her makes her look more Native, more Indian (she hates that word—Indian). But nothing makes her look young. She's Native, and she has trauma. So do I—I'm the one who saw it—but she thinks she has more. She doesn't say that, but she thinks it. Maybe she's right. Maybe older Natives have more trauma than younger ones.

It takes a bit for me to warm up to her. Mom wanted cigarettes, and that morning on the phone she also asked me to buy a pack for this woman here I don't know. Mom said the woman had cash, that she'd pay me. But during our call Mom slipped up, said the woman didn't have the money yet, that she was waiting for her friend to show up who owed her. I wasn't playing that game, I told my mother.

"I'm so tired," my mother says. "I want to sleep, but I can't."

"I'm not even here," I say, starting to warm up to her.

Mom looks at me, then smiles. "Shut up," she says.

"You're so tired I'm a hallucination," I say. I smile a little.

She's laughing now. She lost all her teeth years ago, but she has dentures. Top only. She lost the bottom at a Dysart's Restaurant last year, asked me to call them, which I did, and I asked if they found a pair at the back table. That was where she'd been sitting, she told me, next to an oil painting of green olives in a brown bowl. They didn't find any teeth.

I point at the two packs I brought her. "You're going to reach for those cigarettes later," I tell her, "thinking they're there, but they're not. I never even brought them."

I'm laughing now.

"Stop that," Mom says. She's laughing.

"Then I'll call you tonight," I say, "and ask if you need those cigarettes."

That does it, and we're both laughing hard. It feels good to laugh with her, feels like it scrapes the dark and grimy walls inside me.

When we're done laughing she says I'm a shit. "Always were," she says.

I wipe my eyes of laughing tears and then bring my coffee mug to my lips. It's still hot, and so I blow on it and then set it back down. When I do, Mom's getting up.

"I'm a little chilly," she says. She hasn't even smoked yet.

Inside, we sit across from each other at the long kitchen table. An old man in a tan sweater is sitting there too, but at the end. He's eating a sandwich, hands shaking, and with each bite, his sleeve slides down his wrist to reveal a gold watch. He doesn't talk to us, doesn't look at us, and for a moment—a moment, a single tick of his watch—he becomes familiar. Do I know you, I want to ask. Perhaps he was here the last time I visited.

That woman who wanted cigarettes is in the living room, watching *The Maury Show*, fidgeting with her purple lighter. I wonder if she's mad at me because I didn't get her any cigarettes.

From my seat at the table, the whiteboard and its blue quote snag my attention. If we're built things, I wonder, then who builds us?

Mom and I are quiet. Then she starts asking if I've seen this movie with Adam Sandler.

"I think it's called *Adults*," she says. "Yes, that's it. It's called *Adults*. We all watched it last night." By all, she means the others there with her, the others in crisis.

I blow on my coffee and take a sip. It's warm, but I wish it were warmer. I let it cool for too long. I don't tell my mother that I know the movie, that she's wrong, that it's not called *Adults* but something else. I don't tell her a lot of things, like how I couldn't pay half the rent and so my girlfriend left me and took her spaz cat with her. Mom hated my white girlfriend and would like it too much that she left. I don't tell Mom that I finally got the job driving truck for UPS. My father drove truck for them before Mom and he were married. They're divorced, have been for years. And my father's dead. Maybe that's why I don't tell Mom about the job, don't want her to tell me not to be like my father. She's dramatic like that.

"It's a riot," Mom says about the movie. "You have to see it."

I say I'll check it out, that I bet it's funny, but I know I won't watch it.

These days when Mom talks, she's always looking for words. Something isn't right with her brain. The trauma. It's been that way for years, but she's taking longer than usual.

"Ma?" I say.

She looks at me, doesn't say anything. She straightens the two unopened packs of cigarettes on the table in front of her and sips her coffee.

"I'm so tired," Mom says. "I haven't slept in four nights."

See? First three nights and now four. She's dramatic, has to up everything. I wonder if she has slept or if she's lying.

The front-door buzzer rings and one of the staff—a woman with wide hips and a small head—asks through the intercom who she's here to see. That woman who wanted me to bring her a pack of cigarettes is standing up now, watching the door. I get a good look at her. Her name's Meryl, I think. Mom said that she looks pregnant but that she isn't. I look at Meryl as she peeks at the door. She looks pregnant. I wonder if one of them is lying.

"It's my friend," Meryl says to the staff. The door buzzes and opens. A cold draft rushes over the floor and brushes my ankles like water. I wonder why her friend didn't get Meryl cigarettes.

Mom asks if I want my coffee heated. I say yes. She heats hers too, in the microwave.

Again, when she brings the heated coffee, I blow and blow on it, watch the steam swirl and feel it dampen my upper lip and nose. It's too hot to sip. I don't want the coffee. I want to leave. But I wait before I say anything—she just heated my coffee up.

Mom's talking again, and I'm listening. She's saying she hopes she sleeps tonight. "God," she says. "I need some sleep."

My coffee's too hot to sip, but I want to leave. Want to get home. For what? I lose the place in two days and no one's there. Emptier than the litter box. But I want to get away, and so I drink the hot coffee in four sips and burn the shit out of my mouth.

"I don't mean to rush," I say to Mom. The coffee mug thuds when I set it down. "But I have to get going."

"I know you do," Mom says. "I appreciate your bringing me some smokes." She pats the top of her packs on the table.

Meryl's friend is gone, and Meryl's standing near the long kitchen table. "I have that money," she tells me. "If you don't mind getting me a pack."

I don't know if I mind, but I'll go get the cigarettes.

Meryl looks at Mom. "Is that okay?" Maybe Meryl doesn't know I'm leaving, doesn't know I said I have to get going. Maybe she thinks she's interrupting us.

Mom doesn't say anything, stares at Meryl.

"There's a gas station right at the end of the road," Meryl tells me.

I don't tell her I know that. "I can get them," I say to her. "I'll go right now."

Meryl's looking at Mom though, waiting for Mom to answer her, like my going depends on my mother's letting me. Then Meryl speaks again. "Is it okay if he runs to the store for me?"

Mom's not saying anything. She's tired. I think she's looking for a word.

"Ma?" I say.

Nothing.

Mom doesn't look at either of us. And then slowly her head turns and twists until she's looking up at the ceiling and this noise like a screaming child comes from her mouth, and the next thing I do is say "Mumma?" wondering what the hell she's doing. But then she goes straighter and straighter in the chair, like she's wood, a two-by-four leaning against it, and I rush around the table and hold her. I say, "Mumma? Mumma? What's wrong?" She doesn't say anything, and her arms are tightening, curling up toward her throat. She's convulsing. I yell to the staff, tell them to help. Meryl's standing there, arms crossed, watching. She rolls her eyes—rolls her eyes! Fucking bitch.

The staff run over. One staff woman tells Meryl to go in the TV room. She does. Then the staff woman goes outside, tells the people under the gazebo to stay outside, that there is a problem. They all do. The staff woman with the wide hips and small head is on the other side of my mother, helping me hold her. Hold her in place.

The other staff woman is on the phone with 911.

"She's having a seizure," the small-headed woman says to the other on the phone.

My mother is shaking, frothing from the mouth, spitting. I watch the spit land on the small woman's face. I think my mother is choking.

"How long?" the woman on the phone says.

"About a minute long," the small-headed woman says. "She's coming out now."

My mother's breathing is slowing, catching.

I'm holding on. My mother is loosening, struggling to sit up as if it were the first time she ever rose, ever used her muscles. I'm rubbing her back, and I'm thinking about the cigarettes and the voice mails. The voice mails about the cigarettes she always wants. Right then I tell myself I will always bring her cigarettes; right then I tell myself I'll watch that movie with Adam Sandler.

"Tell them she's out of her clonazepam," the small-headed woman says. "That could be why. A lack of benzos. And she hasn't slept in three days."

I'm rubbing my mother's back. But she has Valium, I think. She told me she has Valium. Different, but a benzo. Why doesn't she tell 911 about the Valium?

My mother is sitting, and I am holding her, rubbing her back. She looks at me, tries to speak. But she can't. She can't find coherence. Her sentences are mumbled.

A puddle is under the chair.

"Who who who," my mother is saying. It's coming, what she wants to say. Piece by piece, she swashes onshore.

She's looking at me. "Who who you?"

"I'm your son," I say.

She's scared, is unsure what I tell her.

I don't repeat to her that I'm her son. I say my name instead, and her mouth and tongue move as if I'd taught her an unpronounceable word, like *isthmus* or *Worcestershire*. But she tries to say it again and again and again, failing each time. Then she gives up and starts to whisper to herself. "I need better . . . I need to get better." It's her first coherent sentence.

The ambulance arrives. Seven EMTs. They ask my mother questions. She cannot answer them, and in that she's truthful.

They put my mother on the gurney and pull her to the front door. Not one of them tells me where they're taking her. They don't know I'm her son; even my mother doesn't know I'm her son. When I try to follow them out the front door, an EMT with thin lips puts his hand up, tells me to stop, says I'm not clear to leave. He thinks I belong here. By a dirty white van—double doors open—the exterminator cleans the black boxes. I can't tell if he watches.

I pretend the EMT's right, and I wait for them to leave. Through the closed front doors, the EMTs load the gurney with Mom into the ambulance, and the doors slam shut.

The woman with the small head is shaking when she asks if I am okay. I tell her I am. Then she says they took my mother to St. Vincent's.

The puddle is still on the floor. It's flowing down and away from the table. A river. Or an ocean. Both packs of cigarettes I bought my mother are gone, and I look through the window out back at the gazebo and Meryl is outside with the others, smoking.

In the parking lot of the crisis stabilization unit, I lean for a while on the green car I borrowed from a friend. Eventually Mom calls my cell from the E.R. She says she had a seizure.

"I know," I tell her. I kick dirt and roll black earth under my foot. "I was there."

"What?" she says. "I thought . . . I thought you left."

I tell her I was getting ready to leave, that Meryl wanted me to get cigarettes for her. I tell her almost everything. How it all happened. But I don't tell her that I thought she was dying. I don't tell her how much my legs shook, how my voice quivered when I said, "Mumma, mumma, mumma." I don't tell her how little and alone I felt. I don't tell her how I'll always bring her cigarettes, how I'll watch that movie for sure.

I do tell her, though, that she didn't know anything when she woke. That she couldn't speak, that she couldn't tell the EMTs what day it was or when she was born or who the president is.

Maybe it's good, I tell her, that she didn't know who our president is, and she laughs at that. I tell her she didn't know where she was. I tell her that she didn't know me, didn't recognize me. Of all the details I tell her, she clings to that one only.

"How did I not know my baby?" she says with a sharp breath.

"It's okay," I tell her, even though it's not.

She says the doctor's coming, that he wants to run some tests.

"I'll be by soon," I say.

"What?"

"The emergency room," I say. "I'll be by soon." We say good-bye, hang up.

I knock on the front door of the crisis center. They buzz me in. One staff woman is cleaning the puddle off the floor, and the other is sitting behind the desk.

"I've lost something," I say, and I go out back to the gazebo. Meryl isn't there with my mother's cigarettes. The old man who was shaking while he ate his sandwich is sitting outside smoking a long Camel 100. I bum a smoke from him and light it with the red of his lit one.

"You don't look so good," he says to me. "You shake like me." He lifts both hands.

I don't say anything. The old man picks up his cup of coffee and sips it.

"Damn cold," he says.

"Let me heat that for you." I set my cigarette on the picnic table, the lit end dangling off. I take his cup. I wonder if he watches me leave. Watches me go inside. I wonder if he gives a shit. I put the coffee in the microwave and set it for forty-four seconds. I walk to the front door and go out and stand in the parking lot. The exterminator is still here, eight black boxes at his feet. They're laced by a rope, as if they were fresh meat.

"You supposed to be out front?" he asks me.

I say nothing and get in the car, start it, and reverse—I throw it in drive and peel out and the back right tire thuds over one or two black boxes that crack-crunch. In the rearview mirror the exterminator throws his arms into the air and he runs to the front door to tell the staff—forget him. Ahead, to the north, I'm drawn to the dark blue clouds like mold, the spray of rain and wind and yellow lightning soon to come over this part of our swell.

It drizzles, and halfway to the hospital I remember my dangling cigarette and the old man's coffee, remember that I was supposed to bring it to him, and I'm thinking and thinking and thinking at sixty-five miles per hour on this smooth residential road, until an empty playground, the red swings rocking in the now-heavy rain, catches my attention, my breath, and when I snap forward and exhale my car clips a brown telephone pole and spirals onto a cracked concrete lot. Glass shatters and the tumbling momentum flings me and the world upside down right side up and the car and me slide with blue skidding sparks and with the taste of rust in my mouth, and then the car rolls scrapes rolls to a stop. The green car is on its side and one small wind could push it on top of me and so no wonder I want to free my leg from where it's trapped under the side of the car and when I do there is no pain not unlike childhood and red swings and returnables of all hard glass and laughter and the good feelings there in the dark, and when I look at my leg the skin is peeled back my pulsing meat in my face and I grab the flap of skin and flip it over my exposed bone and have you ever tried to walk in such a time of great rupture?

The rain is thick, wet, and cold. The car hisses, steams. The trees and their limbs rustle like my fingers shake. I rise and take but one step, and on the ground I drag myself to the road and there is already a hand on my shoulder turning me over and I see the line of cars with people marching to me, a dozen ships of ideas aiming for this shore once again.

As they did with Mom, the EMTs grab me and lift me and settle me and poke me and quiet me and I recognize the man who would not let me leave and I say something something something to him but his thin lips shush me and he pokes me again and I sit up to see my skin covered with a red cloth and time lurches forward with such speed to the emergency room that I'm there in a bustling room white curtain pulled closed and blue soft masks floating about me, and it goes how it should go the pain is hitting and a woman is yelling for her baby, and I feel bad that she lost that baby, hope she finds it, and before I'm put under to the sound of her screaming behind the curtain I grab the doc by the sleeve, say to the doc, "Does my mother know I'm here?"

SMOKES LAST

At the kitchen table, Frick fidgeted with a bag of pork rinds. Mom scrubbed dishes while the oiled pan on the stove got hot enough for her to lay down spoonfuls of batter in it. The sideboard was caked white. The house smelled like the empty sweet-corn can that sat upright next to the sink.

"Back west, when the Minnechaduza Creek froze over," Frick said, sitting perpendicular to the table, "we used to go and wait for the white kids to try and cross. Once they made it halfway"—he raised his arms and looked down the barrel of an imaginary rifle—"pop!—and we'd shoot. I guess our battles were for a different time." He reached into the bag and pulled out a pork rind.

I got up from the table.

"Don't come home blind," Mom said, examining a glass cup and then placing it to dry. "And bring the mail in before you go, gwus. Your father said he finally sent some money up."

Sure he did. The last money we'd seen from him was on my last birthday, when I turned fourteen.

Frick chewed a pork rind and then paused. "That's how I lost most of my vision in my right eye. Rock wars, we called them." He dug in the pork-rinds bag again, feeling for something other than rind dustings and crumbs.

"Well," I said. "If I lose my vision I won't come home."

Frick wiped his hands on his jeans, and Mom slammed a plate down in the sink. "Stop that!"

Frick and I looked at her.

"Wipe your hands on them one more time," she said, pointing at him with a soapy finger. "I gave you a napkin. Use it."

Since Paige had gone to rehab six weeks back, Mom didn't have anyone to snap at, so that left Frick and me. I went for the door.

"Don't forget the mail, David."

I turned the cold doorknob and the November air nipped my fingers. Everywhere, bare tree branches reached at a gray sky. With the ground covered in leaves, it was harder to find good sticks for a battle. I walked down the road past all the same long rectangular homes, the only difference being color. I smelled ash and chalk—somewhere a fire burned. Crows cawed in the distance and the road came to an end. Through the high grass and into the woods, I set off along the riverbank. The river was moving fast, but the cold moved faster. Soon, all would be frozen again.

I trekked along the riverbank until I came to the fallen tree where JP and Tyson said they'd meet me. In rapid bursts a woodpecker drilled on a tree in the distance and the river carried the sound. I unzipped my jacket and reached in my hidden pocket and pulled out a Winston 100 and a red Bic. The cigarette sizzled in the flame.

Smoke clung to the cold air like it clung to my lungs. *Exhale.* The wind off the river was chilled. The crispy fallen leaves crackled behind me. I faced the sound. Tyson was wearing his bright orange jacket.

"You going hunting?" I asked.

He laughed. "It's the only jacket I got."

"Puff?"

He grabbed the cigarette and pulled off it. "Where's JP?"

"Thought he'd come with you," I said.

Tyson looked out at the water.

"What, you want to swim?" I asked.

He looked at me like I was stupid and then pointed with the cigarette to his feet. "I'm not getting my new shoes wet."

"You know you're going to ruin those shoes before today's over."

"Nah." He blew smoke. "My mom will kill me."

"Whatever you say." I took the cigarette and turned back toward the river. "So when's JP getting here?"

Tyson looked at me, startled, and then he laughed. "Oh yeah, he said head down to the spot and he'd meet us there."

"So if I didn't ask, then we'd be waiting here for no one?" I poked him in the chest. "I'm telling JP you forgot what he said. He's going to go after you during battle."

"He's going to go after me no matter what."

Tyson followed me into the deep woods, bending and twisting through tree limbs. "Well, now he's going to go after you even harder."

We had spots all over the Island. Dry spots. Wet spots. Lonely, unvisited spots. Where we were going had been someone else's spot years ago: a rope swing hung from a high branch off a tree that had an old rotting tree house in it. Nothing grew within fifty feet of there.

When we arrived, JP was on the rope swing, one foot stuck in the knothole, the other dangling. The tree branch bent and creaked under his weight.

"I been waiting long enough," JP said.

I pulled another cigarette from my pocket and lit it. "Tyson said you're too heavy to be on that."

"What?" JP struggled to free his foot from the knothole.

"No I didn't," Tyson said.

I said it again. "Tyson said you were too heavy to be on that."

"Heavy? You wait, Tyson. I got a heavy fucking stick coming your way."

Tyson's voice cracked. "I didn't say that!"

"Don't matter if you said it or not." JP freed his foot. "What matters is it was said. And you're done for." We walked closer and JP met us. He then plunged two fingers into Tyson's chest and laughed. "Just messing with you. Let me get a puff, David."

I handed it to him. In between drags JP watched Tyson. JP kept shaking his head.

"What?" Tyson said.

JP ignored him and exhaled. "Here." He passed the cigarette to me. JP walked away from us, and he glanced over his shoulder. "You best get running, Tyson. You got twenty seconds." JP bent over and picked up the first stick.

I took one last rip on the Winston, handed crack-drag to Tyson, and ran, scanning the ground for ammunition.

Sometimes, we had twelve people play and sticks flew from every direction and people quickly got bored; sometimes—most of the time—it was us three playing, and those games lasted hours. Once, Tyson hid so well in the woods that JP and I gave up and left him. He thought the game was on for hours after we had quit.

There was only one rule in battle: submission meant game over for the person submitting. It was a generous rule, but JP never acknowledged it, especially when Tyson said he surrendered.

I picked up some small sticks, and I saw Tyson was following me. "Get the fuck away from me," I told him, and I ran as fast as I could. When I looked back, there was only the gentle rocking of the woods behind me.

I had run toward the riverbank and was trapped against it. While I stopped to catch my breath I searched the ground for better sticks and found a few long and short ones. I walked cautiously, avoiding any twigs that might snap or dried leaves that might crunch. Progress was slow; it seemed as though hours had passed before I made it fifty feet. Crows cawed loudly and the river smelled damp. Off in the distance, a treetop rustled and birds flapped their wings and flew away. Someone was walking.

A row of pine trees blocked the view, but I approached slowly and crouched down behind them. Smells of pine and sap filled my nose. A branch snapped.

He was there, bright orange appearing from behind trees and getting closer. I ducked down and watched with my ears. If Tyson's here, I thought, JP isn't far behind.

I stood, cocked back a thick stick, squinted my eyes, and barreled through the pine tree branches, needles pricking at my face.

SMACK. I crashed into a body and fell over.

"Jesus Christ!" JP said.

I lay on the ground looking up at him. He stared back at me, a look of both confusion and wonder at how he hadn't heard me. Then he lowered his brown brows, battle-mode.

He poked my chest with a long stick. "You're done for," he said. As he pulled the stick back to swing at me, I was about ready to surrender when something smashed into JP's back.

JP jumped and swung around. "You little shit," he said. "You're dead!"

Tyson's laugh filled the air while JP chased him. I rolled over and stood, and then I snatched up my sticks and ran after them. Tyson was leading JP back toward the spot with the rope swing.

JP only slowed down enough to wing a stick at Tyson, who looked like an orange peel running through the woods. When they broke through brush and came to a clearing, Tyson turned, and in one last effort to save himself from JP's wrath, flung a stick hard at him.

JP dodged it.

I dropped to my knees and grabbed my eye.

"I submit!" Tyson screamed.

One final loud crack hit my ears and Tyson wailed.

"I guess I win," JP said, laughing.

"I submitted!" Tyson said.

I opened my eye and I could see, but blood ran down my face and covered my hands. Tyson lay on the ground rubbing his back. JP hurried over to me.

"You all right?" he said.

"Where am I cut?"

JP bent down and looked. "Between your eye and your nose. Man, that's a deep gash. Nice battle wound."

"It need stitches?"

"No, let's go to Tyson's and clean it up and get lunch."

"Fuck you, you can't have lunch." Tyson stood and rubbed his back.

"I can have whatever I want. I'm the winner." JP raised his fist.

"Fucking hell," Tyson said. "Look at my shoes."

Thick mud covered his new sneakers.

. . .

Tyson stood in front of the bathroom mirror lifting his shirt as he examined his lower back. He held his muddy shoe in one hand.

"Would you move?" I said. "Your back's fine."

"It hurts. And I have to clean my shoe."

"There's no scar and you can clean your shoe after. Move so I can clean this blood."

"Where's your mayonnaise?" JP yelled from the kitchen.

Tyson set his shoe in the tub and went to the kitchen.

I looked at my face. Pale skin. Dark bags under my eyes. A thin, tear-like layer of blood streaked down my face. The blood from the gash between my eye and nose had hardened like dried red paint. I turned on the sink. Blood stained my hands and seemed to belong there. I scrubbed my hands hard with a bar of soap and then scrubbed the line of blood off my face. The area around the cut was beginning to bruise.

With a cloth, I dabbed the gash, gently scraping away small bits of crusted blood. It bled again and was watery. I pressed a

Q-tip soaked in peroxide against the wound and winced. I dried the area and put Neosporin on it. Behind the mirror I found a box of assorted Band-Aids and stuck a medium-small one vertically between my eye and nose.

Tyson's parents were working so I lit a cigarette and walked into the living room. I plopped down onto the couch.

"Nice Band-Aid," JP said. "It matches your vagina."

I laughed. "Shut up."

JP finished his sandwich. "You going to make one?"

"I'm not hungry." I flicked my cigarette.

"I call David's sandwich." JP went back to the kitchen.

Tyson stood. "Don't, you've used most of the bologna."

"Relax, you have an unopened package of it in the fridge drawer."

Tyson could do nothing but watch while JP piled on the fixings.

"Sorry about your face, David," Tyson said.

"No worries." I passed him the cigarette.

JP sat in the rocking chair in the living room. "See this, skee-jins." He pointed to his sandwich. "This is an Indian sandwich. We got some nice thick white bread, a thin layer of mayonnaise, a dab of ketchup, some shredded cheddar cheese, and then three slices of bologna." He took a bite.

"How does that make it an Indian sandwich?" I said.

JP looked at me and then at his sandwich. "Because I'm eating it, that's why. Don't ask stupid questions, David."

Tyson and I laughed.

I split one more cigarette with Tyson and JP before I decided to go home. When the smoke was butted I went to

Tyson's bathroom and peeled the Band-Aid from my face. In front of the mirror, the cut looked worse than earlier, but better without the Band-Aid. The chance my mother noticed the cut was less without the Band-Aid, but if she did notice it, I preferred that she see it for what it was: a wound.

Frick's truck was gone from the driveway when I got home. The wind blew, and yellow and orange leaves twirled in the road. I opened the mailbox at the beginning of the driveway. Nothing but a dead hornet that had been there for months.

Mom was sitting in her rocking chair with the TV remote in her hand. "Where's the mail?"

I unzipped my jacket. "There was nothing."

Mom stood, and she walked with a limp. Arthritis. She was as hot as the woodstove. "Where's the phone," she said, but it wasn't a question.

I made it down the hallway to my room before she spoke: "Come back and call your father."

I tossed my jacket on my bed.

"Here." She handed me the phone and I dialed his number.

It rang. Mom hovered not too close, but close enough. I turned my bruised and split face the other direction. The phone rang. Mom looked in the cabinet under the sink where she kept all the poisonous fluids. I wondered how many times she had checked under there today. The phone rang. I hoped he'd answer, an end for today. Like undone chores, these missed calls piled up.

It rang. The kitchen table was clean: not a pork rind in sight. I dug my finger into the small dent in the table, formed when Mom and Dad and Paige and I had all lived together. It was one of the few memories I had of that time, and the memory was as sharp as glass. On top of our fridge, Mom had kept a heavy jar filled with nothing, and it had fallen onto the table and left a perfect, smooth indentation. The jar never broke.

The phone rang and rang. Mom slammed the cabinet shut, and the voice on Dad's automated voice mail said his inbox was full. I pretended to leave a message, to please her, and then I hung up.

"Your father." Mom took the phone and dialed his number again and again, each time hanging up before the automated voice said the machine was full. I turned my face away from her and smelled for the first time the corn fritters she'd made. Not a trace of their preparation or their cooking remained—she had cleaned everything. The only dirty dish was the one upon which the fritters sat, cooling. The garbage bin was empty too, the bag white like fresh snow.

Frick's truck groaned up the road, and Mom set the phone down and watched him pull in. He got out of the truck, and he kicked shut the driver's door. He cradled in one hand a large brown paper bag—the bag wet, the chilled bottle having heated and sweated in the hot truck—and in the other hand he carried a bag of pork rinds.

. . .

Dad called later in the evening, but Mom and Frick were out back of the house around the fire.

"Hey, buddy," Dad said. He was fully awake. "Whatcha doing?"

"Just got done eating."

"What'd you have?"

Dad loved all food. Even if it were a can of tomato soup, he'd spend all day with it on the stove at a simmer, struggling against his weight to get up from his chair every thirty minutes to stir it and add dashes of salt and pepper.

"Corn fritters."

"The ones your mother makes? Those are good. What'd you have with them?"

Peace and quiet, I felt like saying. When Frick had come back, he and Mom went straight outside and I had brought six corn fritters back to my room, shut my window so as not to hear them, and ate.

"Mom made some soup."

"What kind?"

For fuck's sake. "Chicken noodle from a can."

"She's cheap."

"Mom said you were supposed to send money up in the mail."

"What?" He groaned, and I could tell he was trying to sit straighter. "I sent her money two days ago. Did you get any of it?"

Did I get any of it? "No."

He started to cough. "Hold on, David."

I moved the phone away from my ear until he was done with his coughing fit.

"Shit," he said. "You there?"

I told him I was.

"I sent her monthly money and then some."

"Mom said you haven't sent anything since my birthday."

"That fucking liar. I did too. I sent four hundred."

"Earlier this month?" I said.

"Yeah!"

I didn't know what to say, but Dad always said something when I was quiet.

"I can Western Union a hundred dollars tonight," he said. "But I'm sending it in your name."

"Just send it in her name."

"You don't want any of it?"

Frick passed by my bedroom window, and he carried an armful of wood. "Fine," I said. "Send it in my name. You will send it tonight, won't you?"

"Yeah, yeah. I'm going right now."

I put the phone on the hook and looked at the clock. Seven thirty.

Mom came in the front door without Frick and I turned to hide my gash.

"Kwey, gwus," she said. "It's chilly outdoors, but the fire's nice. Come sit outside with us." The last thing I wanted to do was sit outside with the two of them. It was awkward when they started to bicker; I had nothing to do but sit there and listen. If I moved, my mother would say to Frick, *You've upset my boy.*

"I'm all set," I said. She looked hurt. "I mean I would, but Dad called. He's Western Unioning some money."

"Oh? What happened to the money coming in the mail?" She walked to the sideboard, picked up a cold corn fritter, and bit into it.

"I didn't ask," I said. "But he said he sent four hundred at the beginning of the month."

Mom thought that was funny.

"That's what he said," I told her.

"When's he sending it?" she asked.

"Right now."

Mom took another bite of the corn fritter. "I think I can drive," she said.

"No need," I said. "He's sending it up in my name."

She stopped chewing. "Your name?"

I shouldn't have even told her. "I offered to go and get it."

"How much is he sending?"

"Eighty."

She turned away in disgust and threw the rest of her corn fritter away.

"Better than nothing," I said.

"Sounds about right for us."

I went to my room and grabbed my jacket. The back door slammed shut behind Mom and I pulled my cigarettes out. One left. In the kitchen, I looked through the window above the sink at the fire. Mom and Frick were sitting there, guzzling whatever had been in that paper bag. I hurried to Paige's dusty room and turned on the light. I opened drawer after drawer, searching for a loose cigarette. I found one way under her bed, right next to a blue pill and several bobby pins.

Before leaving I wrapped two corn fritters in a paper towel and tucked them in my pocket. Outside, the sky was clear and my breath mingled with the stars. I didn't want to make the walk to Overtown by myself, so I walked down the road to Tyson's and knocked on his door. He was all for it. He didn't even put his shoes on inside—he grabbed them and started walking and put them on as we walked down his driveway.

The Island was quiet and dark. Houses were awake if their outside lights were on; houses were asleep if you didn't see them in the dark, if all they seemed to be were masses of dense black pulsing between the surrounding trees.

We passed the church, and the sign under a white light read "Sunday ass." I pointed to it and we laughed. When we crossed the bridge and were in Overtown I pulled Tyson down a path to the riverbank, and we stood under the cold belly of the bridge. I flicked my lighter, flame casting shadows over steel, and the flame sizzled against the tobacco. I let go of the gas and I wondered what all the shadows were.

I took a drag. "I found this under my sister's bed." I passed it to Tyson. "It's a Newport. Tread carefully."

When we finished the cigarette and were back on the road, I pulled the corn fritters from my pocket.

"Want one?"

Tyson took it in his hand and inspected it under the streetlight. He bit into it. "What is it?"

"A corn fritter."

"It's pretty good." He swallowed hard. "Little dry."

Main Street came into view, and people floated like dust outside the bar. We crossed the street to avoid them and continued the road to Rite Aid. The parking lot was empty except for the dull orange light from the streetlamps beating down on the concrete.

Tyson stayed outside. I squinted in the bright light of the store and leaned on the counter while I filled out the Western Union form. The only ID I had was a tribal one and the cashiers never accepted it, but there was an option to set a security question-and-answer system to verify who you were. If whoever sent the money asked the same question and gave the same answer as whoever received the money, then that was valid enough proof.

What is your favorite color? I wrote. Dad always put blue, but I didn't know if that was his favorite color. *Blue,* I scribbled. Well, maybe he was asking what my favorite color was?

The cash register *cha-chinged* and the attendant handed me five twenties. Three stiff, fresh bills and two floppy, smooth ones. No matter the condition, I knew each bill smelled of a million dirty hands. I thanked her and before I got outside I slid one twenty in the pocket with my pack of one cigarette.

On our way back to the rez, people were outside the bar smoking. We passed by on the other side of the road and Tyson and I felt them staring.

"Hey," a fat guy said. "You got a cigarette?"

Tyson yelled back. "Look in your hand!"

"I'm holding this for someone! Come on, you got a cigarette?" He walked out from under the streetlight and into the dark of the road. "Come back."

Tyson and I kept walking toward the bridge.

"Greedy fucking Indians!" He yelled. A roar of laughter came from all the men. "Can't spare one lick of tobacco!"

We stopped.

"Let's tie our shoes," I said.

We knelt down. I checked my laces and they were knotted tight. I searched the ground for rocks. When I stood, I had a handful.

"Ready?"

We turned back toward them.

"Atta' girls!" Jabba the Hut said. "Bring me a cigarette."

We got as close as we needed.

"What are you dicking around for?" His voice was calm, and he held out his hand. "Come on," he said. "I won't bite."

I leaned toward Tyson. "Throw that rock like you threw that stick at my face."

"I'll throw it harder," he said.

I counted to three and we let them fly. The fat man was the first to duck and the others closest to the bar door tried to go inside.

"You dirty fucking Indians!"

Glass shattered, sprinkled all over the sidewalk. Men rushed out from the bar and the fat man stood. "You're fucked now, girls!"

Tyson turned first and then I followed, sprinting ahead of him. I didn't look back but it sounded like footsteps.

"The swamp, head to the horse bridge!"

I ran so fast across the bridge to the Island that everything was a blur. I passed the church, I knew that much, and soon I found myself near the swamp. I veered off the road and into the woods, twigs snapping and leaves crunching underfoot. I stuck my hands out to protect my face from tree limbs. The moonlight lit the swamp and I avoided the pools of murky water, hopping from one small patch of mossy ground to the other, until those patches got fewer and fewer the closer I came to the river that crept inland and formed the swamp.

A fallen tree closed the gap between the swamp and the path along the riverbank that led to the horse bridge. I was out of breath when I stepped carefully on top of the fallen tree and wobbled across to the other side. Even, flat ground. I took one deep breath and floored it toward the horse bridge.

With hands on my knees, I tried to listen. All I heard was ringing in my ears and my heavy breathing.

I waited. My breath slowly came back to me and my ears stopped ringing. Five minutes passed, then another, and Tyson didn't show up.

I wondered what time it was. Panic crept over me. But soon I heard footsteps coming down the opposite way of the path. It sounded like feet were sliding, dragging across ground.

I hid under the horse bridge and the feet scuffed against the wood above my head.

"David?" A voice whispered.

"Below."

He was breathing hard and the moon off the river divided his face. We stared at each other until we erupted with laughter.

"Oh, man." I wiped the tears away from my eyes. I had laughed so hard I cried.

"I gotta get home," Tyson said, still laughing.

"Me too." I reached in my pocket. "Let's smoke this last cigarette while we walk."

Tyson told me that he couldn't go into the swamp. Someone was chasing him and was too close, so he led them farther up the road before turning down a path. He ran until he was sure he shook whoever it was and then cut through the woods. He'd already overshot the horse bridge and so he found the riverbank and came back toward it.

"I thought you were done for," I said. "My heart was pounding."

"You think we'll get caught?"

"For what?" I asked.

"Breaking that window."

"When did we do that?"

Tyson laughed. He took one last drag on the cigarette and put it out. We came out onto our road and we split off in opposite directions, his feet dragging farther and farther away.

Frick's truck was gone. I looked out back of the house at a dwindling fire. Coals popped and little red sparks died in the cold air. Inside, the clock read ten. It felt later than that. Mom was in her rocking chair, sleeping, her head crooked sideways.

I shook her arm. "Hey," I said. She jumped awake.

"You scared me, gwus," she said, slurring her words. She shut her eyes again. "What time is it?"

"Ten."

She rocked forward and tried to stand. I grabbed her by the elbow and helped her up. I guided her down the hallway to her room.

I gave her a good-night kiss and she shut her door. I went around the house turning off all the lights. On the cedar chest in the living room, Mom had left her pack of Winston 100s and I stole three. I put one in my mouth but didn't light it. In the kitchen, I spread the four twenties out on the table so they covered the small dent. Before I went to bed, I went around the house collecting ashtrays. I dumped them into the garbage, and ashes and filters sifted down over Mom's half-eaten corn fritter.

. . .

The morning was cold, and my heart thumped. The sunlight lit my room, the trees outside too bare to shield this side of the house. Shivering, I pulled my blanket tight around my body and thought of the bar window and all the ways we would not get caught.

I sat up. I had to tell Tyson not to wear his orange jacket today. With the blanket wrapped around my shoulders I dragged myself to the kitchen. The floor was cold through my socks. I looked out the kitchen window at the oil-tank meter. Less than an eighth of a tank. The woodstove wasn't burning, so I filled the base of it with crumpled newspaper and then wrapped kindling in some more, lighting it all up with a grill lighter. When it was ready, I fed logs into the fire.

It was quarter to eight. We were out of coffee filters, so I stuffed a paper towel into the coffeemaker and filled it with grounds, and then I poured eight cups water into the back part. I plugged in the coffeemaker, and it screamed and gurgled.

I heard a quiet voice over the sound of the coffeemaker and the popping of the woodstove. "Gwus?"

Mom was up.

I opened her door and peered into the darkness. Her curtains were blacker than mine and the sun didn't rise toward her windows. "Yeah?"

"Bring me some juice?" She didn't open her eyes.

"You want coffee too?"

"No, just juice. I'm going to rest some more."

I got her juice and set the cup on her nightstand.

She picked it up and took a sip. "Thank you." Her voice was grateful, as it usually was when she needed something.

I poured a cup of coffee and set it on the cedar chest in the living room and while it cooled I went to my room and made my bed, straightened the corners of the red comforter, and when I finished I went back to the living room and sat on the couch and picked up the coffee and blew on it. I wanted a smoke. I didn't know if Mom would get up to use the bathroom, but after tapping my foot on the floor for a long time, I went to my room, shut my door behind me, and cracked the window.

The sun was bright on my face and the first drag brought me to myself. Smoke filled the air and showed the sunrays. I remembered the cut on my face. It was tender, coarse, hard. I picked at it the way my father picked at the sores on his legs. It wasn't ready to peel. Fresh blood dotted the tip of my finger.

By ten thirty Mom wasn't up. I crept in her room, and I shook her arm.

"Hm?"

"I'm going out for a bit," I said.

"What time is it?"

I told her.

"You want to bring me coffee?"

I poured her coffee and put five sugars in it.

She grabbed the cup and sipped with shaky hands. "Thank you, honey."

I inched toward the door, had my body turned sideways so she couldn't see the cut.

"Where you going?" she said.

"To Tyson's."

"You eat?"

"No, but I'll take a few corn fritters with me." I wasn't hungry.

"Come home for lunch, I'll fix you something. What do you want?"

"Grilled cheese?" I said.

"We don't have any bread." Mom laughed. "I'll ask next door."

I dressed, grabbed a corn fritter, and went outside. Out back, frost sparkled on the tips of grass around the fire pit. An open tin coffee can filled with sand and cigarette butts held down an empty pork-rind bag in the wet grass. I took some long-butted Winstons, and then I found the lid to the can and snapped it on. I cut through the woods to Tyson's.

When I showed up to his house, he was eating a bowl of Lucky Charms, and when he finished and brought his bowl to the sink and came back to the couch he turned on his Xbox and handed me a controller and we played three matches of *Halo* until his dad left, and we tried to play a fourth match but we grew sick of it, and so we went on his mother's computer and tried to watch porn, but the videos wouldn't buffer.

"You have Lucky Charms cereal, yet you have shitty internet?" Tyson laughed as he cleared the browser history.

"Let's go smoke," I said, and he was saying his dad might be back soon.

"Boiler room," he said.

We smoked in the boiler room, yet it was so hot we didn't even finish our cigarettes and went back inside. Tyson put on jeans and a fresh black shirt. He asked if I wanted to go to the social, the powwow at the football field. I told him my mom was making lunch, and right then I remembered the bread, remembered his jacket. I persuaded him to wear a different one.

161

At noon, before I left Tyson's, I stole four pieces of white bread and put them into a sandwich baggie. It had gotten much warmer outside. I carried my jacket over my arm and rolled up my sleeves. I rounded the corner of our road. Smoke rolled out of our chimney and into the sky. The door creaked shut behind me, and Mom's hair dryer was whistling from the bathroom. I rolled my sleeves down.

"Ma?" I yelled.

"Be right there." She turned off the hair dryer.

I sat at the table and the money that had covered the small dent was gone. Mom came out. "Oh, shoot," she said. "I forgot to go ask for bread."

I held up the baggie with four slices and smiled.

"David," she said. "What happened to your face?"

Shit.

She took the bread from my hands but didn't take her eyes from the cut.

"A stick," I said.

She put the bread down next to the sink. "I told you. You fucking kids don't listen." She meant Paige and me.

"It's fine," I said. "Relax."

"It won't be fine when one day you're blind. You already lucked out once bef—"

"I know," I said. Don't bring it up, I thought, and she said no more.

She sprayed a frying pan and turned the burner on medium. We were quiet. When the pan was hot she buttered one side of each slice and lay one down in the pan. It sizzled. She put two slices of cheese on top and then lay the other slice down, buttered side up. She flipped the sandwich over and it sizzled, hotter and louder. She turned the burner lower.

While the other side cooked she went in the bathroom and put on makeup. After a while, she hollered at me. "Check your sandwich, David." With the spatula I peeked under the sandwich. It was black. I lifted it out of the pan, set it on my plate, and carried it to the table. The phone rang.

"Pew, you burn that sandwich?" Mom said. She picked up the phone. "What?"

The sandwich crunched between my teeth. Here we go, I thought.

"Why haven't you called?" Mom took the phone to the bathroom with her and on the way she moved the phone from one ear to the other. "What do you mean they only let you use the phone once in a while? You can use the phone all the time there."

Mom listened. "I don't know," she said. "How are you? How's the program?"

"What'd you say?" Mom paused, and she leaned out the bathroom and looked at me. "He's fine. Listen . . ." She was serious. "Hold on." Mom left the bathroom and shut herself in her bedroom.

The house was quiet except for the hum of the fridge. I leaned in my seat toward the hallway, trying to listen. Nothing. I took a bite of my sandwich, set it down, and chewed and tiptoed to the hallway.

I heard words, sentence fragments, incoherent and jumbled. There was no context unless I gave them some. Eventually, I heard all I needed to: "He's stealing my cigarettes."

My stomach dropped and I wanted to puke. Mom had this way to make you want to die. I brought my plate to the sink and then sat in the living room. I looked at Mom's pack and didn't even want one.

Soon, Mom came out of the room and put the phone on the hook. She didn't ask how the sandwich was. "I'm heading to Overtown soon," she said, returning to the bathroom, and in time Mom's makeup container snapped shut, and when she came out of the bathroom she said nothing to me and left. I could do no wrong when Paige was around, but the moment she was gone, the world in which we lived became my fault. I scraped the black burn off my grilled cheese.

. . .

The house was quiet when Mom left, except for the crows cawing outside. I put on my jacket and went out to find JP and Tyson. Crows cawed louder; they were in the trees and on the power lines. Through the woods I walked and smoked. The trees were bare, and the sky above was a piercing blue. The smoke made my eyes water, and it was like I was drowning.

My stomach growled. I hopped over a fallen tree and continued down the path until I heard cars passing on the road. I finished my cigarette and walked onto the street toward Tyson's, but he wasn't home, was at the Social with JP probably. I cut through more paths until I came out on the other side of the Island, where the football field pressed against the river.

No one was drumming and not too many people were left at the Social. People clumped together in small groups that speckled a third of the field. JP and Tyson were sitting on the side of the field tossing rocks into the river. Tyson was wearing a black jacket. I walked over and sat next to them.

"You missed some good burgers," JP said.

"They're all gone?" I wanted one.

He nodded. "A lot of people showed up."

"I'm surprised they're not drumming,"

"Only one drum group came. There's a powwow up north. You got a ciggie?" JP said.

"Just butts. They're good length though."

He wiped his hands together to get the dirt off and stood. "Better than nothing."

"You want to go now?" I said.

"Everyone's leaving."

I didn't want to move, didn't want everyone to leave, didn't want the food to be gone. But it was over. We left, and in the woods away from everyone we huddled together and I gave them each a half-smoked cigarette.

"Damn," JP said. "Butted Winstons are strong."

I nodded and lit mine. JP didn't mention the bar window, so I knew Tyson hadn't told him.

"Let's go down to the river and watch the sun set," JP said.

"That's way on the other side of the Island," Tyson said. "And it's getting cold."

"Shut up," JP said. "If you're cold why'd you wear a wind-breaker? Going jogging?"

I laughed.

"Yeah," I said, "Why aren't you wearing your good jacket?"

Tyson shook his head and smiled. Then we were laughing. Really laughing!

"What?" JP said.

I caught my breath. "Let's walk and we'll tell you."

. . .

The river drained into the setting sun.

"I would've smashed that guy's head," JP said. "At least you broke the window. That counts for something."

I lit another butt. "I feel so much lighter now that we told someone."

Tyson nodded. "Yeah, my dad asked this morning if I saw anything."

"Wait, what?" I asked. "Before I came over?"

"Yeah."

"And you're just now telling me that?" I shook my head. "You're ridiculous."

JP poked Tyson's rib cage. "Why didn't you tell David earlier?"

"I forgot!"

"What'd you tell him?" I said.

"Who?"

"Poke him again, JP."

"Stop!" Tyson scooted over some. "Who?"

"Your dad, dumbass. Who you think I'm talking about?"

"Oh yeah. I said we didn't see anything. Then he didn't ask me anything else."

"That's the most anticlimactic story I've ever heard," JP said.

We were quiet and smoked our butts. After those, I had none left. The sun was setting fast and a few bright stars dotted the sky.

"I wish I'd been there," JP said.

. . .

It was dark when I got home. Frick's truck was parked behind Mom's car. No lights were on in the house. Mom's laughter poured out from behind our neighbor's backyard, where a fire burned hot and fast, and her and Frick's shadows pressed against the edge of the woods, swaying.

The house was cold. I turned on the kitchen light, went over to the woodstove, and touched the icy steel.

I dug in the wood box for newspaper but there wasn't any. On the kitchen table some bills lay sprawled as if they were thrown, an empty brown paper bag upright as if set down gently, and a pile of that day's local paper was neatly stacked. Mom always brought them back from the store for the woodstove.

I put the local papers in the wood box but kept one out, and I glanced at each page before I crumpled and stuffed them in the woodstove. A story about a 5K fundraiser, accompanied by a large picture of a woman running, covered most of the front page. Another story came below, something about a bill for higher taxes, and continued on to a later page. Stories of animal shelters overflowing and grand openings of stores that never lasted and the governor's new plan for more jobs seemed to compose in no order the paper. There were stories on retirement homes and even a story of a car salesman's journey to sales titled "Transformer." They all had stupid titles.

I continued to glance at, crinkle, and toss each page into the woodstove until my eyes fixed on "Crime and Court."

I froze, fingers clenching the paper.

Rock 'n' Roll

Police say that last night a local bar had its windows smashed out in what they're calling vandalism. According to the police report, at 8:45 PM, patrons of the local Overtown Bar stood outside smoking when two teenage boys approached them and asked for cigarettes. When the patrons refused, the teenagers became infuriated and began to harass them, eventually picking up rocks and throwing them toward the establishment.

The two boys have not been identified, but the report suggests that they are from the Panawahpskek Nation. According to the patrons, the boys ran toward the reservation. Overtown police are working closely with Island officers on the matter.

If you have any information about this crime, please contact the Overtown Police Department or the Office of Tribal Corrections.

I laughed, but I was angry, too. I ripped the story out, folded it up, and slid it in my pocket. I reached in the wood box and pulled out every local paper. One by one I crinkled up the "Crime and Court" page and put it in the woodstove and then neatly reorganized each newspaper and set them in the wood box. I took a front page and wrapped it around some kindling. I lit a match and touched it to the paper, and the fire crept and crept over the woman running on the front page, and I watched her disappear in the woodstove's twisting flame. I took the fire poker and prodded the fire, which whooshed. I opened the damper and touched the warm cast iron.

I flicked on my bedroom light, and when I sat on the bed I saw it.

I got up. On top of my dresser stood a pack of cigarettes on top of a note. I held them. Winston 100s. I picked up the note. Mom's handwriting.

Make them last, it read.

I folded the note and put it in my pocket with the news article. I undressed, turned my light off, and crawled under the covers. A small breeze slipped under the cracked window behind me and carried with it the sound of my mother's laughter.

HALF-LIFE

It was Saturday. Early fall. I was sitting up, holding my head, and thinking about my grandmother for not too long before Fellis saw I was awake and asked me how we got down here, in one of the two tall silos at the blue abandoned Olamon In-dustries. Except for us and some dirt and blown wet leaves and crushed cans of cheap beer, the silos were empty. What light made its way this deep showed me my orange-colored hands. Rust from the ladder we'd used to get down here, and it was that ladder I wanted to say was how we got here, but that's not what Fellis meant. The answer he sought had something to do with all the crushed beer cans. Or maybe it goes back further, has more to do with why we crushed those beer cans in the first place.

"Dee," Fellis said. He stood now and brushed dirt off the back of his jeans. "Do you remember coming here?"

I was thinking too much into his question. All he wanted was a memory.

"I don't remember," I told him.

"Me fucking neither," Fellis said.

I stood, and I rubbed my head and neck.

Fellis climbed out first, and I followed. His sneakers on the ladder scraped loose flakes of rust that fell like bloody snow, and so I climbed up looking down at the bottom of the silo. I couldn't see he'd stopped climbing, and so I bumped my head on his heel.

"Wait a minute," he said. "Be quiet."

I sneezed and the noise reverberated through that empty silo.

"Goddamn it," Fellis whispered. "Shut up."

Olamon Industries was out back behind the tribal lumberyard. It had been years since the industry produced anything or stored any materials in those silos. The tribe used to make audio cassettes, but they started in on that when CDs were becoming a thing, so the venture didn't last too long. Then the tribe's business was saved, just for a time, when they partnered with some contractors to manufacture tactical landing light systems for the US so aircrafts could identify landing areas. Not sure why the tribe stopped making those—maybe the US had landed in every possible place so they no longer needed Indians to help them out.

Or maybe we just sucked at making them.

The car Fellis waited for to pass passed by.

We went out and over the edge and climbed down the ladder to the ground.

"Christ, it's bright when you've been in the dark so long," Fellis said.

We stepped into the woods past the lumberyard, the shortcut to our roads home. And we weren't in the wooded path for more than a rock's throw before Fellis asked me to come over for breakfast, said his mom would make us something.

"I got to get home," I said. "I told my mother I'd go see my grandmother this morning up at Woodlands."

"It's still early," Fellis said. He looked up in the gray fall sky and pointed. "Sun's right there. It's not even nine yet."

"Then I'm late," I said, and it was then I realized I was shaking. "Can I get a pin?"

"They're at home," Fellis said, but I knew he was lying. He had them on him last night. "Come by and I'll give you some."

"No," I said. "I have to get home."

We came to the end of the path and out onto the road, and Fellis went one way and I went the other.

At home, the driveway was empty, and I cussed on my way indoors and through the kitchen and down the hall to the bathroom where I threw up in the toilet with the lights off. The phone was ringing out in the kitchen, but I let it go. With my head under the sink faucet I swallowed three Tylenol, and then with some soap I washed my hands of the rust, washed my face and behind my ears and around my nose, and then did it all two times more to make sure I got everything, all of it. I refused to look at myself in the mirror.

The phone started ringing again.

My hands were wet when I answered the phone and said hello, but nobody said anything back. I hung up and was on my way to the bathroom when I looked at the stove clock.

It wasn't even morning; it was half past three in the afternoon.

When my mother came back later, I was in the living room with the TV on low and a lit cigarette I couldn't drag from without getting nauseated. She had some groceries and asked me where I was this morning.

"I lost track of time," I told her, and she said nothing because she was sick of me. How could she not be? It's just been us two for the past six years. *How'd we get here?* That's Fellis's question, but it's mine too. *How'd we get here?* I'm starting to think that each time I ask it, each time I consider an answer, I wind up farther away from where I should be, from where I was. Where I had been. I left a lot of things behind. Or maybe that's not it—maybe it's that a lot of things had left me behind. Friends. Family. Relationships. The future.

I put out the cigarette and stood to leave. My mother didn't care to know where her twenty-eight-year-old son was going, but before I left I asked her when she was going next to Woodlands.

"Tomorrow," she said. She stood at the sideboard with a candle in a glass jar and a knife, lengthening the wick. "Same time."

I told her I wouldn't miss it again. She scraped wax off the knife with her fingernail, which she then rubbed off on a dirty cloth. I waited for her to say something more until I knew she'd said it all.

I walked to Fellis's. His mom, Beth, let me in but didn't say anything to me because she was on the phone telling someone it was all going to be all right. Fellis was sleeping when I went to him in his room. And he didn't wake when I nudged him, so I sat in a beanbag chair and wondered where he put those pins, and when I settled on a place—in his dresser—I looked for them but only found some cash and change and sticks of half-burned incense.

I tripped over a box in his room on my way to the bathroom in the hallway. Again, I threw up, and in the light I saw some rust was still on my hands. I washed it all off.

Fellis was awake when I went back in the room, and so I turned the light on. He was sitting up in the bed with his back against the wall. He asked when I got here, and I said a little bit ago.

"How was your grandmother?" he asked.

"I was late," I said. "Didn't make it."

"There's always another day," he said. He sat up straighter. "What time is it?"

I told him and he whistled.

"This was the fastest fucking day," he said.

"Let me get one of those pins," I said.

Fellis yawned and wiped his face and then looked at his hands and smelled them.

"Rust," I said. "Did you hear me?"

"Yeah, I heard you. Hold on. Christ."

He wiped his hands on his shirt and got up and left the room. He was wearing only his boxers. I could hear him out in the kitchen talking with Beth about something. When he came back he held two beers and dropped one in my lap and set his on the dresser, and then he grabbed his jeans off the floor and squeezed both pockets, and then, still holding the jeans, he kicked at the dirty clothes on the floor, looking. He dropped his jeans and went to his bed and tugged the blanket off.

"You can't find them?" I asked.

He stopped doing what he was doing and looked at me with just a sliver of his face. "Does it look like I can find them?" He started digging again.

Fellis slanted his bed away from the wall and peered in the gap. He didn't right the bed, and he grabbed his jeans off the floor and put one leg in.

"I must've left them in the silo," he said, losing his balance. "Whoa!" He reached for the dresser to steady himself and put his other foot in his pants, yanked up, and buttoned. "Let's go up there and drink anyway. My auntie's coming over soon to cry and I don't want to be around for that shit."

If the pins weren't in the silo, I told myself, I wasn't staying.

Before we left, Fellis shoved eight beers in a plastic grocery bag, which he made me carry while he carried his hand-crank flashlight and a half-gone bottle of gin, and somewhere between his place and the silo, when we were on the wooded path, he told me to hold onto the bottle and flashlight so he could tie his shoe. When he was done he didn't take the bottle or the flashlight back until we were at the ladder, and he only took them because I couldn't carry all that and I told him so. We climbed up the ladder and down into the silo.

Fellis kept his pins in a medicine bottle with the label partially peeled off, which makes sense when you buy from the streets, but he got these prescribed from the doctor on the rez. The flashlight cut the dark of the silo, and I watched as Fellis kicked at the small mounds of wet leaves.

"Here it is," he said, and he rattled the bottle with the little blue pills before tossing it to me.

I knew better than to take a whole one on a pretty empty stomach, but I couldn't snap the tiny pill in half, so I took it.

"You're gonna fall asleep on me," Fellis said, and he swallowed a blue pill with a sip of beer. He leaned back on the silo wall and slid down it to a sitting position. It was all but dark out now. He cranked his flashlight once, twice—thirty times. He propped it up and in the lit space between us I saw our mess of crushed cans and cigarette butts and crumpled cello-phanes and bum lighters and glass bottles.

How long had we been coming here?

Three beers in, I started telling Fellis the story about my grandmother, years back when I was little, when her memory first started to go and she thought I was someone else. I told the story and he said "uh huh" or "mmm" for a time, and when I got to the funny part his hard laughter gave me energy to dig up another about her, which he listened to quietly and with no noise. The hand-crank flashlight cut out in the middle of my story, and when Fellis made no movement to get the light going again I wondered at which part in this second story did he fall asleep? I lay down and used my arm as a pillow, and the sting from the cold metal of the silo against my skin reminded me that she wasn't dead yet and in the morning I better be up and on time.

. . .

I was up in that early, early hour when it feels like anything can happen, that moment right before the sun crosses the horizon in a quick and unexpected burst.

My grandmother.

I left Fellis sleeping. I wasn't feeling as sick as the day before, but I had those heart shivers, where thinking or not thinking both get you nervous. I was halfway up the ladder when I thought to take some of Fellis's pins. I climbed back down and looked for the bottle. I found it and knocked four into my palm but I put one back because he was almost out. I couldn't read when he was due a refill. That bit was peeled off. I swallowed one with no drink and put the other two in the tiny pocket on my jeans, and then I climbed out of the silo and headed home.

My mother was in the bathroom when I got home. I shut the back door behind me.

"Is that you?" she asked.

"Yeah, it's me."

"What?"

"It's me!"

There was coffee left in the pot, and I poured a cup and went to the couch. That pin I took was doing its job: I was for the time being no longer shivering from thinking or not thinking. But I was tired. Real tired.

I lied and said no when she asked if I was sleeping.

"You don't have to come," she said. She sat down on the couch next to me and put on her shoes.

"I said I would," I told her, and I stood up.

On the way off the rez we drove by Fellis walking down the road and in the rearview I watched as he turned around and watched right back.

The only time my mother and I talked during the drive to Woodlands was when she asked me for a lighter and I told her I forgot it. Nothing else was said. And you'd think there'd be some awkwardness in this drive, in this non-talking, but the truth is that we're used to not talking. Or maybe it's just me, since I can't speak for her. But she's never said otherwise.

I wonder if *How'd we get here?* is the wrong question. Maybe the right question is *How do we get out of here?* Maybe that's the only question that matters.

My mother parked the car in the parking lot of Woodlands, and she asked if I was sleeping.

"No," I said, and I got out of the car.

Woodlands was a nice-looking place. But like all assisted living centers or places where the old go to die, there was that empty feeling to it, like every part of the place—the walls, doors, handrails, desks, tables, counters, cupboards, board games, TVs, couches, chairs, plants, everything, all of it—was hollowed out and could so easily break, like that colored plastic used in children's playhouses you see at day cares. If you could squeeze it hard enough, it would be misshapen. And the smell—the smell too had some hollow to it.

A bald man buzzed us in, and a nurse with sharp blonde curls came out from a side office and pulled my mother aside like she had a secret to tell, something to do with my grandmother, but all she said was that my grandmother's been laughing a lot today, and in hearing that I felt something I hadn't felt in a long time. It wasn't quite happiness, but something close to it.

I followed my mother down one long hall. This old white guy whose face sagged and who leaned on the wall's handrail laughed at us, and when I stared at him as we passed he got all serious-like and let out several "whoops" before he laughed again.

"Weirdo," my mother said, and our laughing wasn't fake.

My grandmother's door was partly open, and my mother pushed it and stuck her head in the room and said my grandmother's name.

"Hi, yes," she said. "Come on in."

Even though she could still walk, my grandmother was in a wheelchair, and had it facing the window through which the maples were losing their leaves.

She turned herself around and rolled herself to the center of the room.

She looked at me.

"Hello," she said.

"You know who this is," my mother said. She sat on the bed.

"I do," my grandmother said, but in a way that could have been either a question or a statement.

"This is your grandson," my mother said.

"I know that," she said. "Welcome back, gwus. You know, if you were white it would have been self-defense."

"No, Mom," my mother said. "This is your grand*son*, not your grand*daughter*."

"That long hair could have fooled me," she said, laughing. "But I know who he is. I was just making conversation. Abin, gwus."

My mother pointed to a chair that I did not see. I grabbed it and turned it around and sat.

"I know who he is," my grandmother said again. "He's the one who doesn't do anything."

"Mom," my mother said.

"Well," my grandmother said.

That old white man came to the door and whooped.

"You get the hell out of here!" My grandmother got up from the wheelchair and went to the door. "Go on! Get!"

He didn't leave, so my grandmother shut the door in his face. "Winooches," she said, and then she laughed. She sat back down. "What was I going to tell you?" She looked at her finger, which she rubbed. "Forget it."

My mother's mouth opened to speak.

"Oh," my grandmother said. She looked at me. "Before you leave," she said, "can you check my mail?"

"There's a mailbox?" I asked.

"At the end of the driveway," she said.

Mom looked at me and I just went with it. "Sure," I said. "I'll check it."

"I'm waiting for my check," she said, and then she started in about some bingo game she won recently—"five thousand dollars," she said, smiling, her hands folded—and how with the money she was going to renovate her kitchen, and if there was some left over she was going to fix up her back porch.

But she wouldn't have money left over, because she won that money years back when the tribe first opened Super Bingo. What she won wasn't even enough for the kitchen.

"It's going to look so nice," my grandmother said.

"I bet it will," my mother said.

"You know," my grandmother said, but I stopped listening to her. Wasn't it only twenty-five hundred she won? And didn't part of that get stolen by some rez rats when she was at church? Yeah, I think that's what happened and why she couldn't get the kitchen finished. No—maybe it was five thousand. Yeah, it was five thousand. She gave half of it to the church. Yeah! That was it. I remember. And when the pastor found out about that money of hers getting stolen he didn't even offer to give back what she'd given to the church.

"You sleeping?" my grandmother asked.

I sat up straight and said no. But I think I was.

My grandmother laughed.

"He's tired," my mother said, and then she lied. "He just started working at UPS and they have him on nights."

"Is that right?" my grandmother said.

"Sure is," I said.

"Good for you. Good for you, gwus. You start paying rent now. You're too old to be mooching off your mother. How old are you?"

"Twenty-eight" I said.

"Jesus," she said. "Older than I thought."

"Mom."

"Can I use your bathroom?" I asked.

"Can you?" My grandmother cackled.

In the bathroom I didn't go but flushed like I did, and then under the sink faucet I swallowed another pin.

They were talking about something they didn't want me to hear, because they got quiet when I returned. When I sat down, my grandmother was smiling at me, smirking almost, like she knew the totality of my life, knew where I came from, where I was presently, and where I was going. And she kept on smirking at me, and then she nodded like she was agreeing on something, something about me—about where I was headed—and then she laughed and leaned forward and patted my knee.

"I had a brother . . ." she started to say.

Before we left that day my grandmother reminded me about the mail. "I'll wait right here," she said, and she stood half in her room, half in the hall.

Mom went and started the car and I waited near the front exit for a minute before I went back to my grandmother. She was still at her door, half in, half out.

"There was no mail," I told her.

"Maybe tomorrow," she said, and she cupped my chin in her hands. "Listen now—you be good." She let go and shut the door.

. . .

I'd been bumming pins from Fellis for months. Maybe even close to a year. One every three or four days, then one every other day, then one once a day, then two a day, then three a day. Maybe now is when I should stop bumming them. Or go see the doc. No—I can't see him. But I can't not take them. The world without them feels too muggy. Too stuffy. Like I can't breathe.

"You be good," my grandmother said. It's worth a shot.

On day three with no pins I asked Fellis again if he knew anyone who was selling. I did good the first two days without them, probably because I drank both nights, once in the silo and then once at Fellis's because it rained and the silo was all wet.

"I told you," Fellis said. He was putting in *Signs*, that alien movie with Mel Gibson and that little girl who leaves glasses of water all over the place. "That fucking kid Meekew has some."

I waited for the movie to be over before I left. I needed time to think it through, think about how I'd get the money. When I got up and told Fellis I'd be back, he asked me where I was going, and I lied and said to get some money from home, and he asked if he could come.

"I'll be right back," I said. "Just wait here." I took one of his smokes before I left.

I put my hood up and walked down the road and smoked a cigarette dotted with rain splatter and I thought—no, I asked—should I do it?

Over my grandmother's empty kitchen sink, I busted up the window frame and I pried it open and crawled inside, and I was crying not because I felt bad about doing it but because I didn't feel good one bit.

I drank a glass of water and splashed water on my face.

I didn't think I'd find any money, and so I suppose I tricked myself into thinking that that was a fact, and that that fact would absolve my attempt to take the money I convinced my-self was not in the house.

Then why look? I can't remember.

My grandmother's house wasn't too big. It had an upstairs with two bedrooms and a bathroom, and above that there was a small attic I'd never been in before. The bottom floor had the kitchen and living room and another bedroom, the one my grandmother stayed in even though the stairs weren't nothing for her to climb.

I decided to look upstairs first because I knew if I started downstairs I'd hear above me those floorboards creaking, which my grandmother said were from Goog'ooks walking around, and in hearing it I knew I'd get creeped out and wouldn't go upstairs, just like I did when I was little and refused to sleep anywhere but in bed next to my grandmother. But there was nothing upstairs except dust and boxes of pictures and old frames and empty plant pots and this cedar chest full of baby stuff that belonged to my mother. I did find an empty carton of cigarettes, Mistys, the kind my grandmother said she quit years back but we always knew she kept on smoking.

I found some change near the couch: a dime and two pennies under the cushions, and a quarter way back under the couch near the wall. But there was nothing else in the living room, nor in the kitchen. There was the bathroom to check, but why would there be money in there?

My grandmother's room felt like a display, like everything in it—the brown dresser, the bed with the long blue skirt, the two matching nightstands each with a lamp, and the closet behind whose white-colored doors hung all my grandmother's clothes—was never used but not never used, was just a room in an abandoned furniture store.

The rain outside picked up and hit hard the glass of the bedroom window.

You won't find anything, I told myself, yet I had a feeling I would find everything.

It was in a safe no larger than a cinder block, and it was half under the bed, half sticking out under the blue skirt. I slid it all the way out. The key was in the hole, like it had been waiting for me, like it had been put there for this very moment. Not a test, no. An alignment, an alignment of something I could not name. I turned the key, and its ridges and grooves lifted the cylinders with such assurance it took my breath away.

Papers, documents, pictures. A rosary. A letter from my sister. Pictures, documents, papers. A letter my grandmother never sent to my sister in an envelope with blue penmanship so sharp I could not read it.

The sound of floorboards creaking above me pulled my head like it was on a rope.

And then they were gone like the Goog'ooks themselves.

The manila envelope was about the same size as the money it held, and I counted it but didn't really count it, because the whole time I was saying, "There's supposed to be nothing here." I began again, and I only made it to four hundred and twenty dollars when a car door slammed shut. I shoved everything back into the safe, including the money, all of it, whose envelope I saw had my name written on it in that blue penmanship of hers. I would take no money right then, not because I couldn't and not because I convinced myself there was no money to take, but because the memory has always been that I left everything as it was.

I shut and locked the safe, and pushed it back under the bed as it had been. The front door opened and I opened the closet, and when the front door shut I shut the closet.

The bedroom light came on. Huddled between my grandmother's hanging clothes, lines of light crossing my face, I watched my mother cross the small room to the side of the bed I'd just left. She got on the floor and was out of my vision, but it was like I could still see, could still see what she was doing. She pulled out the safe.

She said something I couldn't hear. She sat up on her knees, looking.

She started in the dresser drawers, moving stuff around, and then she went to the nightstand closest to the safe, pulled open drawers, and she left them open when she went to the other side of the bed, the other nightstand, passed so close by me in the closet that I could smell her sharp perfume. I did not blink.

She left those drawers open too, and she went back to the safe, got back on the ground and out of my sight. Everything she pulled out from under the bed she set on the bed until everything that was under there was on top: old VCRs and unpainted shelves for knickknacks and a basket full of rogue cables and wires and a small plastic tote filled with buttons and sewing string and another empty carton of Mistys.

"Where is it?" my mother said.

Her eyes set on the closet, and she came for it. In my fear I tensed and squeezed each of my hands so tightly shut that I finally felt it.

My gasp made my mother jump back. "Who's there?" she said, and then perhaps to frighten the person behind those closed closet doors my mother declared she had a weapon. "I'll use it," she said.

I stared at the key in my hand.

How did we get here? and *How do we get out of here?* sometimes have the same answer.

"Don't you open that door!" my mother yelled. "You stay right there!"

She stood at the nightstand and picked up the phone and dialed three digits.

"Yes, I need—"

I wrapped myself in the hanging clothes and barged out through the closet door, and my mother screamed and dropped the phone. I sprinted from the room and still clenched most of the clothes to my body, and I ran out the front door and into the pouring rain. The longer I ran the heavier the clothes became, the cotton and polyester and wool of my grandmother's jackets and shirts and pants absorbing the rainwater. When I was on the wooded path I heaved the clothes off me and they plopped in the muddy wet of the earth, and I kept on going until the path ended. I had to cross the street to reach the other path, and I did so just in time. Sirens whirred and whined right past, and I crouched and ducked in a thicket of pines until dark.

. . .

Fellis found me down in the silo that night, and I thought he was the police coming for me. He stayed standing on the ladder and shone the hand-crank flashlight in my face.

"What are you doing down here?" he asked.

I told him what happened.

"That was you?" he said.

"Yeah," I said. "Anyone call you looking for me?"

"Your mom did," he said. "You think if it rains enough we'll drown down here?"

The water pooling at the bottom of the silo had soaked through my shoes hours ago.

"What did she say?" I said.

"She was looking for you."

"What'd you say?"

"That you went home."

"And what'd she say?"

"'When was that?'"

"And you said?"

"I don't fucking know," he said. "I can't remember." He hopped off the ladder and splashed water. "It's not as deep as I thought."

"You got a smoke?" I asked.

He lit one and handed it to me. "What are you going to do? Hide down here all night in the rain?"

"I wonder if she saw me," I said.

"She didn't," Fellis said.

"How do you know?"

"Because she wouldn't have said to me, 'If you see him tell him to call me. Someone broke into his grandmother's house.'"

"She said that?" I asked.

"Something close to it, yeah."

Fellis flashed his light around the silo, and I smoked that smoke down to the filter.

"Let's go to my place," Fellis said. "My feet are wet."

If the cigarette hissed out when it hit the water, I didn't hear it.

. . .

I called my mother when I got to Fellis's.

"Yeah, he told me," I said.

"I'm all right," she said, and in detail she recapped what happened, which was exactly as it did happen. "Why would someone rob an old woman's home?" my mother asked.

"You said they didn't take nothing?" I looked at the key in my hand.

She didn't say anything, and I asked her again.

"Yes," she said. "Nothing."

"Nothing?"

"Just those clothes that person ran off in."

"That was it?"

"That was it."

We were both quiet.

"I'm filling in again tomorrow," she said. "So if I'm not home—"

"You'll be at the tribal offices," I said.

"Yes," she said. "And give your grandmother a call tomorrow."

"I will," I said.

"Don't forget. And don't mention her house getting broken into."

"I won't."

"All right."

I ate some leftovers of moose meat and rice, and when I finished the plate Fellis and I went out back of his house under the awning and smoked to the sound of rain drumming above us.

"Did she have any money?"

I was surprised it took Fellis so long to ask.

A flash of light blinked in the sky far off, and I counted twelve seconds until the rumble.

"Thunder's coming," Fellis said, and he flicked his smoke that was half done.

I walked home at three in the morning. I thought Mom was up when I got home, not because the bathroom light was on but because I could have sworn she was standing right there in the hallway, looking at me. I was so convinced it was her I asked, "Are you all right?" But she wasn't there; I was just seeing shit between the light and the dark.

I turned the stove light on in the kitchen, and then I went down the hall to the bathroom and turned that light off. Back in the kitchen, I again thought I was seeing things that weren't there: my grandmother's safe rested on the kitchen table, and it didn't get any more real when I put my hands on each side of it and carried it like a watermelon to the living room and sat down on the couch with it in my lap. No. It got real when I took out that key and again had my breath sucked from my lungs when I twisted and pulled open the small door.

Forty-seven hundred dollars was in that small manila envelope with my name on it. I counted it in the dim light that stretched from the kitchen to the living room where I sat, and I thought I miscounted—forty-seven hundred dollars?—and so I counted it again but had got it right the first time. Forty-seven hundred dollars.

I took it. I did. Not all of it, and not right then. I sat on it, literally. Sat on what I took. I didn't even know how much I grabbed. Just some of it. I put the envelope with the rest back in the safe and closed the door and locked it and carried the safe back to the table where it was when I found it. Back on the couch I put the money under me as I sat for a few hours, thinking, really thinking if I should take what I already had, kept thinking about it and thinking about it and thinking about it until it grew light outdoors. And I only moved twice from the couch that whole time, once to make sure the key I held was real and that the safe door was closed and locked, and the second time to make sure none of that money I sat on got dragged with me when I went to check the safe, check to see the key in my hand was real.

Mom got up at quarter to six. I shoved those bills under the couch cushions. Just as I had scared her when I burst through the closet, I scared her again, not meaning to, when I said hi from the living room.

"Jesus fucking Christ," she said. "I thought you were at your friend's?"

"I came home last night," I said.

"You slept out here?"

"Yeah," I said.

She didn't say anything more. I smelled the coffee she poured, could taste the hazelnut creamer she used, could taste it thick on the air.

"There's coffee," she said, and she took her cup to the bathroom with her.

I poured too much in a mug. My hands shook and I spilled some all down the sides and on the counter, and to get rid of some of it I sipped it and burned my lip and tongue.

I put the TV on just to have it on, and the news was playing. Mom watched it from time to time, when she was taking breaks from getting ready, always standing, never sitting, holding a small white plate with a toasted English muffin with strawberry jam on it, leaving, coming back and standing there again in my periphery, putting earrings in, leaving, returning, asking if she missed the weather, leaving, returning, looking for her cigarettes, her wallet, her purse, coming once more to ask about the weather.

"More rain," I said.

"Don't forget to call your grandmother later."

When her car pulled out of the driveway, I pulled the money out from under the cushion and counted it. Six-hundred and forty dollars. Maybe if I'd felt better I could do the math, but I got a calculator to figure out how many pins I could get. Enough. I could get enough, enough to last and make plans for next steps, next steps that maybe included going to the doctor. And, I figured, I could even get myself more time, more time to make more plans.

I left Mom's to go to Meekew's. He doesn't live on the reservation—he lives in Overtown in an apartment his parents pay for. Maybe that's why Fellis hates him so much: he's got everything taken care of for him, so I don't even know why he sells drugs. It might be one thing if he took them, but he doesn't use at all. He's got that type of future where he knows he's going places. Everyone knows he's going places. Because he is.

I get why Fellis hates him.

Before going to Meekew's, I stopped off at Jim's Corner for a pack of smokes and a Slim Jim, which I ate in the store up near the door because it was pouring hard. I finished it and was thirsty so I bought a short can of Sprite for fifty cents. I drank it in five swigs. I couldn't find a garbage so I just put it in the stand with all the potato chips. The rain didn't let up when I left.

Meekew's apartment is across from a bank, and the bank's digital clock outside said it was only going on 9:00 AM. I wondered if he was still sleeping or if he was up. The lobby door was open, and I took the stairs up to the fourth floor to apartment 409. I knocked several times, but he didn't answer. Maybe I just need to give him time, I thought. I sat down in the hall with my back against the wall and waited and waited and waited, but I didn't hear any noise from that apartment.

The hallway smelled like cigarettes, so I lit one up and stayed sitting on the floor. I had no idea how long I'd been sitting there, but I was committed to waiting. Hours must have gone by. I put my head in my knees and took drags from cigarette after cigarette until I heard the noise, not from the apartment but from down the hall and through the doors, and, when they opened, I saw Meekew.

I stood up and felt how wet and heavy my clothes were.

He stopped walking for a moment and looked at me, and when he figured out who I was he walked down to his door.

"Put that out before you come in," he said. He took out his keys and looked for the right one.

I put the smoke out in the puddle of water my clothes left on the floor.

Inside his apartment, I told him I was sorry to show up like this.

He didn't say anything. "I have to be back for my next class this afternoon, so you can't stay."

"Yeah," I said. "I get it."

"So what do you need?"

I told him.

"How many?" he asked.

I said I had five hundred.

He looked to be counting in his head, and then he left the room. He was gone for a minute or two, a minute or two in which I took in how clean his place was, except for where I stood, a puddle of muddy water under my shoes.

When he came back he had a bottle with the label peeled off. "I only have seventy-eight," he said. "That's three eighty."

I paid him, and before I left he said he should have more next week. "If you're looking."

I left and wondered if this, this looking, this constantly looking, is the future my grandmother's smirk seemed to suggest she knew about.

And then I figured it out. I had the fucking question all wrong. It had nothing to do with us. It had everything to do with me. How did *I* get here, and how do *I* get out?

I took three pins before I left the building and walked out into the rain, which got real, real warm by the time I made it back to the rez. I took the path that ran along the river and split through the swamp, and when I passed through that, I realized I was walking slow, so slow, and so I stopped and sat on a fallen tree and looked out at the river and the millions of drops of rainwater plopping on the surface.

I tried to think about what my grandmother saw, what made her smirk, and when I started to feel down about it, that I didn't know and couldn't figure it out, I didn't want to remember it anymore, so I took two more pins, settled into that fallen tree, and I thought I was sleeping until the rain hit my open eyes, the only part of me awake, and I didn't shut them. Floods. If it keeps raining this whole place will flood. All of it. If I stay here long enough the water might rise up, brush my feet, recede, come back higher, to my knees, recede, come back higher, higher, to my neck, gone again, higher, higher, higher, over my head, and it will go back the way it came but not empty-handed: it'll have me with it, right out there in the water too murky to see through at first but it'll keep filling with that rainwater, diluting the pollution, until it's crystal clear. But it'll be too late for me to see—I won't be breathing.

"Fuck," I said. I burned a hole through my jacket, right down to my arm, and melted my skin like plastic to a flame. I smacked at the red embers of that dropped cigarette, and then I shut my eyes and felt the rain stop.

. . .

I was shivering when I woke up in the morning, which I knew was morning by the way the horizon was over the river, how the light rose soft like blood from a scratch. I cleared my throat and tried to stand but fell back from the weight of my heavy clothes. I tried again and was up. On both feet. Barely. Two, three steps—I got it, but I sit back down, give myself more time. I check my pockets for that bottle of pins, but I can't find it. *You be good,* I hear her say. *You be good. You be good. You be good.* Her voice is everywhere but nowhere.

I was supposed to call her. Fuck. I said I would. The sun has come up now, and I got up and walked the path, going only where it was taking me, to the road, the road home.

But no one was there: Mom's car was gone, the lights all out in the house but lit up bright from the sun shining through the windows.

I picked up the phone but couldn't remember the number to Woodlands, so I had to look it up in the phone book. I found it and dialed and a woman answered, and I asked her to connect me to my grandmother's room. She asked if I was family, and I told her I was her grandson.

"Hold on," she said. "I'm transferring you."

Static. A low beep, beep, beep. Crackle of answering.

"Who is this?" the voice said.

"Who is this?" I said.

It was a nurse supervisor, and she said her name.

"Well, put my grandmother on," I said. "Or is she sleeping?"

She said it and I heard it and she asked if I was coming up to Woodlands.

"Are you there?" she asked.

I ended the call and put the phone on the table, and I reached in my pocket for that bottle of pins. But I remembered I lost it— somewhere—and instead I pulled out that key. I stuck it in the safe, which, like the key, didn't belong to anyone anymore.

EARTH, SPEAK

Fellis drove with his knee and lit a cigarette. Over the top of the high hill, morning fog hovered above miles of pines like the nests of fall webworms in the crooks of brown branches. I jerked backward as Fellis let off the gas and we coasted downhill and into the fog.

We were going to see Daryl. Not because we liked him—Fellis hated him for what he'd done—but we were going to see him because Daryl's uncle ran the tribal museum, and for years he'd let Daryl clean the place on the weekends for a flat rate of twenty bucks. Fellis and I wanted the alarm code. Yet I was convinced Fellis wanted more than that, and the closer we got to Daryl the more I worried that Fellis would mess up.

"You ain't going to do nothing to him, right?" I said.

"Right."

We drove past a dirt road that I thought was the turn.

"Don't ruin it," I told him.

"Dee, I said I won't." Fellis flicked his ash out the tiny cracked window.

It would have been easier to get the code if Daryl hadn't been banned from the rez. We could have gone up to his place, brought a thirty-rack of shit beer, got him drunk, and talked the numbers out of him. But instead we had to drive an hour north, all the way out to his uncle's cabin where he was staying.

We drove by another dirt road. "Wasn't that it?" I said.

"No, it's up a ways."

I kicked the blower motor under the glove compartment to shake up the dirt and grime. The fan clicked and rattled and a gentle heat blew from the dashboard vents.

The fog finally thinned down and Fellis slowed the truck. "This is the turn," he said.

The road led to a borrow pit.

"Next one over," Fellis said.

Down that next road, Fellis drove slow. I smelled the wood-smoke before I saw the cabin. Daryl's uncle used to hunt deer and moose, but as he got older he couldn't keep up with the cabin's needs: fresh water, shoveling outhouse shit, chopping and stacking wood in the woodshed, plowing the dirt road, and sweeping the roof of snow in the winter months. Come winter, I couldn't picture Daryl tending to the place.

Fellis parked the truck and we got out.

"What's that smell?" Fellis said.

Two deer, twisted, half gutted, leaned against the small woodshed.

"Fucking waste," Fellis said.

We walked up to an upside-down orange bucket, and I stepped onto it and knocked on the cabin door.

"He's there," Fellis said. "Keep knocking."

Fellis went around the cabin while I stayed on the bucket. I looked in, squinting through the misty white curtain over the door and to the cabin's other window at the opposite end. It was hard to see exactly, but the table by the back wall was cluttered with what looked like Daryl's pill bottles. He probably had some good stuff.

At the far end by that table and back window, a head rose and looked at me.

"Fellis!" I yelled. "I see him! I see him!"

"That's me, you dumb shit," Fellis said.

Fellis came back around the cabin.

We leaned on the truck, quiet.

"Maybe he ain't here," I said.

"He's here," Fellis said. "That chimney's going too hard for him not to be."

Birds chirped in the pine and oak trees. Squirrels and chipmunks crunched dried leaves and snapped tiny twigs around us. The sun shone through clouds for a moment before the gray sky swallowed it. It felt and smelled like rain was coming.

"Let's go in," Fellis said, and before we pushed away from the truck, a man groaned and something metal clanked. The outhouse door opened. Daryl fastened his belt and looked at the ground as he walked. He was wearing white earbuds.

Fellis picked up a glossed acorn and tossed it at Daryl, who saw it fly by him. When he saw us, he tripped and tumbled down, his earbuds popping out of his head.

"This is private property!" he said. "Help! Help!"

"It's us," I said. "Daryl, it's us. Dee and Fellis."

Daryl looked pale, thin. A small red cut ran across his forehead. His black shirt hung off one shoulder like he'd been beaten up by two men, a tug of war. The tongue of his belt was too long, his waist too thin.

"What are you listening to?" I said. I gave him my hand, and his felt sweaty.

He didn't answer me. He watched Fellis.

"I don't know why you're here," Daryl said, "but I wasn't myself."

Fellis took out his cigarettes and opened the pack. He didn't light one, and he put the pack back in his pocket. He looked at Daryl.

"I know you weren't," Fellis said. "I ain't here to do nothing."

"Then why'd you come?" Daryl said.

"Ain't seen you since before you were banned," Fellis said. "Just checking on you."

I nudged Daryl on the shoulder. "And the tribe's talking," I said.

"Talking?" Daryl said.

"About letting you come home," I told him. "Council held two meetings these past months."

"Oh, yeah," Fellis said. "They're voting sometime soon."

Daryl scratched his nose. "Why didn't my uncle tell me?"

Fellis opened his pack of smokes again and this time he lit one. He went to the cabin door and grabbed the orange bucket. He brought it near the truck and sat.

"Maybe he likes having someone out here," I said. I walked toward the truck and Daryl followed. "You know, someone to take care of the place since he can't." I sat on the hood.

"He wouldn't do that," Daryl said.

From his pocket, Daryl took out a pink iPod. He wrapped the headphones around it.

"Where'd you get that?" Fellis said, pointing with his cigarette.

Daryl didn't say anything. He stared at the ground. Then at the trees. A breeze blew and leaves shivered and twirled down. Daryl's hands shook.

He looked at me. Really—stared at me and didn't blink. His lips were chapped and he licked them. He rubbed his head.

Fellis and I glanced at each other.

"So," Daryl said. "Why'd you guys come out here?"

"Told you already," Fellis said. "To check up on you."

Daryl stared at a line of thick pine trees behind us.

Fellis waved his hand in Daryl's line of vision.

"What are you on?" Fellis said. "He's gotta be on something." He handed me the cigarette and I took three drags.

I nudged Daryl. "Here," I said, holding out the cigarette for him. "What are you on?"

Daryl whispered, "I ain't on nothing." He shut his eyes as he took a drag of the cigarette, and as he exhaled the smoke he mumbled something unintelligible.

The orange bucket tipped over when Fellis stood, and he right-hooked Daryl so hard the cigarette ember exploded and Daryl fell to the ground.

"What the fuck did you say?" Fellis said, kicking him in the side. "Say it again."

"What did he say?" I asked.

"Say it again," Fellis said, now stomping on him.

Daryl licked his lips.

"I I I I I," Daryl said.

"You you you you what?"

"I I I I home."

Fellis shook his head real slow. "The rez don't want you," he said. "You think the council would meet for you?"

Daryl squirmed on the ground. He flailed and turned and rolled over, and on his knees he pushed himself up so he was on all fours. Dirt and leaves stuck to his back. "I home," Daryl said directly to the ground. "I home."

Fellis kicked him in the side. Down. Then again. Daryl's body may not have deserved it, but Daryl did. Fellis kept kicking and I watched the trees rock in a wind.

"Piece of shit," Fellis said.

Finally, I told Fellis to stop. But he wouldn't. He kicked and kicked and kicked at Daryl's side and stomach and at his head. Once again, Daryl's body tensed and he screeched and cried. Fellis couldn't see that Daryl's body was crying out for help. Something that was Daryl, something that rarely communicated, was signing to me in a language I didn't know, like an earthquake speaking for the earth.

Fellis tired of kicking him and set the orange bucket upright. He spat on Daryl, sat, and wiped the sweat from his forehead.

Daryl was barely breathing. A clump of wet dirt clung to his face, and the brownness of the earth's soil so close to his mouth and nose nauseated me.

"You deserve much worse than this," Fellis said. "You ever come near my family again—especially my cousin—and I'll set you on fire."

I didn't doubt it.

Fellis opened his pack of cigarettes but it was empty. He crinkled the soft pack and stuffed it in his pocket.

Crouching down, Fellis reached in Daryl's pocket and took the pink iPod, and before he stood he slapped Daryl across the face. I didn't understand Fellis's anger—the only family I had left wasn't talking to me—and it wasn't like Daryl got after Fellis's little cousin. Sure, the dead crow and love note written in purple was fucked up (tucked it right into her dresser drawer too), but Daryl could have done worse. Maybe that was why Fellis did what he did to Daryl—because Daryl could have done worse, since men can always do worse.

Fellis made for the truck.

"Let's go," he said.

"Hold on," I told him. I felt sick.

I brought the orange bucket to the cabin door, stepped up, and went inside. The room was dark and warm and smelled of Pine-Sol, and I wondered how Daryl—the Daryl out there on the hard ground—kept the place so clean. Maybe he could manage the place come winter. A fire burned in the woodstove. The bed was made neatly and the wooden counters were sleek, the clean dishes stacked in the dish rack, the unclean ones in the sink covered with the customary red cloth to tell the spirits to stay away, that there was no food for offering. I moved the cloth and dry-heaved once and then twice over the half-full sink. I wiped my mouth with the cloth and draped it back over the dishes.

On the small wooden table by the back wall, a cribbage board was set up, the middle of a game paused. The blue pegs were winning against the red, two hands of cards lying on opposite sides of the table. I imagined Daryl playing against himself in that dark, warm cabin.

Next to the cribbage game were what I thought I'd seen: pill bottles. Same ones Daryl always kept out and about. Heavy stuff like lithium. I didn't want that, didn't need that. My therapist years back cut me off everything when I got on methadone. "Can't mix this, can't mix that"—bullshit. I picked up each bottle and read the white labels, searching for his benzos.

Then I found some. A bottle of Klonopin. No wonder Daryl was a wreck—the prescription was full, hadn't been touched.

Fellis honked.

I put the pills in my pocket.

Fellis honked again. I stepped down on the orange bucket and glanced at Daryl. He had rolled over. I got in the truck. Fellis drove in reverse all the way down the dirt road and looked behind him the entire time while I faced forward shaking the bottle of pills in my hand and watching the puffs of smoke coil out of the chimney and up into the sky. Daryl probably didn't even remember the code anyway.

. . .

"Fuck" was the first word Fellis said. It was quarter to twelve, and we were on the main road heading for the highway.

"We'll make it," I said. "We have an hour before it closes."

I kicked the blower motor.

"I ain't worried about the methadone clinic," he said.

Fellis pulled the truck over on the side of the road. His hands shook.

"Fuck!" He punched the steering wheel.

"Forget the code," I said. "It's a stupid idea anyway."

"We're not forgetting it," Fellis said.

I opened the bottle of pins and held a blue one in my palm. "Here," I offered. "Take it."

Fellis swallowed it with spit.

"Can you drive?" he asked.

"I hate driving," I said, and I scratched my leg.

"That don't stop you taking the truck when you want beer or smokes."

"When's the last time I drove this truck?"

"Last week," Fellis said. The tires kicked dirt and dust and Fellis pulled onto the road. "I gave you twenty bucks and you drove to Overtown to get beer and crappy cigars. I didn't want cigars. I wanted a pack of Camels. You wanted cigars so that's what we smoked."

"I asked if you wanted cigars and you said yes."

"I thought you were going to get me smokes too!"

We were quiet for fifteen, twenty minutes. I watched the trees as we zipped by them. Fellis hit a pothole and the radio turned on. He turned it off. "Damn," Fellis said. He laughed. "What milligram are those?"

I looked at the bottle. "Two."

"I feel like fog," he said.

On the highway, I didn't have to kick the blower motor. The truck shook at eighty-five miles per hour and hot air barreled out of the vents. I was still cold.

Fellis rolled down his window.

"Put that up," I said. "I'm getting warm."

"You got something wrong with you," he said.

When we got off the highway in the little city, Fellis rolled up the window. Saturday traffic thickened the road. Blowout sales at Macy's and JCPenney. Fellis drove by Burger King and McDonald's and Wendy's and then he turned on Myron Avenue, passing Home Depot and Walmart and this little Bible store that made its money from gelato. At the last set of lights before the methadone clinic, the light turned yellow and Fellis slowed and when it turned red he stopped the truck and rested his head back on the seat and closed his eyes.

We waited. Cars zoomed in the intersection. Turned. Sped. I coughed. A car honked.

"It's green," I said.

Nothing.

I backhanded Fellis. "Wake up, it's green."

Fellis drove straight, turned into the clinic, and parked across two spots.

Inside, the line wasn't long. Fellis was in front of me. Tabitha—an asshole everyone at the clinic knew who threw up her liquid methadone and sold it—stood in front of Fellis, her arms crossed, a lockbox in her hand. She bounced on her feet, and then she turned and faced us. She always pretended she didn't know me, like we weren't something at one time.

"Can you back up?" she asked.

"Why?" I said. "You have to fart?"

Fellis backed up even though he wasn't close to her. Tabitha looked past him at me. "My boyfriend's out in the car," she whispered.

The line moved.

"You're holding us up," I said.

"Fuck you, Dee." She faced forward and stepped closer to the counter. "You're nothing."

"I wasn't nothing in the past, was I?"

"Okay, minuteman." She said that loud and Fellis laughed.

Fellis dosed first and he didn't wait for me. I drank my dose, that pink syrup, and it tasted different than the last time, as if the methadone were incomplete, like some chemist and a man in a black suit were in a white sterile room still trying to right the recipe. I wish I hadn't lost my take-homes and didn't have to come here every single day—you miss one appointment and they get all upset and act like you fucking murdered someone. I have to get off this shit.

Outside, Fellis sat in the passenger seat, snoozing, the keys in the ignition.

"Sneaky bastard," I said. I started the truck, wondering if he'd feel bad if I wrecked both his truck and myself. I left the clinic with Fellis snoring.

. . .

Fellis still lived with his mom, Beth. I lived with her too. Rent-free. I found it funny how Beth was a schoolteacher but also a cold-blooded gossiper. She knew everything, and what she didn't know she made up and it became so. She told people I paid rent, but that was only a front. She knew I had the real stories about her, like how much of Fellis's bullshit she covered up throughout the years.

My own mother didn't talk to me anymore. Beth had run into her at the grocery store one weekend, and she told Beth to tell me that she sold all my stuff. Mom had owed me money, and so I hadn't seen the big deal in selling the small ash baskets she kept in the shed, as well as the picture frames and jewelry she didn't even wear. That was what happened, why I was at Beth's—Mom was pissed at me, wouldn't let me stay with her anymore. But the story Beth told everyone who asked was that my mom was charging me too much rent, and that was why I left her place for good. That became the story. Sometimes I believed that version.

I parked the truck in the driveway behind Beth's car. Fellis's aunt Alice had parked her blue Elantra alongside the road. Her daughter was probably with her too. No one left Lily alone since the Daryl crap.

I shook Fellis. "Get up," I said. "Look awake for your auntie."

Fellis rubbed his eyes. "I should have took a half."

Fellis's house was cluttered. Beth wasn't a hoarder—just depressed. Empty boxes and years of student papers were stacked in the living room. In the kitchen, dirty dishes filled the sink, always left uncovered at night. One night I woke Fellis and told him I heard noises—Goog'ooks, I said, spirits wanting food—and he told me to shut up, that it was the pipes in the walls.

Fellis opened the front door. Beth stood at the stove, laughing while Alice shook her head, proud of something she'd said. Lily sat at the scratched kitchen table, her head propped up by her hand, bored out of her nine-year-old skull.

"What you cooking?" Fellis said.

Beth was too busy laughing to answer.

"I bet his jeckin smells like garbage too," Alice said.

Beth stirred a white ladle in a metal pot. "The council's going to evict him," she said.

"It isn't hurting anyone," Alice said. "If he wants to live in filth, let him."

"Who you talking about?" Fellis said. I leaned on the wall.

"That Nelson and all his garbage." Beth took out a pan. Melting yellow butter slid and pooled.

"Say hi to your cousin, Lil," Alice said.

Lily turned and said hi real quick.

"Where you been?" Beth said.

"Nowhere important," Fellis said, and then he took the pink iPod from his pocket. "I got you a present, Lil."

Beth and Alice watched as Fellis handed the pink iPod to Lily.

"Where did you get this?" Lily said.

"Was out walking this morning," Fellis said. "Found it in the woods."

Lily turned it on. "This is mine," she said.

"Yeah, I know," Fellis said. "I'm giving it to you."

Lily stood. "No," she said. "This is actually mine."

"I'm sure it's different," Alice said. "Let me see." She held it, looked it over. "Didn't yours have stickers on it?"

"Yeah, but look," Lily said. "You can see where they were peeled off."

Beth left the stove and looked over Alice's shoulder at the iPod. "I don't see any sticker marks," Beth said.

Lily reached across the table and traced with her finger. "Right there," she said. "See?"

"No," Beth said. She returned to the sink and washed her hands. "I don't see anything."

Lily pestered her mom for headphones.

211

The pan sizzled and spit hot and Beth rested two moose medallions in the pan. "Can you chop some wood?" she said to Fellis.

"In a bit," he said, and he started for his room.

Fellis's door didn't have a doorknob. It broke, and since Beth didn't like anyone coming into her house—the boxes, the student papers, the dirty dishes—she wouldn't call Housing to come and fix it. She'd asked Fellis to fix it, but all he did was tie a checkered scarf around the hole so the cloth held the door shut.

Fellis opened his dresser and grabbed an unopened pack of cigarettes. He sat on his made bed and scooted back.

I took out the bottle of pills, shook them, and sang Native gibberish but stomped each foot twice real good, and then I set the bottle on the dresser. I sat in the beanbag chair in the corner.

"You think he's going to tell his uncle about us?" Fellis asked.

I shrugged. "Probably not."

"I think he will."

We were quiet, and I wondered what Daryl was doing, if he was on the ground out there among the animal feet. I remembered his twisted body and I wondered what it felt like to have something speak on your behalf.

"We have to do it tonight," Fellis said.

"With no code?"

"And then we're out of here."

I counted my fingers. "We got no money, your truck's a piece of shit, the next arts festival ain't till October, and we haven't weaned off our doses."

"We got money."

"Yeah, okay," I said. "You bummed twenty yesterday from your mom."

Fellis stood. "I've been bumming from my mom for thirty-one years." He pulled the bed away from the wall. In the corner, he peeled back the carpet and picked up three envelopes from the cold wooden floor. He emptied all three on the shifted bed.

All these late boring nights we didn't do anything because he was broke!

"Twenty-eight hundred bucks," Fellis said.

I knelt in front of the bed and felt the money, some bills soft like velvet, others stiff and fresh.

"I got money," he said.

"Your truck's still a piece of shit."

Fellis took the money from my hands. "You don't want to do it, do you?"

I said nothing. The whole thing was my idea. We'd been watching *Antiques Roadshow* one long boring moon-night last week and some old dusty lady brought in an old root club that was worth five grand. Five grand! I said, "Fellis, the museum has tons of those!" and we looked at each other and got off the couch and walked fast to the head of the Island, right near the bridge. We went out back of the little museum whose only visitors were white people wanting pictures. Looking through the window, Fellis had seen the alarm box blinking green.

"Do you or don't you?" Fellis said.

"What about our doses? I ain't getting sick if we're on the road."

Fellis waved the envelopes at me. "You got Tabitha's number?"

"I'm not drinking puked-up methadone," I said.

"She don't puke it up," Fellis said. "You're retarded if you think that."

"I've seen her do it," I said, even though I hadn't.

"You're full of shit," Fellis said. "She gets full take-homes. You think that lockbox is her purse?"

"Even if she sells to us," I said, "where are we going?"

"Down south to sell it all."

"Why don't we just learn how to make our own root clubs or baskets and sell them?"

Fellis stuffed the rest of the bills into the envelopes and put them back under the carpet. He straightened the bed.

"I ain't got time for that," Fellis said. "I'm doing it my way."

I stayed sitting as Fellis left the room, and before he made it out of the house I heard Beth ask him nicely once more to chop wood. But Fellis ignored her and opened the front door and slammed it shut so hard the bedroom wall shook.

"That boy," Alice said, and Beth told her never mind him.

I finished Alice's thought for her—"is something else." But then I wondered if she meant me.

The beanbag chair creaked when I sat up. I pulled the bed from the wall, peeled back the carpet, and took three twenties, one from each envelope. I stuffed them down into my sock and laced my shoe back up.

Neither Beth nor Alice said anything to me as I passed through the kitchen and living room and out the front door. Out back of the house, the sky had cleared enough for the sun to set red like light through a fingertip.

I picked up the axe and stood a log wobbling on a wide-cut oak trunk. I swung, picked up the split wood, and tossed it in a pile. Beth bought hardwood—ash—and so her house was always warm. My own mother bought softwood and sometimes late at night she'd shake me awake and we'd get in her white car and go down to the thick woods and I'd hurry through it to the tribal lumberyard on the other side and carry eight good logs back and dump it all in Mom's trunk.

I wondered what she was doing.

"You didn't have to do that," Beth said as I brought in an armful of wood and dropped it in the wood box next to the woodstove. Alice and Lily were gone.

"He wasn't going to do it," I said, but Beth simply stirred a pot of something.

"You hungry?" she said. "I'm making fiddleheads and salted pork. And there's moose too."

I told her no, that I had to be somewhere. "Maybe later," I said.

"If there's any left," she said, and she banged the ladle on the stove.

I snagged three more twenties from Fellis and left.

The woods were that dark shadow of dusk, and I followed a jagged, rough-rocked path, heading to the back of her house. I passed by a large boulder—rolled and placed back when the reservation was a burial ground. Couldn't tell that to anyone, though, because people talked *Pet Sematary*. But it was true— this reservation was for the dead.

At her house, the lights were on, the blinds swept aside. I caught a glimpse of her. She was at the sink, her silver hair tied back. Then she was gone. Sitting on the cold, leafed ground for hours, I didn't see her come back to that window.

I was hungry when I left. The closer I got to Fellis's, the more I felt bad about the money, Mom's ash baskets, Daryl's pills. No, not Daryl's pills—he wasn't even taking them.

From the woods, the streetlamps glowed orange. My sneakers scraped the concrete as I walked and I thought about how good those fiddleheads with salted pork and a slab of moose meat would taste after popping a pin or two (not three, then I'd pass out). The road bent and I looked up to see Beth's house. The driveway was crowded with police cruisers and a black van. An officer shone his flashlight in Fellis's truck, and another talked to Beth in the driveway. Headlights poured over the trees—another tribal cop—and he pulled by Beth's house.

I turned my ass around and split into the woods.

Star- and moonlight hit the water. Down by the river, I sat on a rock, wishing I'd eaten and grabbed those pills and had a cigarette. Wishing I'd never heard of *Antiques Roadshow*. Maybe even wishing I was a winooch and didn't live on a reservation whose history was in a little museum and could be stolen for a buck. Didn't make any sense that parts of us were worth so much and at the same time we were worth so little. "You're nothing."

I grabbed a twig off the ground and pretended to smoke it. "Fuck you, Tabitha," I said, and as I said it, the first dog barked.

I had nowhere to go, but I ran like I did. The paths all met at some point, right in the heart of the reservation, right behind the tribal lumberyard. I couldn't hide in someone's garage, because that would mean I'd have to get on the roads, so I stayed in the pitch-black woods. I kept going, stopping only to listen for growls and to look behind me for light.

No dogs barked and no light shone. I slowed, thinking: deny, deny, deny. You weren't with him. Those pills? You never seen them. The iPod? You don't know. He says you kicked him. You say he's a liar.

I denied all night until the sun came up. I had to hide all day until the sun went down. A stench rolled off the river, and not knowing where else to go, I followed it to Nelson's.

Ralph Nelson owned the most land on the rez, and on that land pressing against the river he kept junk. Cars that didn't run. Piles of sheet metal and garbage and electronics like old computer monitors. Next to his house, twenty-five years' worth of deer and moose antlers tangled and hooked in a tumbleweed of bone. Somewhere among that stuff Ralph had a sweat lodge, one that was built into the ground. No one ever sweated with him because of the garbage smell.

The sweat lodge wasn't hard to find. Between the piles of bone and sheet metal, a small blue tarp blanketed a wide mound. Under it, a passage with hard dirt stairs spiraled down into the earth.

Ralph's sweat lodge ran deep, and at the bottom—a fire pit in the middle, needle of light pricking through the top where smoke escaped, dirt seats, cold earth walls barred by a man-made wooden rib cage giving structure to the circularity of the mound—I stood without my head touching the roof and even when I tiptoed I didn't hit my head.

Sitting down, I pulled my arms and head inside my white shirt and breathed long and hot, warming myself. I dozed like that, too, inside my white shirt, but never as deeply as those buried down below all over the rez. Each time I woke I forgot where I was. When I took my head out of my shirt I thought I was buried alive but then I remembered what I was supposed to be doing—hiding—but I didn't know why, didn't exactly know what for.

It was a long, cold day in that sweat lodge. I didn't know what time it was, and I couldn't feel my hands or feet. I climbed back up the spiraled stairs and moved the tarp over quiet-like and then untied some twine holding patches of deer hide over the wooden rib cage and flipped it back enough for the sun to shine through like a spotlight and light poured over my neck and down my arms like hot water.

Back down under I was in a half sleep when voices startled me awake. They were not dream voices but real voices. Men. I crawled in dirt away from the light and pressed against the earth wall. A tree root stuck out of the dirt and scratched at me. My head throbbed like I'd held my breath too long, and down in that cold earth hole I was a barely beating heart.

Outside the lodge people were coming. Sheet metal wobbled thunderously. A dog barked.

"Don't touch my stuff," a man said. It was Ralph. "I ain't said you can touch. You can look, but don't touch."

The men walked around up above. Every so often Ralph spoke, saying he saw no one and that no one was here.

"Why you looking for him?" Ralph asked, and I listened but all the police would say was that they wanted to talk to me to find out where Fellis ran off to.

"What that michigun do?" Ralph said.

The officer ignored him. "What's that over there?" he said.

Like a great eye searching, a flashlight shone down through the peeled-back hide. I pressed against the wall and then Ralph told them to stop.

"Don't violate the sanctity of this place," he said.

"We need to look down here," an officer said.

"You're not going down there," Ralph said. "I blessed it yesterday for a sweat I'm running tonight. You're more than welcome to come later and sweat, but until then no one goes down."

Ralph flipped the hide back and tied the twine. They walked away, and a cop started asking if Ralph had permits for all that garbage.

"Get off my property," Ralph said.

I huddled in my shirt and rocked back and forth, breathing hot. How long had I been down here? How long would I be down here? I whispered those questions over and over again until the crinkly tarp and floppy deer hide flapped back and exposed me in the earth's chest. Ralph said, "You leave at sundown," and he set something on the stairs.

A glass plate wrapped in tinfoil. Under it, steaming brown rice and hotter-than-hell peas and a slab of tough meat. A spoon, too. I held my hands over the food as if it were a fire and when it stopped being warm, I ate the meat first and then mixed the rice and peas together and ate. I picked at my teeth until the sun was down.

Before leaving, I popped off my shoe and peeled back my sock for a twenty and left it on the plate and set the plate on the top of the stairs. I pocketed the spoon. Out in the woods looking through pine needles I waited for the pure dark and I watched Ralph walk back to the sweat lodge and take the plate and he looked right at me. He fanned the twenty in my direction and I knew I owed him more.

I started for her house. Halfway there the soul-shivers started and when tree limbs brushed me they scared me and my chin trembled and my nose ran as fast as I was right then, trying to get to her.

The light was on but she wasn't at the sink through the window, and I crept up the hill behind her house and opened the boiler-room door—flicked the light—and I shut myself in with the warmth but I was cold-sweating.

The metal chair was too warm to sit on so I sat on the concrete slab floor and slept with the light on until my soaked body woke me and I could no longer sleep to the boiler's never-ending machine breath. I scanned the *fuck*s that Fellis and I had scratched into the walls over the years hiding in this room from the winter cold and that was what I said—fuck. The machine breath blew steady and my stomach hurt. Something squeezed me in my gut and out came more sweat and I bit my fingernails for a while and spit them on the concrete around me and when I bit too close to the skin I wiped the blood on my white shirt and I tried to fan cool air in my hot face but it was all warm air and I wanted to hit something so I hit the wall but it was loud and so I slapped the concrete floor around me and then I kicked and kicked and kicked the boiler and it whistled and hissed at me to stop and so I stopped and curled in a dirty dusty corner and I yelled to her.

I slapped at the walls and yelled to her again and again and again. The door flung open and the cold hit me and the dawn light shut my eyes. She was there one minute holding a root club ready to beat someone and then the next she was gone and back again with a blue Pendleton blanket. She lifted me up and covered me and I saw it was her favorite blanket and so when I threw up I pushed the blanket away and spilled rice and peas and meat onto the ground.

"Make it stop," I said. My head fissured open and Mom said so softly into it that she would and she put the blanket back over me and we went up the steps and through the door where no machine breathed but the clock ticked slow and loud and the fridge hummed and down the hallway Mom opened my bedroom door and all my stuff was there and she pulled back the blankets on the made bed and she took off my shirt and stripped me to my underwear and slipped me under the blankets and she was gone for a moment and when she came back she set a wastebasket lined with plastic next to me on the floor and after she'd gone again I threw up in it and she came back and changed the plastic and then brought a kitchen chair and sat next to my twisted body in the bed.

She put a warm wet washcloth on my forehead.

My joints hurt and I wanted to roll out of bed and onto the floor and I did try but Mom pushed me back and I told her to fuck off and I started crying and Mom left and returned with a warmer washcloth and when she set it on my forehead I took it off and flung it across the room and it splattered against the wall.

I yelled at her all day and then all night and then all day and then all night and when she brought me barley soup I slapped it out of her hands because I thought it was that root club and I thought she wanted to swing at me but then I said I'm sorry and she brought me another bowl which she spooned in my mouth is that Ralph's spoon and I wondered once and only once if I'd remember this moment and then I threw it all up and rubbed my sore throat while Mom rubbed my head.

For days coming off that methadone I fought with Mom and I cried to her and she shushed me each time I sat up and tried to get up and at some point Mom spoke to me—not to my body—and she said, "You'll be back soon," and the next thing I knew I envisioned Fellis's truck reversing to a stop in front of Daryl on the ground who laughed and pointed at me and said "earthquake" and I split in half.

Mom was in her chair, sleeping. The washcloth on my forehead was cold.

I touched her knee and she lazily stirred. She put her hand to my forehead.

"Did they find him?" I said, and she said yes, that Beth bailed him out and he's home, sick like me.

My lips were cracked and peeling. "What they get him for?"

"Burglary," she said.

"What he steal?"

"Like you don't know," Mom said.

My nose ran and I wiped at it.

"How far did he get?" I asked.

"Boston," Mom said. "It's all over the news."

I laughed and so did Mom. She left the room and came back with a newspaper.

"I can't read that," I said.

"'Native Man Steals History,'" Mom read. She placed the newspaper over something wet on the floor. "He was caught with over one hundred thousand dollars' worth of tribal memorabilia and a month's worth of methadone from someone named Tricia."

"Tabitha," I said.

"Whatever."

I sat up in bed.

"They looking for me?" I said.

"I showed you to them," Mom said. "Brought the police right in here and they saw you were sick. You told one of them to go fuck themselves."

I laughed.

Mom coughed. "It's not funny. They got your friend. You were lucky."

I was quiet.

"Take off my sock," I said.

She did, annoyed, tired of taking care of me. The bills were stuck to the soles of my feet.

"Take it away," I said, and Mom peeled the twenties off me.

. . .

Another week and I wasn't feeling better, but I was well enough to get up and walk around and help Mom clean the house and wash the vomit from my clothes and bed. Mom splurged and ordered burgers from Overtown but I could only take small bites, and I threw the burger away after it got too soggy and the lettuce all burned and shriveled from so many nukes in the microwave. Mom bought me a few packs of smokes and a package of white T-shirts and when she came back from the store she sat with me on the cold concrete steps.

It rained lightly.

"Can you give me a ride?" I said.

"Where in the world do you need to go?"

"Ralph Nelson's," I said.

Mom asked what for.

"Can you bring me?"

She went inside. From the steps I yelled to her. "Did you see a spoon?"

"A spoon? What do you need a spoon for?"

"No, did you see one when you found me out back?"

"Are you all right?"

"Did you see a spoon or not?" I yelled.

"I didn't see no goddamned spoon, David."

"Well would you get me one of yours?"

"One of my what?"

"A spoon!"

Mom started the car and I sat passenger holding the spoon and the wipers swiped the rain and she drove me to Ralph's in the woods and parked in his muddy driveway. I got out and smelled garbage and went up to his door and knocked but he didn't answer. I knocked again.

"Over here," Ralph yelled. He was by the sweat lodge, his shirt off, kindling in his hands.

I walked toward him and waved Mom away, thanked her and yelled to her that I'd walk home and that tonight I'd make us dinner and we'd watch TV—maybe *CSI* or *Criminal Minds*. "Whatever's on," I said. She waved, looking forward as she reversed out of Ralph's driveway.

I took off my shirt and pants and stood in my underwear and Ralph said, "What's that?" and I handed him the spoon, told him it wasn't his but it'll do and he looked at me and laughed. He took the spoon and threw it and it clanked and bounced off the pile of sheet metal. "Grab some wood," he said, and I did. I followed him down the spiraled earth stairs to a hot molten core.

Ralph held a small handmade drum, and when I asked him how he made it, he said he'd show me another day. "Today we sweat," he said, and down in the earth's chest the red glowed unbearable and Ralph beat the hand drum and he sang songs I didn't know if he made them up but they sounded and felt as real as the heat between dirt walls and in my windpipe, and right then my body sweated all that was left in it, which really wasn't very much at all.

NIGHT OF THE LIVING REZ

When the bus arrived in Overtown, it parked and hissed and sank in the cracked concrete lot. The woman sitting beside me—thin brown hair, worn brown skin, puffy brown mole on her neck—did not stand, and she did not look to want to leave the bus.

From South Station in Boston to Overtown—through dark tunnels lit by passing headlights and orange bulbs, through highways green with pine and pressed below gray sky—the woman had sat in the same position: upright, hands folded over the blue-and-white-striped handbag on her lap, and her eyes set straight ahead much like a driver, like in her mind she was traveling somewhere and could not take her gaze from it. She had a used Gatorade bottle. *Cool Blue*, the label read, yet the contents were not Cool Blue but instead looked to be apple juice. She didn't drink from it, and every once in a while, my eyes shut, I'd hear her shaking the bottle, my eyes open, and then she'd set it back in the cupholder.

The woman had coughed on occasion during the trip, and she spoke only twice. A man in faded jeans and a paint-speckled shirt had leaned from his seat across from us and said, "That's a nice gun." He said it so loudly that everyone turned to look at the woman—the bus driver watched in the mirror, eyes flicking behind sunglasses to the road to the woman to the road to the woman to the road—and the woman opened her blue-and-white bag and pulled out a bulky orange water gun, and she raised it into the air. "Super Soaker," she said, and for a time everyone admired the orange frame and blue handle and the barrel with six holes for water to spray through. The woman put the Super Soaker back in her bag and the man who asked the question said, "For your child?"

"No," was all the woman said.

The bus was clearing out, and the woman would not move. She looked straight ahead. I stood, thinking she'd see me trying to get out, and I bumped my head on the overhead TV that Greyhound never used. The woman looked at me, and she put up a finger. *Hold on.* Through the window, Mom's white car was parked in the parking lot. Her window was down, and how she saw me through the tinted bus windows was beyond me, yet she did and she was waving.

The back of the bus cleared out and the woman stood with her bag, grabbed her Gatorade bottle, and went to the bathroom in the back of the bus. I got off the bus, and as I descended the steps I wondered if Overtown was that woman's stop.

The air was chilly for August. But then again, each time I came home from Dad's the world got a little colder, more so now than ever: I hadn't spent the summer with my father in four years—I was thirteen the last time I saw him, when Mom let me see him or let him see me—and he looked so sickly this time. All summer he smoked and barely moved from his recliner, and before I left to catch the cab that took me to the bus station Dad hugged me as tight as he could, his cigarette smoke going up my nose, and said, "I'll see you, buddy."

Mom leaned over and unlocked the car door.

"Welcome home, gwus." She patted my leg and then she put the car in drive. Her freshly dyed brown hair darkened her skin. She had grown her hair out and it went past her ears now. The last time I saw her it was short and speckled with grays around the rims of her ears. "Your father behave himself?" Mom ran a red light leaving the parking lot.

"You got a cigarette?" I said.

She gave me one. I wanted to tell her how the one and only time Dad and I went someplace he fell asleep driving on the highway and I had to grab the wheel and guide the golden Saturn to the emergency breakdown lane. But why say anything about it? We survived.

I lit the smoke, and Mom said, "Well, did he?"

"I don't know why you're prying so much," I said. "Since when do you care if he behaved himself?"

"A mother can't be concerned?" she said.

I knew something was irking her—she never gave a shit what Dad did.

"Why are you annoyed? I said.

She coughed and cleared her throat. "Your sister," she said. She lit a butted cigarette and the car swerved. I gripped the seat.

"What'd she do now?" I asked.

"You'll see."

"What do you mean, 'you'll see'?"

"There's something wrong with her."

"There's always something wrong with Paige."

"No, I'm serious," Mom said. "She's gone wacko." The car hit a pothole as we drove onto the bridge to the Island. "She believes in zombies, David."

I wasn't sure why, but I defended Paige: "Don't you believe in stone people?"

"Those are different," she said.

She wasn't wrong: they were different. But I asked anyway. "How so?"

"Stone people have hearts of ice, and they were chased off for trying to destroy the earth. Zombies don't run off too easily, do they? They come for you all slow like." She flicked her cigarette.

"Well," I said, "they sound different, but have you ever seen a zombie's heart? For all we know it could be made of ice."

She laughed smoke. "You're a little shit."

I stared out the car window. Weeds and cattails tangled in the pond. Dead sticks and large debris, blown from a storm, crawled out of the water, reaching at us as we puttered by and up the steep hill and past the few abandoned houses on the rez. At the top of the hill, Mom took the long way home. We drove on Wabanaki Lane toward the busy section of the rez: the small health clinic, the community building with its yellow-stained walls from cigarette smoke, the tribal offices tucked behind thick pine trees, the tan-brick school, and the football field, where red tents covered part of the green grass and the sacred fire burned in the corner. People tended the sacred fire, and a film crew stood next to its blue van, camera rolling, even though almost half of the tribe had voted not to let them make a documentary about our Community Days.

The road was blocked off and Mom slowed the car.

"For real?" she said. "All this for a stinking movie?"

She turned the car around, and I asked if Paige was home, yet she must not have heard me right because she started talking about Frick.

"I don't know where he is," she said. "He's been weird for weeks now. Last Friday—in the middle of the night—I found him shivering in the kitchen with a tablecloth over his shoulder. He was sleepwalking, and he kept saying the Jesuits were coming."

"He's always been weird," I said, and I laughed. Mom didn't.

"David," she said, "I'm not in the mood."

"I'm just saying," I said. "So if Frick's shivering in the kitchen, then where's Paige?"

Mom smiled a little. "She's home. Was on the couch watching those stupid apocalypse shows when I left to get you."

We rolled past the stop sign and turned onto our dead-end road, heading up to our little yellow house. Mom pulled into the driveway, and people walking out back of the house in the woods caught my eye—JP and Tyson.

"Did you see that?" Mom said, and I told her who it was.

"Of course," she said. She put the car in park and unbuckled her seat belt. "I'm glad you're home, gwusis." She reached over and hugged me, and kissed the top of my head. "Now," she said, "stop coming home with your hair short. It's bad medicine." Dad never liked my hair long.

I grabbed my duffel bag and went up the crooked steps to the house. I was excited to see my sister. The TV in the living room was on. The end credits to a movie were playing with slow, low piano notes, drawing out something suspenseful.

"Paige?" I checked the living room. The imprint of a body indented the empty couch. I turned off the TV.

Mom came in the front door. "Get your shoes off."

"Sorry, I was going to drop my bag off and head out."

"So?"

My socks were damp from having my shoes on all day and my soggy feet marked up our old linoleum floor as I walked down the hallway to my room.

"You going to find your friends?" Mom said from the kitchen.

I asked if she minded—after two months away I had this feeling that I was supposed to visit with her. I unzipped my bag and pulled out a new pack of Camels and returned to the kitchen.

"No, I don't mind," she said. "Just tell them I know they been going in the shed most nights."

"How do you know?"

Mom leaned over the stove, inspecting the burners for crumbs.

"Crows. You know better than anyone. They talk."

Before I left the house I asked if she could get me smokes at the store—told her I had ten bucks and it was in my bag in my room—and she said she would. I left the house and the door slammed loud behind me. I jumped off the front steps and headed out back of the house. I slipped in mud but caught myself. My feet felt heavy the more I trekked through the woods, leaves sticking to my soles. I scraped the bottom of my shoes on a log, and I heard JP laugh in the distance. I saw Tyson first. He was wearing a bright orange jacket that barely fit him now. I thought it was impossible for him to grow anymore—the kid was pushing six foot three and he was so skinny that if he got any taller he might disappear.

In a clearing beyond the trees, JP threw a rock at Tyson, who was telling him to quit it. JP had his long hair pulled back, something he couldn't do at the beginning of the summer. He raised his big arm and threw another rock at Tyson.

At the sound of my crunching leaves and twigs, JP turned around.

"David," he said, pegging one last rock at Tyson. "We were starting to think you weren't coming out. Give me a ciggie butt."

I handed one to JP, who then sat on the giant boulder that forked the path.

JP pointed to Tyson, who was rubbing his arm. "He was doing it again," JP said.

"Doing what?" I said.

"You know, he invites you over to hang out and then stuffs his skinny ass with food while you sit there and watch."

"I didn't know you were hungry," Tyson said.

"Bullshit. I'm always hungry. Anyway, David, lots has happened since you've been gone. We have to go find a new spot. The last storm that came through took out the lean-to."

I lit a cigarette. "Why don't we rebuild there?"

"The spot's shot. We're too close to the swamp and the rain's been making it all muddy. And Tyson's convinced the swamp lady's after him." He flicked his cigarette.

"No, I'm not."

JP and I crept toward him.

"Oh, you ain't scared, Tyson?" JP said.

"Yeah," I added. "You don't think the swamp lady will bother you tonight while you're sleeping?"

"Fuck you guys."

"Better be courteous when she comes by." JP poked Tyson hard in the chest and he tripped. "You'll get more than a rock peggin' if you don't!"

We all laughed, and we headed up the path. I started thinking about that woman—she could have been Native, could have been Puerto Rican, could have been Mexican—on the bus. I wondered if she got to her destination.

"Do either of you know if the Greyhound has another stop after Overtown?"

"How the fuck would I know?" JP said. "You're the only one of us who takes the bus."

When we left the path and stepped onto the road, JP flicked his cigarette and then cupped it in his hand to hide it from on-coming cars. "Oh yeah, David," he said. "We have to come back down here tonight to the boulder. Have to show you something. And Tyson, you're coming. No crying about it again."

"Show me what?" I asked over Tyson's declaration that he never cries.

JP turned to face me. He lowered his voice to a whisper.

"A pugwagee."

"Get out of here," I said. "Really?"

"Swear to God," JP said. "We were down at the boulder and we saw it far away in some trees. Right, Tyson?"

Tyson nodded.

"See? Even Tyson knows what he saw. I basically have drag him through here at night to get to your shed."

"Yeah," I said. "About the shed—my mom knows you two have been going in there."

"How does she know?" JP said. "We go late."

"Crows were talking, she said."

There was a pause and we stood. "I don't know what's scarier," JP said, "the swamp lady or your mother."

We laughed and kept on going.

"But for real," JP said. "We saw one and chased it."

"You chased it?" I laughed in disbelief.

"Yeah, but we were so far away that it was gone by the time we got to where we saw it. I'm surprised Tyson followed me."

"I wasn't waiting there by myself," Tyson said. "I had no choice."

"Well, Tyson," I said. "Now you'll wake up to the swamp lady and a pugwagee. You can cook them dinner."

"Don't forget the tobacco," JP added.

On the side of the road we stood, staring into a path that could bring you about anywhere. The last glimmers of day covered the rez roads, but the trees shrouded the path in darkness, a tunnel of never-ending night.

"Let's go before it gets too dark," JP said.

He stepped into the path and I told him to wait. "Where are we even going?" I said.

"I don't know," JP said. "Let's go all over the place."

I followed his shadow into the woods.

. . .

That night, we waited in the same spot where JP and Tyson had said they saw the pugwagee, behind my house in the woods at the giant boulder. We sat quietly, but all we saw were tree shadows under the moon while mosquitoes pricked us.

After we quit waiting, I went home. Frick's truck was in the driveway. I hadn't seen him since I got back.

I climbed up the crooked steps and went inside. It was late. Mom sat in her rocking chair and watched the eleven o'clock news, her eyes barely open as she tried to fight off her pain pills and wine so she could stay awake and eat her dinner.

"Gwus," she said, slurring her words. "Where you been?"

"Out with JP and Tyson." I took off my shoes.

"You lying?"

No," I said. "Where you think I been? Making plans with the devil?"

"Just thought I'd ask."

There was some rice in a pot and I scooped some out onto a plate. Mom had baked some haddock, and I took a square of it. Standing near the sink, I ate the food cold.

Mom laughed.

"What's funny?" I said.

"This woman on the news," she said.

"What'd she do?" A piece of rice got stuck in my throat.

Mom slurred her words bad. "Went into that grocery store, the one up—oh, you know."

"Save 'n Shop?"

"Yes."

I set my plate down on the sideboard and I poured some water in a cup from the sink, and I drank it and then set the cup down and picked up my plate.

"And?" I said.

"And what?"

"The woman?"

"Oh," Mom said. She laughed again slow and tired. "Fuck." I looked at her. She'd dropped a piece of haddock onto the floor.

"Leave it," I said. "I'll get it."

But she picked it up and set it on her plate.

"You were saying?"

"Went into the store with a water gun and sprayed people with her own piss."

I went into the kitchen.

"A woman did that?" I didn't take another bite of my food.

"Fucking crazy white people," Mom said, and she didn't mention it again.

But if it was her she wasn't white. Or maybe she was. I set my plate in the sink.

"Where's Frick?" I said.

"Who?"

"Frick!" Christ, turn that TV down.

"In bed. Doesn't feel well."

Mom tried to stand with her plate, but she wobbled and the plate almost fell. I went to her, told her to sit down and that I'd take it and rinse it.

"Did Paige leave?" I said.

"What?"

237

I turned down the TV. "Did Paige leave?"

"She's not in her room?"

I went down the hall and checked. The light was off, and her room was clean as it always was, her pink-and-red duffel bag set on her dresser next to her small mirror and incense sticks.

"No, she's not there," I said.

Mom stood. "Then she must be out. Give me baasus. I'm going to bed."

I gave her a kiss good-night. She stumbled, and I helped her down the hallway to her room.

The house was quiet, and so when the ashy fire poker that leaned on the wall next to the woodstove slipped to the floor the noise scared me. I picked it up and set it on top of the woodstove. I wanted to tell Paige about the pugwagee, that JP and Tyson saw one, but I'd have to wait. I wouldn't tell Mom about it, because I knew she'd be disappointed. "You leave them alone," she'd say. "I don't want no little-people spirits following you home, stealing stuff and causing trouble. We got enough trouble in this house already. They're dangerous. And they're not called pugwagees—they're mikumwaso to us."

. . .

Pugwagees were children when they were cursed. A woman was out collecting sweetgrass in her swamp. She had lived under the shadows her entire life. Each morning she left the hollowed-out tree that was her house and covered her body with fresh pickings of dark green moss and small ferns that she squashed together with muck from the murky water and then tied around her body with twine from young trees. When she finished dressing, she spent all day searching for sweetgrass and stopped only when the last bit of her clothing had slipped out from under the twine.

The only animals to know better than to stare at her throughout her day were crows, but many thought she controlled them, because they remained quiet, black dots perched up high in the cedar trees. Crows were never quiet, which was why they were created: the Creator got sick of them cawing and cawing, telling secrets in his head, and so he spoke their name into the world.

Unlike the crows, pugwagees were not spoken into the world: they were born in it, a product of the first people, who were made from ash. Nobody, it was said, watched the children.

One day, when the sun barely penetrated the thick swamp, the swamp woman woke and dressed in fresh clothing. She placed her deer-hide medicine bag on the ground and marched around the swamp, pulling up the grass that grew so she could let it dry. When she could pick no more she returned to her bag, fists full of damp sweetgrass. She picked up her bag. It was light and empty. Nobody had ever stolen from her. Infuriated, she stomped back to her hollowed-out tree to think.

In the morning, dressed in swamp regalia, she informed the crows of what had happened. They puffed out their black chests with each caw and she told them to be quiet and listen. She pointed to her bag on the ground and then to her eyes, saying, *Watch this.*

Confident in the crows' ability to talk, she set off and began picking. Soon enough, the crows cawed. Too far away to see, the swamp woman straightened, tightened her grip on the bundle of sweetgrass in her hand. She ran to her bag, the swampy earth squishing and squashing and squishing until she stopped. Three little back-ends stuck out of her bag.

She got closer. They fumbled around with the bag's contents, tossed strips of birch bark out onto the ground, and ooh-ed and aah-ed at the shiny objects for which she had traded.

She stood over the bag and realized they were children. With one giant swoop she scooped them up, shoved them in her bag, and slung the bag's strap around her shoulders.

The little children screamed and the crows cawed louder.

She held the bag up to her ear and heard the children crying. Off in the distance she heard the faint sound of tiny feet running away through the woods.

"Jiistowks!" the swamp woman yelled at the crows. She needed to listen.

She followed the sound, marching through tall grasses until she stumbled upon flat ground. She stood over the children, swamp muck slipping off her, and they cowered in her shadow. They were little and fragile, dressed in nothing but the deer hide that they pulled tight around their shoulders, hiding. The swamp woman was too angry to blink, too angry to ask why. While we know she cursed those children in that clearing, to forever be little people for their thievery, no one knows what happened to the children she scooped up in her bag.

. . .

The next day—after a long night of dreams of the Greyhound parked outside my house honking its horn repeatedly, made all the more eerie when Frick woke me in the middle of the night to sleep-tell me the Jesuits were here—JP, Tyson, and I spent the afternoon resurrecting the lean-to. It had rained overnight, which made it easier to stab sticks into the ground to give extra support to the structure. We sat on the damp earth when we were done, and we smoked cigarettes until darkness filled the trees and mosquitoes swarmed and buzzed and poked at our eyes.

"Let's get a fire going," JP said.

We split off into the woods and collected firewood. We assembled a giant pile of sticks and logs, wet and dry, and piled them a few feet from the growing fire.

"This should last us till about twelve," JP said, "then we can go look for that pugwagee again."

"I don't want to go up there," Tyson said.

"Shut up," JP said. "You're coming."

I threw them each a cigarette. Mosquitoes hovered beyond the fire's smoke; hemlock popped and sizzled, and the river flowed and gurgled.

"How's Paige?" JP asked. "My mom said she saw her walking down the road and she didn't look too good."

"I have no idea," I said. "She hasn't been home. Well, she has, but not when I'm there. I don't even remember the last time I saw her. Last year sometime."

We didn't feed the fire. Tyson put another hemlock branch with its needles on top of the little flame. It popped. I wondered about Paige, what she looked like now. The last time I had seen her she was gaining weight and had stopped laughing so much.

Tyson said he was going to head home.

"Sit down," JP said. "We have some hunting to do tonight."

"We're not going to see it," Tyson said.

"Yes, we will. David, let me get another cigarette."

"Let's split one, I'm running low."

We passed the cigarette between us. Three-drag pass. Tyson, as always, took crack drag, pulling off the cigarette until the cherry fell to the ground, smoking part of the filter. The fire slowly died and we stood. Our eyes were used to the dark. Thick trees blocked out the full moon. We didn't need to see—the woods knew us. We moved effortlessly over the path. We knew all the ups and downs of the ground, where all the roots stuck out and reached for our feet.

Concrete. The streetlight on the road was bright, its orange light making me squint, the bulb buzzing and mingling against the sound of crickets. Headlights turned the corner of the hill, coming for us.

"Get in the woods," JP said.

We tucked ourselves in a small ditch and mud sucked our shoes.

"Council passed a curfew ordinance," JP whispered. "No one under eighteen can be out after ten unless they're walking home."

The vehicle drove by us. It wasn't the police—it was the van with the film crew.

We hurried up the hill. Behind my house the path was lit, the ground aglow from the moon perched in the sky and through the trees. We followed the lighted path to the giant boulder that forked the path.

"Keep your eyes open," JP said. He held a stick.

"What are you going to do with that?" I said. "Beat it?"

"What if it comes after me?"

I became more and more nervous at the thought of chasing the pugwagee. I didn't want it to follow me home, wake me up in the middle of the night with its bangs on the walls and its little voices whispering down the hallway. I didn't want to hear Mom yell and tell it to go away, the way she did with the Goog'ooks that knocked on the cabinet doors when she'd forget to put a cloth over the dirty dishes. I didn't want Mom to complain to Frick, who would then light aflame his blessing and fill the house with thick smoke. I didn't want the need to expunge.

I bit my nail too close to the skin.

"I don't know if this is a good idea," I said.

"Shut up," JP hissed. "What is that?" He pointed with his crooked stick.

Under the blue moon, small trees in the distance parted and a black outline of a body tumbled through. Tyson turned to run and JP grabbed him by the neck.

"I'll smash this stick over your fucking head if you ruin this," JP whispered.

"It's coming at us," I said. The dark body tripped and tripped over the earth. It grunted and then cried out into the sky. Tyson broke loose from JP's grip and ran the opposite direction. JP didn't stop him.

From behind the boulder, JP and I watched this thing trip and stumble. Every broken branch and twig snapped under its feet and the pops echoed into the night.

"That's no pugwagee," JP said. "It's too big."

"What is it?" I asked, but it was too late. The thing picked up speed and pushed thin trees out of its way. As it screamed the body burst through thick brush and landed facedown in front of JP and me. It looked up at us. It was her.

"Fuck you," Paige slurred and laughed. "Give me a cigarette."

I stood and wiped my pant legs off. I lit a cigarette and headed for the road.

JP dropped the stick and followed after me.

"Give me a cigarette!" she yelled.

The orange streetlamp floated above us on the road.

"Shouldn't you help her home?" JP asked.

I wanted to say no, but I couldn't.

"You're just going to leave her there?"

No, I wasn't. In the path she was sprawled out on the ground. I stayed back from her. "Go home," I told her.

She raised her head. "Who are you?" she said. "You got a cigarette?"

"No, go home. It's up there." I pointed to our house through the woods. An inside light shone through the kitchen window and it reached for Paige and me.

She got to her feet and wobbled in place. "Please," she begged. "One cigarette."

I didn't want her to know it was me. I lit another cigarette and handed it to JP, who brought it to her.

"Now go home," I said.

"You're the fucking best." She stumbled away from us and tripped again and again up the path to our house.

"Fuck!" She dropped her cigarette but found it. Its bright red dot made all kinds of dying patterns in the air as she kept her balance, swearing and saying loudly, "That motherfucking pig." Finally, she made it out of the woods and fell to her knees. She crawled into our shed.

"Close enough," I said. I needed to get away from there, from the woods, my house, that place.

"Where are you going?" JP hurried behind me.

The air outside was an uncomfortable mix of hot and cold. The taste of cigarettes was in my mouth and so I lit another.

"Everywhere," I said.

In silence we moved together over the Island. I wanted to lock Paige in that shed, leave her there until the slab of concrete cracked below her body and the earth made her better.

"You want to go find Tyson?" JP asked. "We can kick his ass."

I laughed away some of the heat in my face. "I'd probably kill him."

"Well," JP poked me gently. "I'm going to find Tyson and then head home. I'll give him a punch for you."

At home, Frick's truck was parked where it had been in the morning, and I leaned on it, flicking chipped paint and rust while I looked at the house. The small lamp next to the couch was turned on, and Frick sat on the couch with Mom, and he was raving about something. One hand in the air, then another. He stood once, had that man-stare looking down on a woman, and Mom pointed at the couch and he sat his ass back down. He rubbed his head, and then his eyes.

I left the truck and went to the shed. The door was open and I looked in. Paige was face-first on the cold concrete. Her body was close to a metal fold-out chair that she probably fell off of. I flicked my lighter and searched for something soft, which wasn't difficult since Mom hoarded all kinds of old quilts and pillows and sheets and curtains.

Paige snored. I tucked a garbage bag filled with some blankets or sheets under her head and then draped a quilt over her. I left the shed door open a crack so in the morning the sun would bother her awake.

The screen door squeaked when I pulled it open, and squeaked when I closed it. "Hey," I said.

Frick stood and looked at me. "Time is it?" he said. "Ain't you got school tomorrow?"

I kicked off my shoes, flinging dirt over the kitchen rug.

"You that drunk you don't know what month it is?" Mom said.

He stood and mumbled something. His braid was undone, and his hair stuck to the sweat on his cheek. When nobody said anything, he walked to the kitchen sink and splashed water on his face. He reached in the cupboard and took down a pill bottle, twisted the lid off, and shook two into his palm and popped them in his mouth. He put the bottle back into the cupboard, and then he stuck his head into the sink and drank from the faucet. He forgot to turn the faucet off after he dried his face and hands. He walked down the hall—a shoulder bumping into the wall—and disappeared into Mom's room.

"Christ," Mom said. She stood from the couch. "I was starting to think he'd never go to bed."

"What was he yakking about?"

Mom went to the sink and turned off the water. "I don't know—I think something's wrong with him. He's been taking Ambien for sleep, which would explain his sleepwalking."

She went into the living room and checked how much wine Frick had drunk. She poured herself a cup and sipped it. In the kitchen, she looked at the glass of wine and then she dumped it down the sink. She washed a few plates and bowls, and the ones that were extremely dirty, food stuck like cooled lava, she left in hot soapy water.

Mom dropped a fork.

"Oh," she said, and she went on to say the old saying about strangers showing up.

"Hopefully it's Publishers Clearing House who shows up with a big fat check," I said, even though that wasn't the first thing that came to mind. I thought of the woman on the bus, how still she was, how intently she looked ahead for the whole ride.

Mom picked up the fork. "With our luck they'd come here by mistake. Either that or it'd be the repo man coming for the car."

"Is the car payment late?"

Mom let out a real sigh. "I shouldn't have said that. You don't need to know about that shit. I get my check in a few days anyways."

In the kitchen chair, I sprawled out and stretched my legs.

"We have to get you some new pants," Mom said. "You're growing right out of those."

"They got another year," I said.

"Another year will be here before you know it."

Mom dried her hands, and before she could wipe down the counter I told her no, said that I'd do it.

"If you insist," she said. "Give me baasus—I'm going to bed."

We said good night, and when she made it to her bed-room door she turned around and spoke to me. "Have you seen Paige?"

I told her no.

The house was quiet as I wiped down the counters. The floor creaked under my feet and the clock ticked. It was late. I covered the dishes that Mom left exposed. Watching myself in the reflection of the TV as I walked closer, I grew larger—my body, my ill-fitting pants, and the kitchen behind me disappeared as I flicked off the lamp.

. . .

The morning after I put Paige to bed in the shed I woke to find her gone. For two days, it rained and I never saw her. She'd slip out. I didn't know why she wanted to be out in the rain, but she did. When the skies finally cleared—sometime around four in the morning, because I'd gone to sleep to the sound of heavy rain thumping the roof and woke to Frick watching TV loudly in the living room—Tyson, JP, and I planned to take canoes out onto the river, which was high and moved fast. I left home early in the morning. Frick had taken two Ambien and finally gone to sleep and Mom said not to stay out late, that she was leaving for a big grocery shop and was going to bring back a surprise for dinner. Before I met up with JP and Tyson down by the river, the van with the film crew had stopped me and asked if they could get footage of me walking down the road, hands in my pockets, and I told them for sixty bucks they could film a few of us canoeing, but they said they were on schedule, had to be somewhere. I was pretty sure they filmed me walking anyway.

In the sun, JP, Tyson, and I paddled against the river for a few hours, and JP and I poked Tyson's canoe with our paddles, and we laughed while he kept his balance in the vast river that was our blood. We canoed past all the land that the state owned until we finally arrived at the marshy islands that have always been our traditional hunting grounds.

We pulled the canoes on land and the earth sucked our feet. We walked inland for forty minutes, away from all the black ash trees, searching for less muck.

"There," JP said, pointing to dry ground. "That looks good."

The fire blazed. JP pulled some beers out from his backpack. He dropped one on the ground and handed it to Tyson.

"Gee, thanks," Tyson said.

"You don't want it?" JP said. "Give it back then."

Tyson tapped the top of his beer and cracked it open.

"That's what I thought."

I took a sip and grimaced. "'I don't always drink piss, but when I do, it's High Gravity.'"

"Shut up," JP said. "It's the best I could do. My brother left these in his room. We could ask Paige to buy us some, but she might drink them all."

"That shit ain't funny," I said, and before he could say sorry I finished the beer. "The bottom of the can is as good as the whole thing."

"'Some days,'" JP said, adopting Thomas's voice from *Smoke Signals*, "'it's a good day to die. And some days, it's a good day to have High Gravity.'"

"'Thomas,'" I said, "'you are so full of shit.'"

"Yeah," JP said. He shook the foam from his can onto the ground. "It's never a good day to have High Gravity. Tyson, if you don't drop out this year you'll be able to watch *Smoke Signals* twice in US History." JP burped and went on. "Excuse me. You get to watch it the first time after you briefly cover the Trail of Tears and then again when you finish talking about our Settlement Act."

"We did watch that twice, didn't we?" I asked.

"Nothing says Native better than 'Hey, Victor!'"

"And fry bread," I said.

The beer hit as quick as I'd drunk it. The fire was warm. Fry bread was on my mind—they'd be selling it at Community Days. Maybe I had enough change in my room to get some. Maybe Paige had some extra change somewhere, under her bed or in a drawer. Frick might have some too, in his truck. Although last time I checked he had nothing but pennies and a two-dollar bill that was too cool to spend. Mom had no money, and I knew better than to look. What money she ever came into she blew. Money—it was everywhere but nowhere.

The pile of logs and thin branches ran out, and so too ran out our buzzes. We all pissed on the fire and then headed for the canoes. Each of us was settled in the quiet downer of drink, and so we said nothing as we got into the rocking canoes and stabbed our paddles into the earth to push off, and down the river we didn't have to exert any force, we simply let the river take us home, and during part of the float the river had spaced us out so Tyson was far to my left, and JP far to Tyson's left, and when we came to the bend of the river its meandering pull brought us together and it was then that we paddled four strokes to the shore and the canoes slid up on the soft dirt bank, a wall of vines dangling down like wet hair. We tied the canoes with rope to some trees, and with aching, lowered heads we walked the darkening woods to the street.

. . .

Mom's car was gone when I got back home, and Frick's truck was parked in the same spot along the driveway in the grass. Tyson said he was going home to eat, and JP said the same except not to his house but to Tyson's, and all the way down the road JP kept telling Tyson he was full of shit, that he knew for a fact there was enough dinner to go around because he had helped Tyson's mother bring in the groceries the other day.

From outside the house I could hear the TV blaring. Strange, unnatural guttural sounds poured out the windows and onto the front lawn, and they got louder when I went inside and into the living room. A zombie movie played—*Land of the Dead*—except nobody watched it, and it was playing with the volume so high, and no audience made the movie more frightening.

The cedar chest that served as our coffee table was covered in ashes, and strewn wrappers of Hershey's chocolate and cellophane littered the floor. The black back to the remote control stuck out from under the cedar chest, and I grabbed it and found one battery under there too. Smooshed between the couch cushions I found the remote but I could not find the other battery. The movie played on, and a man wearing headphones and carrying a rifle was grabbed by a young boy zombie in a filthy black suit, and the man screamed and rolled back on the skateboard he rode for whatever reason, and then zombie after zombie appeared, a dirty clown biting the man's wrist like chicken, another ripping the skin from his neck, and a horde of the dead tackled him into a shed where he fell onto his back and the bunch of them ripped him in half and ate his intestines while he died gasping.

I stuck the one battery into the remote and set the remote and its back on the cedar chest, and I went around to the TV and turned it off, and as I did the quiet revealed her screaming and scared the shit out of me.

"What's the matter?" I yelled. I hurried down the hall to Paige's open door and went in. Her room was trashed—the dresser was flipped over, the mirror shattered into small and large sharp pieces on the floor. An incense stick, burning, blackened the white linoleum. Nobody was there.

She screamed again. Mom's room. I opened the door to Paige on the bed crying and on top of her was Frick, in his clothes but ripping Paige's off. She yelled my name and Frick hit her and then he looked at me over his shoulder and called me a fucking Jesuit.

Paige screamed while Frick came after me slowly, bumping into the wall and rubbing his fingers together. I backed down the hallway and watched him, and he mumbled that this was his wigwam, that white people weren't welcome, and I led him down the hall and through the kitchen and then I opened the back door and stepped onto the concrete steps, to get him to follow me outdoors. He must have thought I was leaving, because he turned around and started back up the hall.

That van with the film crew drove by up the road, and I wanted to yell to them to call the police but they passed by too fast and didn't see me. It was a dead-end road, and so they'd have to come back.

I grabbed my shoe by the front door and threw it at Frick, and he turned around and pushed the fridge over and stepped over all the sprawled foodstuff and shattered condiment jars and he came for me. He took only one or two steps before Paige hit him over the head with the woodstove's ashy fire poker. She screamed and shook and swung and screamed and shook and swung and screamed and shook and swung, and when I stepped over to her bashing his head she stopped and then swung once at me but then lowered the thick metal stick and said, "Don't tell her," and I grabbed the metal and took it from her hands and dropped it with a bang onto the linoleum.

A car honked, and Paige looked to the window. She pushed me aside and went out the back door. I followed her—I didn't look at him lying there—and standing on the steps I watched Mom's trunk pop open. Mom got out of the car, and she said to me, "Get some bags, gwus," and to Paige—who walked down the driveway toward the car—she said, "I got your favorite, doosis. It's already de-shelled. Wasn't cheap."

I walked toward the car but stopped and stayed on the steps. Plastic bags were crinkling as Mom grabbed some from the trunk.

"Don't go inside, mumma," Paige said.

The plastic bags stopped crinkling.

"Don't go inside."

"What's the matter?" Mom said, and Paige started sobbing and tried to hang off Mom like a child, but Mom could not hold her up.

"What's all over your face?" Mom said.

I didn't realize it until then—and I didn't know how long I'd been doing it—but I had my hand over my mouth and I was biting my palm. I was bleeding, and I wiped my palm on my jeans.

I walked down the steps but did not go to them. "She didn't mean to do it," I said. "She didn't mean it."

"Didn't mean what?" Mom tried to escape Paige's holding. The van with the film crew came back down. Paige was screaming, crying, saying, "Don't go inside!" The van stopped and the window rolled down, and the driver—an old white man with a gray beard—asked if Paige was all right.

"You mind your fucking business," Mom said to him. "You're a little far from the sacred fire, aren't you?"

The driver took great offense to that and he kept talking— "I'm trying to help, does she need help? Jace, call someone, she needs help—" but Mom ignored him and grabbed Paige's face in her hand and Mom said, "What did you do?"

"Frick did it!" I yelled, and Mom twisted loose from Paige and hurried down the driveway and she didn't look at me as she walked up the steps and into that yellow house, and she shrieked and wailed walking backward back out of the house and down the crooked steps and she collapsed onto the hard, hard driveway.

Paige was crying to the van driver. "He came after me," she said. "He came after me."

"Someone's coming," the driver said. "Someone will be here soon. He won't get you."

Mom threw up.

One man was filming, and I told him to turn off his fucking camera.

Mom wiped her mouth and said "Jesus Christ" over and over again. "Jesus Christ, Jesus Christ, Jesus Christ." I rubbed her back, tried to pick her up and move her from her vomit, but she said that wasn't how it was supposed to be, and she crawled toward Paige, kept saying and flapping her hands to the white driver, "Give me my baby, come here, come here," and Paige went crying to Mom and Mom held my big sister on her lap in the driveway, and she rocked Paige and said, "Where's my other one, where's my other one?" and I went to her just in time, crawled beside her in the dusty gravel right before the world and its purple sky and red setting sun faded to black.

THE NAME MEANS THUNDER

I am no longer blind, but there was a time many years ago when I lost my vision. Next week I'll see the eye doctor for my cataracts, and he'll ask if my eyes were ever damaged. I don't know how these things work, but should I go in for surgery—should it come to that—I feel that withholding any medical information, any important details, might lead the doctor's sharp tool in the wrong direction.

I want to get the story right for my sake, so I think it should begin here: I was ten, and I sat in a hard chair, pushed in close to a desk too high for me. Every so often Jane, the principal's secretary at the rez school, got up from her big brown desk and walked over, looked at how little I had completed of the map test on the solar system, and said, "You know that planet, right?" She smelled like cinnamon, the flavor of the Nicorette gum she chewed. "It rhymes with *birth*."

I knew where the sun was, obviously, and I knew the location of two planets orbiting it: Pluto—which was way, way out on the perimeter—and Earth. Today, I could probably locate only those two, but then again it's been fifty-some years since Pluto was demoted—cast out from the solar system—and so it no longer matters. But in that chair back then I couldn't write the answer—any answer—because looking on that white paper with different-size circles, I saw Earth and wondered how my sister Paige was getting on.

Mom was there with her, and so too was Frick, who drummed and sang to welcome the child. (He'd either taken the day off from working maintenance or this was around the time he had stopped showing up.) If I recall correctly, even Paige's caseworker, Marla, was there, or at least she was at some point, because Mom would tell time and time again how at first she thought Marla was a nice woman but that she was wrong. When I was older, I'd tell Mom that Marla was doing her job, which, of course, my mother disagreed with. I wanted to be at the hospital with them all, but I'd had a coughing fit that morning—I swallowed water down the wrong hole was all—and Mom instantly thought I was sick and would get the child sick. So I had to go to school.

Jane smacked her gum. "David," she said. "*Birth*. It rhymes with *birth*."

"Earth," I told her.

"Very good," she said. "Write it down."

She returned to her desk behind me and I wrote *home* below the planet, which was right but also wrong, the type of answer a cool teacher might give half points for and write *clever* next to. But those cool teachers did that only for the students who knew all the answers, the students who did all their work, the students who never had caseworkers and went to school each and every day.

That day—it was the start of September, a gray and cloudy afternoon—Frick picked me up from detention. Or maybe it wasn't detention. I don't know. Detention came about with your name on the chalkboard as well as a check mark next to it, both of which I never received. I was good, well-behaved. I had trouble with exams, with studying, with getting work done in school or at home, so oftentimes at the end of each day, when the long dull bell ended yet echoed in the ear, the science teacher—she had the biggest hips I ever saw—would wave me over and tell me she had extra work for me. I'd sit in the front office listening to Jane type away for an hour while I completed an assignment or two and ate animal crackers and drank water from waxy cups.

Frick's truck rumbled in place in the parking lot, the exhaust pipe blowing fumes into the air. The door was locked and Frick had to reach over and unlock it. I climbed in, and as I did he took my backpack and set it in the small space behind the gray seats.

"Is the baby home?" I asked.

Frick put the truck in drive and pulled out of the parking lot. "No," he said. "He's sick."

And the child remained sick for some days. Each day I sat through detention unable to finish a test, wondering if the child would be home when Frick picked me up. He was brought home eventually to our little yellow house. Years later, when I would visit Mom on Sundays at the elder apartments on the reservation, she would tell me—in this low, gentle voice she found in old age—that the boy suffered terrible seizures from methadone withdrawal, a revelation that explained his horrible screeching wails. At the time, I thought his cries were because Paige refused to hold him—she was depressed, quiet, always on the couch with her arms crossed and a cigarette smoldering in the ashtray. But no—the boy's pain was from withdrawal from the methadone his mother had taken to fend off the desire to wash down those blue pills with drink, the desire to numb the memory of that terrible touch of a man's hands on her body on this planet I could not name. It's funny that at the time I knew all of that—that she was on methadone because of her using, which was because of that man who ran back to the Mohawk rez (Frick chased him)—but I didn't know, or couldn't conceptualize, how dependency transitioned from one body to the other, how all those actions had consequences.

When the boy came home, Mom cared for him the most since Paige couldn't. Mom would wrap him in a small, white, soft blanket that the nuns had given us—along with diapers and spare towels and vouchers for the grocery store, all of which were delivered to us in an ash basket the boy slept in, the only other place besides my mother's arms where he tended to be quiet. Mom would rock and hum to him as they sat on the couch with the TV turned low and Frick in the kitchen, holding and flicking an unlit smoke. And that is where we were—Mom and the boy on the couch, me on the floor watching TV, Paige sleeping in her room, and Frick pretending to smoke at the kitchen table—when the first of many calls came from the hospital demanding the child's name.

Paige refused to name him, and the only reason we were eventually able to take him home without a name was because Frick lied to the doctor, told him there needed to be a naming ceremony to take place on sacred ground. Maybe it wasn't a lie, but I remember no ceremony taking place, and I remember one night Frick laughing about it on the phone with his brother who lived out West. Nonetheless, perhaps to avoid a lawsuit or to fulfill a commitment to cultural sensitivity, the doctor agreed to let the boy go home after his stint in the ICU and the doses of phenobarbital that he took in the mornings.

But before Frick told his lie, as the days passed with no name given, the hospital began to call and call. "Next week," Mom would say. "We have to wait a week for the ceremony." Mom paused, listening. "Because," she said. "It has to do with the position of the planets."

When she hung up, I asked her if she knew where Neptune was.

"At the bottom of the ocean," she said.

The days passed, and with each call the hospital grew more impatient. "He needs a name," they said, "or we'll name him. You can change the name when you have one." I'm curious now to know what they would have named him; Google says that a hospital will enter "Baby boy" or "Baby X" on the birth certificate. All I know is that they didn't name the child, but they kept calling us every day at around the same time—four in the afternoon. We knew when to expect the call, and Mom would take the boy, bundle him up (the nights were getting colder), and Frick and I would follow her outdoors where we'd sit on the concrete steps and for an hour get fresh fall air.

It was one of those days outside when we gave him a name, or we called him something. Frick came up with it. A small rainstorm blew through and we waited it out in the shed— Mom and the baby, Frick and me. For not long it downpoured and the green leaves flipped over and shivered their white pale-green undersides while the sky lit with sharp white light and the ground below us rumbled. During it all the boy did not cry. The storm was ending, the rain pattering gentler and gentler on the shed roof; Frick took one more puff of his smoke, then held it out the open shed door under some dripping water where it hissed out and he flicked it to the earth.

"Bedogi," he said, blowing smoke. The name means *thunder* in Panawahpskek, and so that was the name we gave him, or the name we thought we'd use until Paige emerged from that dark place.

I didn't hold Bedogi too often. I usually held him when Mom and Frick and I were outside on those steps, avoiding the hospital calls. Mom would hand him to me so she could have a smoke in the shed, and Frick always followed her. With Bedogi born, Mom was different. She didn't smoke in the house, and she stopped drinking and began to sip tea. Frick too, but only because Mom told him to or he'd have to leave, and the only place he had to go was his unfinished camp some miles north off the reservation.

When I held the boy I whispered to him, gave him hope about his mother. "She'll get better," I said to him on the steps. I remember the first time I told him that. How could I not remember? It was a cool night in late September, going on 9:00 PM, and I held him while Mom and Frick were in the shed, arguing about something. (It was Frick wanting to go out, to drink, but she kept telling him he didn't need it.) As I told the boy his mother would get better, Mom came out of the shed and asked what I had said. I told her what I said, thinking I had said something wrong, and Mom took Bedogi from me and said the same exact thing.

"She'll get better is right. Come on, David, let's go inside."

We all went indoors, and the kitchen lights were bright and I squinted. Bedogi had fallen asleep in Mom's arms and still slept when Mom called for Paige. He stayed sleeping when Paige didn't respond, when Mom called her name again, louder. The third time Mom yelled for Paige, Bedogi woke and gurgled out a thick yelp.

"David," Mom said. "Go wake your sister."

Paige wasn't there—not even an outline of a body pressed into the tightly made bed.

"She's gone," I said to Mom. I stood in the hallway, like I was going to go back and check her room one more time as if my eyes had missed her.

"What do you mean she's gone?" Mom said. She yelled Paige's name once more, and Bedogi let out a loud shriek.

"Shh, shh," Mom said.

Mom got up from the couch. I moved out of her way as she came down the hall to Paige's room and peered into the darkness. She said Paige's name again.

But Paige was gone. Her bedroom window was closed, but the screen was popped out and lying on the front lawn.

Frick went and got it, but Mom told him not to put it back in, that Paige might come back later and she wouldn't be getting in through the locked doors. "How dare she?" Mom said. "How dare she?"

"Do you want me to look for her?" Frick said. He tucked the window screen into Paige's closet. "Drive around?"

"No," Mom said.

Bedogi cried for an hour or so. Mom tried her best to soothe him—she rocked him and hummed louder and louder until he heard it over his screams and quieted. Soon, his breathing slowed, and he fell asleep. It was then, when I think Bedogi was dreaming a dream he'd never remember, that Mom went to put him to bed, telling me to pick up the blanket on the couch and follow her. When I got to Paige's room Mom had the light on and stood staring at the empty space on Paige's bedroom floor. The ash basket Bedogi slept in was gone.

"Bitch," Mom said.

"Do you think she was drinking?" Frick said, but Mom had no answer.

Mom made up her bed and put Bedogi in the middle with two pillows on each side. She came out of her room, didn't say anything, and walked outdoors. Frick followed, but Mom looked at him once and only once, so he stayed indoors with me and didn't speak, sat at the kitchen table while I sat on the linoleum in the living room. When Mom came back in, she washed her hands, scrubbing the smoke from her fingers.

"Do you want me to find her?" Frick said.

The sink thumped off, and Mom dried her hands on her jeans.

"I know what you want," she said. "Just go. If you find her, you find her. If you don't, then I know where you are." Mom turned and went into the bathroom.

Frick put his boots on, laced them up, and was gone before Mom even flushed the toilet. She didn't say anything to me when she came out. She turned off all the lights in the kitchen and living room, then with careful steps walked down the dark hallway and into her room.

. . .

I would tell this story a few times as I got older, and sometimes in the telling I would say I stayed there on the floor all night, but other times I'd say I put myself to bed. In the later attempts to tell it—once to a therapist and once to a girl I would be married to for a few years—I began to mention this detail, that I couldn't remember if I sat there all night or put myself to bed, in order to make the account more truthful. And so I don't know if I stayed there all night or put myself to bed, but I now question whether or not this detail makes the story any more honest.

The next few days, with Paige and Frick gone, the house was quiet. With the exception of the phone, which began to ring and ring for long intervals at least four times a day. I don't know how many times I went to school during those days with them gone, but I know it was at least once. My science teacher talked about the solar system, and she told the class that in four to five billion years the sun will explode—she drew giant chalk scribbles over the chalk Earth she'd drawn on the blackboard. But she assured us that we, humans, wouldn't be around to see it, that in the few million years before the sun explodes, it will first expand and swallow the Earth like food.

I asked my mother about it. She was sweeping with one hand and holding Bedogi in the other.

"I heard about that," she told me. "It was on PBS one night." She held the dustpan with her foot, and standing upright she swept the dirt onto the red plastic pan. "Would you dump that in the garbage?"

"So it's true?" I said. "It'll happen?"

"We'll be long gone," Mom said.

"But it will happen?" I asked again.

"So they say."

"But do you think it will happen?"

"I think you need to come and get this dustpan and dump it, that's what I think."

Each day Bedogi stayed in Mom's arms, and each day Mom sat on the couch or puttered in the kitchen cooking lunch and dinner for herself and me. I stopped asking about the sun, but I began to scrutinize it. Each evening, when it was setting and the woods golden, Mom walked the short path out behind our house with Bedogi, walked the loop, and showed him the oak and maple and birch trees, showed him Frick's sweat lodge, and even brought him in there once. The whole time she was gone I tried with quick glances to make out the roundness of the setting sun through the trees to ensure it was still round, not swelling toward us. When Mom finished the loop she would give Bedogi to me, and I sat on the steps holding him while Mom repeated her walk alone. While she was gone, I told the boy that the sun looked round and fine.

For a week Paige and Frick didn't show, and neither called. Or if they did, we didn't answer. Mom had answered the phone once that week, and it wasn't them or the hospital: it was Marla, Paige's caseworker, wondering why Paige had missed her appointment. "I'll have her call you when she's back," Mom said. "She's out right now." Marla never got the call, obviously, because Paige didn't come home that night.

On a Saturday it had rained all night, and in the morning the house smelled of the wet grass outside. When I came out of my room in the early dawn, Mom was at the kitchen table, dressed in black pants and a jean jacket, keys in her hands, purse on her lap. She was going to find one of them.

"Where's Bedogi?" I said.

Mom stood. "In bed. I fed him this morning, but you'll have to feed him again. His bottles are in the fridge. Remember to heat them under warm sink water, but not for too long."

"Why can't we come?" I said. "Can't we come?"

"No," she said. "Stay with the baby. I won't be gone long." And then she turned to the shoes lining the wall and picked up her rubber boots, and I knew she was going to get Frick at camp.

"What if he poops?" I said.

"You've seen me change his diaper," Mom said. "Don't answer the phone while I'm gone and don't answer the door." Through the living room window, I watched as she backed her white Toyota out of the driveway and then pulled away to find Frick.

I don't think of Frick too often. He's been dead for years, and I never went to his funeral. Few people did. Why would they? But sometimes I can't help but feel I should have gone. Like it would have made something I cannot name not so lonely. In my own loneliness, I thought a lot about that, about if I should have gone. After his death, I went down south for a time, North Carolina way, and painted military vehicles for cash. It was there, on my knees spraying the trucks, that I thought about him. There is that terrible memory, surely, but so too are there sweet ones, the tiny memories with the tiny details that are milder in climax, no doubt, but equally powerful, like how Frick would pick me up from detention and take my backpack from me so I could climb into his high truck, and how I would always forget my backpack there, yet by some point in time the backpack would always be in my room. Or how my bike's chain was always kept greased, or how if my toy men broke he would fix them, glue their legs or arms or heads back on. Or how, even when he was drunk, he would carry me to bed if I fell asleep on the couch.

Mom loved him, and I guess it was for that reason she went to get him that day, but why she left me to tend to the boy I did not know. Once, about ten years back, I asked her why she left me there with the baby. I had brought her a Coffee Pot Sandwich and over soggy bread in her smoky elder apartment she told me she hadn't, that she took Bedogi and me with her, that it was so long ago and I was a child, so I couldn't remember. But I remember, and that's not the story I know, not the story I tell or have told, and not the one I will continue to tell—although I tried out Mom's story once on a therapist, the version where Mom brought us with her, and it ended where it was supposed to. I have to tell it how it went, and it went like this: she didn't take us. But I can see how she'd believe her version, because she had to believe it.

While Mom was gone, I occasionally checked on Bedogi. He slept most of the morning, and so I kept quiet in the house, listening for him to wake, dreading the moment he would cry and I had to do something about it. But he didn't cry. From the living room I heard him sneeze, and when I went to him he was kicking the air, his hands in fists as small as cotton balls. I sat on the bed, and it jostled him, maybe even scared him a bit.

"It's me," I told him. "Mom—well, Grammy, your Grammy, not my Grammy—went to find Frick. You'd think she'd go look for your mom, wouldn't you?"

In my memory he kicked, a little *Yes*.

"She'll come back," I told him, meaning his mother. "And she'll be better."

While I spoke to Bedogi in that way, I kept my fears to myself, particularly that none of them would come back, ever, and that the sun would blow up.

I sat with him for a few hours until he began to whimper, and I thought maybe he was hungry. I got his bottle from the fridge, turned the sink on warm, and held the bottle under the running water. I'd watched Mom test the bottle, watched her tip the bottle over and drip the formula onto her wrist. I tried it, but I didn't know if it was the right temperature, didn't know if it was too hot or not hot enough. With the bottle of formula, I went back to the room, set it on the nightstand, and while the formula cooled I made faces at Bedogi, made farting noises with my mouth. When I went to feed him, when he reached with his little mouth for the bottle's rubber tip, somebody knocked on the back door.

The woman had her face pressed to the window, hands like a tunnel on each side of her eyes, and she saw me down the hallway, looking at her. She knocked again when I dipped back into Mom's room, and kept knocking when I didn't answer.

It was Marla. I dream of her at that door often, more so now that Mom is gone. Up to that point in time, I'd met her twice: once when I was in detention—or homework hall, whichever—and she came to ask me questions about home. The Native Studies teacher, a short skeejin guy who told funny stories about Gluskabe—"the man from nothing," who had supposedly created us after many attempts—actually made her leave the school premises because my mother had no knowledge of the meeting. I met her the second time when she came to see Paige and the boy. She sat at our kitchen table while

Paige was trying to think of a name for the child, and I asked
Marla if she remembered me.

"I don't think we've ever met," she lied in a sweet light
voice, and she shook my little hand. It was the right move,
surely. That day, Mom decided not to like her. As Marla sat at
our kitchen table writing down a lot of notes in cursive, Mom
asked what she was writing, and Marla turned in the little seat
under her legs and said, "The conditions here."

I would never hear the end of that story. Mom brought it
up for days. I didn't blame her and I still don't. I never saw a
cleaner house than ours—Mom scrubbed everything spotless,
and maybe used too much bleach when she was mad, as she
had after Marla left that day. Mom had gotten on all fours and
scrubbed the floor, saying every minute, "Did you see those
legs? That winooch needs to look into *her* condition."

I would encounter Marla a total of four times in my life,
the day she knocked on the back door being the third. She
only stopped knocking to yell my name and to tell me to open
the door. "David," she yelled. "It's me, Marla. Open the door,
honey."

I remember picking Bedogi up from between the pillows
and cradling him, and maybe I'm misremembering this next
part because of guilt, but I was so frightened that I thought
about opening that door for her. But I didn't open it. *That's* a
detail that cannot change. As I sat there cradling him, I told
my scared self she could knock and yell and knock some more
until she couldn't stand on her fat legs any longer. My and Bedogi's condition was fine, except he started to cry a bit at Marla's
knocking and yelling.

To keep pretending we were not there, even though Marla had seen us, I had to quiet him. I reached for the bottle on the nightstand, and when I brought it to his mouth he latched on to the rubber tip, and I tilted the bottle upward.

Neither he nor Marla took a break: he sucked, she knocked, he sucked, she knocked, he swallowed, she yelled, he sucked, she knocked and knocked and knocked. She didn't let up one bit, and kept on through my burping Bedogi and his throwing up on my shirt and my wiping his mouth clean and my laying him back between the pillows. When I took my dirty shirt off and tossed it to the floor, Marla finally quit knocking, and the screen door slammed shut.

Bedogi dozed off between the pillows, and I looked down the hall at the door: no Marla behind it. (I would dream of that too—being in a house and hearing somebody knock, only to find nobody at the door, nobody searching for me.)

With her gone, I slipped into my room and grabbed a new shirt, put it on, and then crawled down the hall and into the living room. I stayed low and moved slow to the curtains draped over the window. I peeled back part of the curtain, and in the driveway was Marla's red Dodge, her in it and on the phone. I watched her talk, and then she hung up.

I remember hesitating as she got out of the car and walked down the driveway again. I'd had time to get back to Bedogi in the room, but I didn't go when I should have. I ended up stuck in the living room, and each time she knocked I pressed my back harder and harder into the wall as if it would take me in, absorb me, let me move around and through the insulation like the Goog'ooks—evil spirits—that moved among our house and spoke a language only we could hear, the Goog'ooks that Frick could never smudge away. (He always blamed me for their arrival, said they came because I once whistled at night.) If only the house could absorb me, I'd dive down under where the pipes rattled in the cold, and I'd go to Bedogi, slither back up the insulation, and reach my arm through drywall and take him with me, tell him that Marla was here for our condition.

Again, she eventually stopped and the screen door slammed shut again. I crawled back to the living room window, peeked between curtain and sill. Marla was there, behind her car, talking to the tribal police.

There were two of them, and they had come in one cruiser. One was white, a man named Mitch who had pulled Mom over once for going the speed limit—or at least that's what she said. The other cop was Native, a man named Charlie. Everyone called him Choggy, though. He'd once come to Frick for medicine when his wife couldn't get pregnant, but Frick told him he didn't have any medicine for that.

Marla and the cops were still talking when I decided to move. I crawled to the hallway, stood, and hurried to Mom's room.

I knew Marla meant to come in, to enter the house. She'd seen me, no matter how much I pretended she hadn't. I wonder now and then why Marla didn't barge through the door and save us. I wonder if things would have turned out differently.

Back in Mom's room I opened her closet, but it was full of clothes and blankets and broken metal hangers. I looked under her bed and saw I couldn't fit between the floor and the bed frame.

Bedogi, startled, twitched when I took him from between the pillows, but he didn't cry, just looked at me as I looked back at him, and I smelled the stinky, milky sweet of the formula roll off his breath.

I glanced down the hallway, saw their heads as they ascended the steps to the back door, and I hurried to Paige's room. They started to knock, a rapid three-rap, and I opened Paige's closet. It was as full as Mom's, a dense wood of clothes hanging, the floor cluttered with boxes and Bedogi's car seat; a soft, smiling star dangling from the handle began to play on its own and beeped happy notes too loudly. I grabbed it and buried it deep down in the closet, and as I did something fell on me: the window screen Paige had removed, the one Frick had never put back in place. I looked to the window, heard the doorknob jingle in the kitchen, and had no choice—I was not to open that door.

. . .

The withered grass was cool on my bare feet, my heels pressed hard in the dirt, and I turned back only once—to shut the window. Then I hurried over the grass and onto the stony concrete, cradling Bedogi, his little arm coming untucked from the blanket. My feet scraped and burned all the way down the road, and they stung numb when I made it into the woods and onto the brown-green earth where sunlight scattered through leaves and thick pines onto the ground.

Down in the woods, holding Bedogi to my chest in the green blanket, I watched my steps over sharp rocks, avoided poison ivy, ducked below grabbing branches. I headed back to the house that way, stopping every few feet to look up and see if I could be seen. I hid behind a tree when I saw Marla standing on the steps, Choggy pointing his finger at her, gesturing with a nod that no one was home. And then she argued with him, pushed him aside and entered the house, searching. She came back out and Choggy yelled that she'd imagined it.

Maybe I imagined his saying that, but I don't think so.

I moved away from that spot behind our house. I walked farther into the woods until the path forked, and I took the rocky one to the river that rushed past the reservation.

The wind blew enough for the crowns of the trees above to part and give me a glimpse of the sun. I stopped walking and looked directly at it until the wind quit and the trees closed up, shadowing the woods again.

"Did you see it?" I said to the boy. I watched the sky, hoping to see the trees and leaves part again for the afternoon sun, to check that it was not swelling, that it was still round and healthy.

"It'll come again," I said to him, wanting to make sure the world would live on. And the longer I waited for the wind to rip the trees apart the more I felt Bedogi in my arms.

This is where the details get harder to remember. I don't remember what happened between my saying "Hey, hey, hey, wake up" and when I pissed myself. I don't remember how long I stood in the bright woods, feet in the hard mud, holding the boy. I don't remember making it back to our empty house, don't remember how I knew where I lived. I could not see. I don't remember doing it, but when he died—for he did die, a detail that can't change or be altered—I must have stared too long at the ball of burning life in the sky, searing my cornea and lens and making the world a black blur.

In the grassy ditch that Frick never mowed I waited, and I felt the wet in my pants growing cold, felt the boy's dead body in my arms. There is a real memory here—as if for a brief moment I could see again—where I watched Mom park her car behind Frick's truck, as if to seal him in, to never let him leave again. I couldn't see—I know that—yet the visual memory exists in my brain: Frick gets out of his truck, the three medicine pouches made of deer hide he wore only for ceremony swinging across his neck as he shuts the door. He grabs all three with one hand to stop them, and then he takes one off. He hands it to Paige, whose hair is messy, part of it dried stiff, part of it stuck to her face—I would never ask Mom how they found her or how all that happened—and she puts the medicine bag over her head and then hides it under her shirt. Mom goes to the end of the driveway and checks the gray mailbox.

Frick is on the steps, head down, keys jingling, looking for the right one. Paige is behind him, waiting, but then she returns to the truck, reaches in the bed, and pulls out Bedogi's ash basket. She carries it over her shoulder like she's carrying a sleeping bag, like she's erected her tent to mark the ground her own, like she has finally arrived at the place where she plans to stay.

She sees me. Paige sees me. By the woods, her earth and ground upturned in my arms. She sets the basket on the hood of Frick's truck and comes to me, comes to Bedogi. She stares at him until she turns blue, and all I can say is that I cannot see, I cannot see, yet I can see me see her.

She says nothing when she pulls him from my arms, the blanket dropping to the ground, and carries him past Frick standing at the bottom of the steps, and past Mom who takes me by the shoulder and picks up the fallen blanket and says, "This didn't happen, this didn't happen, not like this," and she says it until it's made true for the story. Inside, she sits me at the kitchen table and for a long while there is nothing but Mom's crying and a toilet flushing, and when Frick returns he says he will call, but Mom stops him with such a loud scream. Mom is the one who picks up the phone, and she is the one who lies. "They're not taking my baby," she says, dialing 911.

The police and ambulance arrive. Paige sits on the couch with Bedogi in her arms, and she stares at him so intently that the police and EMTs standing around her asking questions do not exist. The house is quiet, even with all the EMTs and police talking and questioning. I stare at the kitchen table the entire time. I don't change my wet pants. I sit there, head down. My eyes hurt and water (it feels like sand is back there), and when I begin to cry I wonder which pain is eliciting the tears.

Mom tells the officer taking the statement that we were all at camp having a ceremony and prayer for Paige. Mom says Bedogi was awake when we left camp, and when we got home we thought he was sleeping. When she finishes the story—the story she would believe, that Bedogi and I were with her the whole time, that he died in his sleep sometime on our way back—Paige speaks.

"He can't see?" Paige says. "What does he mean he can't see? He can see, right?" Whether or not somebody plans to ask for clarification, we are all interrupted by the phone ringing. Everyone stops—Paige, Mom, Frick, myself, the officers with pens and notepads, and the EMT crouching down, hand on Paige's shoulder—and we listen to the phone ring on the kitchen table. We wait for it to end. But it rings and rings and rings, and regardless of how our own story's details will work us for the rest of our lives, I cannot have been the only one to know who it was, why they were calling, and how much it stung and still stings to hear a phone go off.

. . .

The doctor said there was nothing to do about my vision, but that it would return. He was right, and I was lucky. It came back slowly over the next few days, and I think that moment—that blindness—is the cause of my cataracts. It's what I'll tell the eye doctor when I see him in a week. However, I don't know how much of the story he needs to know—I guess I can tell him that as a boy I looked too long at the sun.

My vision returned fully when we got Bedogi's body back. It was cold that day, and I remember bringing in a lot of wood with Frick for the woodstove while Mom made whole corn and bean soup. During one trip out back to the blue tarp covering a cord of wood, Marla showed up for the fourth and last time. She waved the coroner's report and said she wanted to talk with us, said that she had some questions. But we ignored her. She wouldn't leave, kept yelling from the steps into our home: "He was here, wasn't he? Say he was here!" Mom wouldn't. I brought this detail up to Mom once, and all she said was that Marla was out to get her, that Marla was wrong, that I was wrong. But Marla was right, and maybe that's why Mom flung open the back door and chased her down the driveway with Frick's skinning knife, screamed she had no business here—"This is a ceremony for the dead!"

Marla left, and on that cold day we buried the boy out back of the house by the tree with the red, white, black, and yellow flags that Frick had tied around a coarse oak. We were supposed to pray for peace, but I don't remember what I prayed for. It was a long time ago, and somebody else now lives in that yellow house. I wonder if they know a child is buried out back? I once called Paige and asked her that. "Let it go," she said, and hung up. I know that the family who now lives in that house ripped down the sweat lodge and built a swing set in its place.

When the ceremony was done, after we'd said our piece and the last dirt was spread, Paige stayed outside the longest. It was dark when she finally came inside. Mom and Frick were smoking in the living room, sipping wine, and I was on the floor, a cold washcloth over my eyes, which still hurt, and Paige went to her room. She came out with the ash basket under her arm. The steel door whined when she opened the hot wood-stove, and when she shoved the basket into the fire a log hissed and popped. With the steel door open, Paige knelt in front of the twisting flame. Mom butted her cigarette and was the first to kneel next to Paige, and then I followed, cold cloth in my hand, then Frick, and together we all watched the boy's basket burn, the sweat on our faces growing cooler and cooler as the basket smoldered and collapsed like the sun one day will, its core blasting out to a great silence not unlike the one huddled around the orange-red coals dimming in the woodstove.

A NOTE ON PENOBSCOT SPELLING:

The Penobscot language was, historically, an oral language. Over the years, it was given an alphabet and spelling system. I have chosen not to use that system and have opted instead for phonetic spelling in this book for a couple of reasons. In writing the Penobscot language phonetically, I have strived for accessibility—so Penobscot and non-Penobscot alike can pronounce the words. I do not want to discredit the immense amount of great work that has been done to revitalize the language, which was almost lost due to colonialism. Still, while the spelling is phonetic, I want the phonetic spelling to be a representation of *my* knowledge of the language. My grasp of the Penobscot language is rudimentary. I have a lot to learn and so too do the characters I write about. What I know of the language has come from family members using Penobscot words here and there and being taught the language in school at a young age (I wish I had listened better!). When I spell a Penobscot word in my writing, I'm actively spelling it phonetically. In many ways, my choice for phonetic spelling—which has to do with accessibility and my knowledge of the language—is a record of the language as my present self and others in my tribe know it.

ACKNOWLEDGMENTS

Stories in this book have appeared in the following journals and magazines:

"Burn": *Narrative*, Summer 2018

"In a Jar": *Granta*

"Food for the Common Cold": *Narrative*, Fall 2020

"In a Field of Stray Caterpillars": *Arkansas International*

"The Blessing Tobacco": *TriQuarterly*, Winter 2020 and Lit Hub

"Safe Harbor": *Narrative*, Winter 2019

"Smokes Last": *The Whitefish Review*, Fall 2017

"Earth, Speak": *Shenandoah*, Fall 2019

"Night of the Living Rez": *RED INK*, Spring 2017

"The Name Means Thunder": *The Georgia Review*, Fall 2019

My deepest thanks to the wonderful people at Tin House: Win McCormack, Craig Popelars, Elizabeth DeMeo, Alyssa Ogi, Diane Chonette, Jakob Vala, Becky Kraemer, Alex Gonzales, Nanci McCloskey, and Sangi Lama. You all feel like family. Special shout-out to my wonderful editor, Masie Cochran, who helped make these stories as good as they can be.

Thank you to the University of Southern Maine's Stonecoast MFA program for being such a stellar place to grow as a writer. Thank you to Justin Tussing, Robin Talbot, and Matt Jones, and thank you to my mentors, Rick Bass and Aaron Hamburger. Without this program, I would not be where I am today. It afforded me the time to write and develop my craft. Thanks, too, to the Elizabeth George Foundation, whose generosity allowed me to finish this collection.

To the editors and publishers who published my stories throughout the past years—thank you. To my *Narrative* Magazine family—Tom Jenks, Carol Edgarian, Mimi Kusch, and Jack Schiff—thank you for what you do. It's so important.

This book wouldn't exist without the support of so many people. To start, I have to go back to my beginnings. Thank you to the folks at Orono High School: Claire Moriarty, Karen Frye, and Chris Crocker. What would I have done without your continued support and care?

Thank you to Carol Lewandowski and John Goldfine. You were the best teachers a student could ask for. I return time and time again to the things you taught me. I'm forever grateful. And thank you to my professors at Dartmouth College, those in the English department and Native Studies department, for pushing me.

I'm compelled to say "agent," but she's family: thank you, Rebecca Friedman, for being the best "agent" a writer could ask for. And many, many thanks to Cara Hoffman. First a mentor, and now a friend and family member, it's like we've known each other forever.

I am indebted to the Penobscot Nation—and to all my ancestors who came before me, who endured and persisted for us to be here—for its immense support. Tribal resources allowed me to pursue my dreams in higher education, which undoubtedly helped get me to where I am. Thanks must also go to the Penobscot community at large: you all have cheered me on and have always encouraged me. Thank you. I would also like to extend special thanks to Gabe Paul and Carol Dana for putting up with my occasional questions about the Penobscot language. I'm just a beginner, and I know I need to be a better student.

To Jake, Tyler, Ethan, Julian, Dylan, Yuma, Chad, Emily, Darby, and Athena—who would I be without having grown up with you all?

My family has always supported and cared and loved me, and so my biggest thanks go to them. Thank you to my mother, Carol Morgan, who I wish could be here when this book comes out. Same goes for my father, John Talty. But I know you both are proud, as I imagine Grammy is and all the others that went before you. Thank you to my sister, Jessica Moores, for always being supportive and reading everything I write—I love you, Jess. Many thanks to my aunts and uncles: Aunt Linda and Uncle Mike; Aunt Susie and Uncle Tom; Aunt Dot Dot and Uncle Albert; and Aunt Barbara and Uncle Conrad. Thank you to my cousins

Stephanie, Mike, Jade, Julie, and Lily. A special sweet thanks to my nieces and nephews: Joao, Josie, and Lizzy.

And lastly, thank you to my mother- and father-in-law—Linda and Kevin—for all you do and continue to do. To my brother- and sister-in-law, Keven and Melanie, and to their son, Cole, whose very presence is a constant reminder of how precious life is.

And finally, to my best friend and wife, Jorden.

MORGAN TALTY is a citizen of the Penobscot Indian Nation where he grew up. Named one of *Narrative*'s "30 Below 30," Talty's work has appeared in *The Georgia Review*, *Granta*, *Shenandoah*, *TriQuarterly*, *Narrative*, Lit Hub, and elsewhere. A winner of the 2021 *Narrative* Prize, Talty's work has been supported by the Elizabeth George Foundation and National Endowment for the Arts. He lives in Levant, Maine.

Made in the USA
Middletown, DE
16 December 2022

18936644R00166